Murder Casts a Spell

Nancy Curteman

Cover Art:
Select-O-Graphix

Dedication

Larry, Jerry and Juli

Acknowledgements

First, my sincere appreciation to my husband, Larry, for his loving encouragement.

Special thanks to members of my writing group: Art Carey, Carol Hall, Jane Lester and Sol Tetebaum. They taught me the basics. I couldn't have written this book without their powerful suggestions.

Thank you to members of my book club, aptly named Champagne and Chapters: Laurel Gonzales, Sandy Grandbois, Janyce Hummel, Kim Kelly, Trudie Mathiesen, Trish Murray, Catherine Rost, AnneMarie Sylva and Carol Wilson. They were my cheerleaders. They gave me the courage I needed to try.

I owe an immense debt of gratitude to those who took time out of their busy schedules to read my entire manuscript. Art Carey, Carrie Cassidy, Sandy Grandbois, Kim Kelley, Norma Lipman, Trudie Mathiesen, and Trish Murray were my test team. They provided the finale thrust that sent my novel to publication.

Chapter 1

The screech of a bird hidden high in the thick, glossy-green leaves of a South African Yellowwood tree drew the attention of a gangly brown-skinned boy. He searched the leaves as he ambled along a sandy trail on his way home from school. At a sudden rustle of leaves the boy's head tilted straight up. Eyes locked on a flash of gray feathers soaring skyward, he didn't notice the deep dip in the uneven ground beneath his feet until too late. A hard tumble caused him to scrape his knee on a sharp stone. He rocked back on his haunches and swiped sand from his throbbing knee with the shirttail of his white cotton school uniform shirt. When the scrape looked clean to him, he examined the small crescent-shaped wound just below the hem of his short, gray pants. In anger, he grabbed the stone and threw it as hard as he could.

The boy surveyed the tree branches and the cloudless sky beyond in hopes of sighting the bird again. He imagined a Peregrine Falcon had flown from Cape Town's distant Table Mountain in search of prey on Ikhaya Township's sea level terrain.

He waited.

No Peregrine appeared. Disappointed, he tore his eyes away from the tree and struggled to his feet.

That was when he saw something almost as exciting as a Peregrine.

He blinked several times then squinted at the familiar hut he skirted past everyday. The scary medicine man's shack looked the same as always—a small round, mud-walled hut with a cone-shaped thatch roof.

Except today—the door stood ajar.

The boy paused, licked his lips and considered his options. Should he ignore it and continue on his way? Maybe it wouldn't hurt to just take a quick peek inside then run. Who'd ever know?

In less than an instant, curiosity triumphed over caution. He crept up the dusty path to the threshold, locked his hands behind his back, and without touching the door, snaked his head through the narrow opening. The putrid smell made him cough but he persisted. Just enough light streamed through the opening to make out the contents of the shadowy interior.

His hungry gaze inched around the room. A shelf stood against one wall, stuffed with bottles of oil and various sized jars containing red, black and white powders. Beneath the shelf he counted three flat baskets of what looked like crushed roots. Dried herbs and animal carcasses dangled from ropes overhead. Bones and stones lay scattered on the floor. Close by the door stood a can blackened from the dead flame of what used to be a candle. A thick dirty-yellow mixture oozed from a bowl that had tumbled from a heavy overturned table.

So many interesting things to explore in this hut with its old-fashioned dirt floor and strange collection of objects. Maybe he could step inside for just a moment to have a closer look.

He raised one foot over the wood threshold. It froze in midair. The boy's pupils dilated, a high-pitched gasp escaped his lips and his heart thudded. He reeled as if struck by a blow. He tried to tear his eyes from the sight before him but couldn't blink it away. He tried to run but had lost power over his legs. He tried to scream but his voice caught in his throat.

On the dirt floor a few feet from where he stood lay a thin body, mouth slathered with white froth, eyes turned toward the boy in a fixed stare.

Fear of his mother's whipping stick overcame his immobility—he backed away, whirled and ran. A battle raged in his brain all the way home. Should he tell his mother or not? He'd broken a rule. *Two rules.* His mother's warnings shouted in his ears. "Come straight home. Never go into strange houses." He'd disobeyed both rules.

The thrashing he anticipated made the decision for him. He would not tell his mother what he saw in the hut. He wouldn't tell anyone. He would pretend it never happened.

Maybe it didn't.

Chapter 2

Lysi Weston gazed out the cab window as the bright red taxi chugged along the foothills of Table Mountain toward the quiet Cape Town suburb of Oranjezicht. She turned when her friend, Grace Wright, nudged her. "Look, Bosch Lane. We're almost there."

The cab turned off Rugby Road onto tree-lined Bosch Lane. A few seconds later, it pulled up in front of a saffron-colored house with ochre shutters and three ochre garage doors. Lysi admired the formal look of the two well-pruned Japanese Barberries that stood in blue pots on each side of the garage; and the low boxwood hedge that separated a small front yard from the sidewalk.

The two women slid from the stuffy atmosphere of the cab into the sweet-scented air of the park-like community of Oranjezicht. A bird's eye view of Cape Town and the shimmering Atlantic Ocean greeted them. A warm breeze fluttered through Lysi's short, blonde hair and tousled her already disheveled curls. Her brown eyes widened at the great expanse of sea and sky. "It's more beautiful than I could have imagined."

"Umm," Grace said.

The young cab driver lifted two bags from the trunk. He massaged his sparse growth of mustache and waited. After a moment he cleared his throat a couple of times and eyed the stylishly dressed women. Lysi caught his impatient message, walked around to the trunk, paid the fare, slipped the driver a few extra rands, and rejoined Grace.

"I never dreamed someday I'd spend Christmas in South Africa," Grace said. "June's the only time I've travelled here."

"*You* never dreamed!" Lysi said. "I'm still shocked I ever let you talk me into this."

Grace draped a long arm over Lysi's shoulder. "You lighten up, girl. You promised to go with the flow. Remember? Now take a deep breath and get centered."

"Don't worry, I'm fine." Lysi's eyes crinkled into a smile. "It's just that I'm not used to jumping on a plane two days after it enters my mind that I *might* consider a visit to some place as far away as South Africa. Some people like to plan a little you know."

"Yeah, yeah." Grace waved a dismissive hand and walked away.

Lysi watched her statuesque colleague stride with feline grace toward the saffron-colored house. Her long silky black hair rippled in the cool breeze. Grace's iridescent turquoise silk skimmer and four-inch stilettos shouted flamboyant personality while Lysi's tailored burgundy sheath and two-inch matching pumps whispered conservative.

It seemed to Lysi her life had turned upside down since she met Grace two years ago. She remembered the day Stellar Corporate Development, a management training company, hired Grace to replace Lysi's previous co-presenter, Cristin Holden. Lysi missed Cristin who was murdered while on assignment in Eastern Montana, but she'd liked Grace immediately.

Grace, a tough, street-wise child of a gigantic African-American father and a petite Puerto Rican mother, grew up in Harlem. At six feet tall, she had the regal bearing of an empress. With her long slim body, flawless cinnamon complexion and high cheekbones the color of ripe plums, Grace reminded Lysi of Lladro's Watusi Queen. A university graduate, Grace was just as comfortable among a corporate board of directors as she was hanging with ghetto gangs. Lysi thought of her as a cross between a Shakespearean actor and a gangsta rapper. Friendship with Grace had transformed Lysi's life from a predictable carousel round to an erratic roller coaster ride. Lysi hadn't decided how she felt about it.

Lysi looked up when the house door opened and a short-legged, full-busted woman scurried down the steps wearing an orange and gold cotton dress adorned with decorative black braiding. She almost toppled her bountiful Santulo headdress when she threw her plump brown arms around Grace.

"Grace, it is so wonderful to see you after all these years." The woman took both Grace's hands and held her at arms length. "Well look at you. You have not changed at all." With a rich round of laughter she added, "Watch out Africa, Grace Wright has arrived!"

Grace kissed the woman on both cheeks then grabbed Lysi's arm and pulled her forward. "Lysi Weston, meet my old college roomie, Amele Butshingi of the proud Xhosa Nala Clan."

Amele pumped Lysi's hand. "Welcome to South Africa."

The trace of a Bantu click in Amele's throaty low-pitched voice reminded Lysi of the famous Black South African-born singer, Miriam Makeba, whom she'd seen perform at the Orpheum Theater in San Francisco. "So happy to meet you. Grace has told me everything about you," Lysi said.

"Oooh, I hope not." Amele clapped a hand to her chest and cast a censuring glance at Grace.

A giant black man with a shaved head appeared in the open door at the top of the steps. He wore an embroidered African Dashiki shirt that couldn't conceal his massive expanse of chest muscles.

Grace looked up at him. "You must be Luvo." She nudged Amele with her elbow. "You're right, he is one good looking Zulu."

Luvo chortled. In a voice so bass it seemed to come from deep inside his huge body he said, "Amele, I like your friend already. She is very discerning and I must say has excellent taste in men."

"Do not let it go to your head, dear." Amele winked at Luvo.

Luvo loped down the steps taking two at a time and shook hands with Grace and Lysi. They both had to look up at him. Amele is so short and Luvo so tall, Lysi thought. It must turn a few heads when they walk together down the street.

Amele stood on tiptoes and kissed Luvo's shiny black cheek. "Now be a darling and take these bags to the guest room."

Amele led the way up the steps through the shiny ochre door into a spacious living room. A light scent of musk incense greeted them as they crossed a deep-pile blue carpet where a couch and three matching chairs nested around a small coffee table.

Gold draperies with dark blue flowers divided the dining room and living room. On one wall of the dining room stood a small white Victorian fireplace. A wedding portrait of Amele and Luvo perched on the mantle between two candles. Six leather chairs encircled a large mahogany table. Lysi eyed the inlaid wood sunburst medallion in the middle of the hardwood floor. "Magnificent. You don't often see floors like that these days. I've only seen a few in San Francisco."

"That floor is one of the things we love about this house. Luvo's grandfather built it in 1904. It has been in the Butshingi family for three generations. We could never afford such amenities if we had to purchase it now," Amele said. She gestured with an open palm toward a set of French doors. "Shall we take our refreshment in the garden?"

On the way out, she called over her shoulder to Luvo. "Would you mind, dear? The drinks are on a tray in the kitchen."

Grace grinned at Amele. "Boy, is he well trained."

6

Amele arched both eyebrows and tucked her chin. "Oh, he gets lots of fringe benefits, if you know what I mean."

Leaning close to Amele's ear, Grace whispered loud enough for Lysi to hear, "Bet he likes a little dominatrix stuff."

"Grace. You have now hit bottom." Amele tried to stifle a smile. "I met Luvo when he was headmaster at Seaside Primary School in Cape Town. He hired me to teach third grade. He gave the orders then and he still does." She winked and added, "or…thinks he does."

"Did you spend much time in his office?"

"Stop, Grace, Lysi said. "You're enjoying your fantasies too much."

The three women eyed each other, laughed and followed Amele out to a wooden deck that was partially covered by an arbor of green leaves. They sat on cushioned chairs at a round teakwood table.

Amele smiled at Lysi. "So tell me, Lysi, what are your passions?"

Before Lysi could answer, Grace said, "Aussie sheep farmers."

Lysi's mouth dropped open. "Grace!"

"Come on, Lysi. It's just us girls here."

Lysi turned to Amele. "Well, I spent a little time with a detective who owns a sheep station in Outback Australia near Alice Springs—"

"Tell her the important part." Grace leaned her head close to Lysi. "When you e-mailed your sheep farmer you intended to visit Cape Town, where did he say he planned to spend his vacation?"

"He's not a sheep farmer. He's a grazier." Lysi pushed Grace away and spoke to Amele. "His coming to Africa has very little to do with me. He's actually going to Namibia to visit his son."

"Come now, Lysi," Grace said. She turned to Amele. "This awesome Aussie adores her and is willing to traipse all the way to Cape Town just to be with her."

Lysi ignored Grace and continued speaking to Amele. "His son is an Advisory Teacher in Australian Volunteers International."

"Mmmm." Amele nodded. Her lips curved into a slight grin.

"It's like the Peace Corps." Lysi knew she was speaking faster and explaining more than she needed. "His son runs workshops in rural areas of Namibia on how to teach multi-age students. He's had lots of experience because as an Outback teacher he taught in multi-grade classrooms."

Amele leaned forward. "You say he is coming here? To Cape Town?"

Lysi nodded, a resigned expression on her face.

"He will stay with us of course. Luvo will love talking with him about his sheep station."

Luvo walked through the door carrying a tray of drinks. "Did I hear my name?"

"We are going to have a houseguest from Australia. A sheep farmer—I mean a grazier—who owns a sheep station. Lysi's friend," Amele said.

"Really." Luvo's eyes lit up. He set the tray of shimmering red glasses of iced Rooibos tea in the center of the table. "A sheep station is it? When does he arrive?"

Lysi felt her face redden. Thoughts of Detective Maynard Christie still brought a bit of color to her cheeks even though she hadn't seen him in over a year.

She'd met him in Sydney when she and Grace attended an international conference on sexual harassment of males. After she returned to San Francisco, they'd exchanged a few casual letters and e-mails, but she hadn't encouraged his obvious attraction to her. His response to the e-mail in which she'd mentioned going to Cape Town, surprised her. He'd hit reply and typed in "I'll see you there."

7

Things had changed so much since she'd met Maynard. When she was in Australia, she was still very involved with James Tennyson, a detective from Sage Deer, Montana. In fact, she'd almost made a decision to marry him. But James tired of her vacillating and married a woman from Billings. His announcement stung like a deep paper cut, but in the end it was for the best. She couldn't have traded her life in San Francisco for a mere existence in Eastern Montana.

Lysi averted her eyes and directed her words to the tea tray instead of Luvo. "I'm meeting Maynard at Cape Town International day after tomorrow."

Luvo set napkins and glasses of Rooibos on the table in front of Lysi and Grace. "I'll be happy to drive you. I'm most interested in meeting your Maynard and learning about the Australian Outback."

Lysi took a sip of tea. Like Luvo, she looked forward to seeing Maynard but with a mixture of trepidation in her anticipation. The son of a mixed-blood Aborignal mother and a white-blonde Swedish father, Maynard was a tall, fair-skinned octoroon with an easy-going, earthy manner that fed Lysi's desire to explore the exotic side of life. She had to admit Maynard Christie had been on her mind quite a bit since his surprising e-mail.

"Well, it's settled, then. Your Maynard Christie will be our guest," Amele said. She gestured with her glass toward Lysi. "Here's to a bit of an adventure, eh?"

Chapter 3

A pearl of sweat trickled down Mandisa Nala's forehead and dripped on the open Themba Daycare Center attendance book. She leaned an elbow on her laminate-topped steel desk, a worn relic from a local school. It squeaked as if in protest under her weight. She ran her finger down the list of children's names and stopped at the empty square next to five-year-old Saba's name.

"Absent?"

A frown dulled Mandisa's polished mohogany face. Saba hadn't missed a single day since she started at Themba four years ago at the age of 3 months. Zodwa, her mother, never missed a day of work cleaning hotel rooms in Cape Town. Not everyone in Ikhaya had a job. Zodwa protected hers.

Mandisa reached into an apron pocket, pulled out a lace-trimmed handkerchief, and swabbed her brow and neck. She checked the centigrade wall thermometer and moaned. Thirty-six degrees. Already the corrugated metal building radiated heat like a furnace, and the sun hadn't even hit its zenith. She gulped down a glass of water, upped the desk fan speed to high and directed the air toward her face. Is Saba sick? Or Zodwa? But wouldn't Zodwa have called? More likely that silly Lindani neglected to mark her present. Mandisa guessed she would have to check for herself.

Mandisa's eyes strayed to the framed photo of her son, Sipho. He smiled back at her from atop the unpainted board that served as a shelf above her desk. Why had he started traipsing off to Cape Town for 2 days every week? She just could not manage the work with him gone so much. She had even considered closing the Center, but knew Ikhaya Township mothers had to work. Children had to be minded and protected. Themba was the only childcare center in Site C, one of the poorest sections of the Township. So two weeks ago she had to hire Lindani. Now it felt like that girl just made more work for her. Why couldn't Lindani remember even the simplest instructions?

Mandisa blew frustrated air through her lips, placed her hands on her knees, pitched forward and pushed to her feet. At 48, rheumatoid arthritis had slowed her and burdened her with extra pounds. She glanced at the photo of her son again. Sipho should be here doing this. She would have a serious talk with him tomorrow when he returned.

Mandisa plodded into the Blue Room where Lindani herded a gaggle of fifteen green-uniformed four and five-year olds to a rug. The room smelled of warm-skinned children seasoned with scents from their homes and Ikhaya streets—barbecue and kerosene smoke, dog odor, dust. She watched while Lindani set a small bowl of breakfast pap porridge in front of each youngster.

To Mandisa, Lindani resembled one of those skinny, dirt-colored hounds that rummaged through the garbage heaps that lined the township's dusty streets. Long boney arms and legs jutted from her undernourished body. Her greased-down hair accentuated a flat nose. Thin lips didn't quite cover her buckled teeth. Only her big brown eyes and long lashes lent a morsel of beauty to her face. Mandisa sighed. She is a little girl in a woman's body. She tries.

Mandisa scanned the room—blocks, legos, puzzles, books and games lay scattered on the floor. How many times did she have to tell Lindani to make the children pickup before eating?

A quick glance at the squirming children told Mandisa little Saba was not seated with them on the rug. Was she in the toilet?

While the children attacked the pap porridge like a bunch of hungry slurping puppies, Mandisa approached Lindani. "Where is Saba?"

Lindani looked around the room. "She is not here?"

"Lindani, please." Mandisa could not keep irritation out of her voice. "I am asking you. Do you know if she is here or not?"

Lindani shrugged, eyes blank, lower lip thrust out in a childish pout.

Mandisa shook her head. Sipho should be doing this. Why does he have to go to Cape Town? He should be here. It never used to be this way. Sipho always loved helping with the children. He knew just how to cajole them into obeying all the rules. He never yelled. He always smiled. He dreamed of someday going off to teachers' college with his friends.

Everything changed when Sipho turned 19. He still loved working with the children in the center, but he did not smile as much. He quit going with his friends. Every night he stayed home reading or watching television. He no longer talked about attending teachers' college. Then he began spending too much time in Cape Town. Why?

Both Mandisa and Lindani started when the door swung open and Zodwa burst into the room holding five-year old Saba's hand. Her son Philani trailed behind, tear tracks on his cheeks. Frustration and anger creased Zodwa's face under the brown doek wrapped around her hair. She grabbed Philani by the shirt collar and thrust him toward Mandisa. "Suddenly he will not walk to school by himself. I do not know what has got into that boy. I got to catch the bus. Could he go with your students? Just today?"

Mandisa eyed the tall, stringy-limbed boy. "What is the matter with you, Philani? Eight years old and suddenly you cannot walk to school by yourself?"

The boy lowered his head and spoke to the floor. "I just do not want to."

Mandisa looked into Zodwa's harried eyes. "Leave him."

With one hand Mandisa pushed Philani toward her office door. "Go sit on the bench by my desk." With the other hand, she nudged Saba toward the circle of children. "Go see Lindani."

After Zodwa left, Mandisa walked into the office. Hands planted on her ample hips, she frowned down at Philani seated with his head bowed. "Now Philani, what is this about?"

The boy picked at a scab on his knee and wouldn't look at her.

She swiped his hand away from his knee. "Stop that. You will make it worse." She took a disinfectant spray from a desk drawer, sprayed the scraped knee and covered it with a band-aide.

"Now Philani, a big boy like you does not suddenly decide he cannot go to school by himself for no reason. You tell me the reason?"

No answer.

"Well, I guess I will just send you off to school alone since you refuse to answer me."

Philani jerked his head toward Mandisa. "No, please." Tears welled up in his eyes.

Mandisa eased down next to him and put an arm around his shoulders. "What is it, Philani?"

"I saw something."

"What did you see?"

"No, please do not make me tell. My umama will whip me."

"I will talk to umama." Mandisa knew whippings came easily from exhausted, overworked Ikhaya mothers and she had found it necessary to intervene many times. "Tell me what you saw."

Philani trembled. He pressed closer against Mandisa's big soft chest. "The house of the old witch doctor. I looked in the open door. That is where I saw it."

"Saw what?"

"The man. On the floor with white stuff on his mouth. Not moving. Just looking at me," Philani said, taking a short gulp of air at the end of each sentence.

Mandisa squinted and looked sideways at Philani. "None of this smells good to me. Are you telling a story?"

"No." Philani started to bawl.

"Stop it. Do you want the other kids to hear you crying like a baby? Stop it, now."

Philani buried his face in Mandisa's lap, quieted but kept sniffling. She stroked his close cropped hair and in her mind cursed the witch doctor.

Mandisa knew about that old witch doctor's hut and the wicked old conjurer who lived there. Was he still dabbling in that black magic drivel? Could Philani be telling the truth or was he making up a story to hide some mischievous thing he had done?

"Now you listen to me. I am going to walk you to school myself. We are going to look inside that house." Mandisa shook her index finger at Philani. "The man had better be there."

Philani's eyes widened. He shook his head back and forth and opened his mouth to howl. Mandisa shushed him by pressing her finger against his open lips.

"Oh, yes. You will show me what you saw." Mandisa stood. She tried to ignore the arthritic pain in her knees.

She took Philani's hand and dragged him out the door of the pink building toward the sandy path to the school. They passed a pile of scrap lumber, loaded clotheslines, oil barrel barbecues and community toilets. The road led them through a maze of corrugated metal lean-tos and iron shipping containers that served as houses and shops.

About fifteen minutes later they found the witch doctor's house a few steps past a huge Real Yellowwood tree. Philani stopped, yanked his hand from Mandisa's grip and ran to hide behind the thick trunk of the tree.

"Philani," Mambisa shouted over her shoulder as she continued towards the hut. "You stop that silliness and get over here." Philani would not even peek from behind the trunk.

Mandisa pushed open the hut door and peered inside. At first she couldn't see much, but after a few seconds her eyes transitioned from the bright early morning sun to the dim interior.

An instant later, her heart crashed. She uttered a low guttural cry and dropped to her knees. "No..."

Chapter 4

Lysi savored the finale sip of Arabica coffee and watched the morning sun evaporate the last bits of silver fog turning the sky into a blaze of sapphire. She nodded when Amele gestured with the half-filled coffee carafe. "Delicious, but three cups does it for me."

Amele pointed the pot toward Grace.

"No more for me, either. You'll have me strutting my stuff on the ceiling."

"I would like to see that." Amele poured herself another cup and set the pot back on a trivet. "Well then, this morning we go to Ikhaya Township to see my children in the Themba Center."

Grace answered Lysi's puzzled look. "Amele is a volunteer teacher at Themba, a kind of preschool." She squeezed Amele's hand. "This lady has decided to foster ethnic pride in every Ikhaya Township kid by teaching them about their history as Xhosa people."

"Grace exaggerates," Amele protested. "But you will see for yourself. You will meet Mandisa Nala who runs the center. I am the godmother of her adopted daughter, Nambeko."

Grace punched Amele's shoulder. "How did you end up being a godmother? I can't quite picture that."

"I did not plan it," Amele said. "I fell into it. Baby Nambeko's birth mother gave her up for adoption because she already had three boys and no husband. Mandisa had no children but desperately wanted them. She adopted Nambeko and asked me to be godmother."

Grace laughed. "Well at least you're not a grandmother, yet."

"Since Luvo and I have no children of our own, I will adopt Themba kids for my grandchildren some day." Amele dropped three sugar cubes into her coffee and took a couple of big gulps. "Funny how life is. After Mandisa adopted Nambeko, she gave birth to her son, Sipho."

"Does Nambeko know her birth family?" Lysi asked.

"Her birth mother died of AIDS before Nambeko reached five years." Amele took one more drink of her coffee then carried the breakfast dishes to the dishwasher. "She knows her three brothers but will have nothing to do with them. This is good because they are ruffians. They have tried more than once to extort money from Mandisa."

"What about Nambeko's father?" Lysi asked.

"No one knows. Not even Nambeko's birth mother," Amele said. "It is just as well. Mandisa has raised a fine young woman. She is now Doctor Nala and practices in Ikhaya Township. You will meet her."

Lysi knew little about African townships. What she did know she connected with Johannesburg's Soweto where Nelson Mandela and Archbishop Desmond Tutu once lived. She knew Soweto meant South Western Townships and wondered about Ikhaya. "Tell me about Ikhaya?"

"It is a large township located in Western Cape Town on the Cape Flats. Over 500,000 people live there—mostly Xhosa, mostly poor. The name Ikhaya means home." Amele finished clearing the butter and jam from the table.

On the way out the door, Lysi started to ask more questions but Luvo's deep voice interrupted. "Amele, I remind you that Ikhaya is not safe for pretty ladies when the sun sets." He trailed them down the steps to the street, his face stern. "Do not make me worry. Come home early."

"Of course. Of course, dear. We shall return early. I would not want to miss your barbecue," Amele said. He leaned down and Amele kissed his glossy cheek then hurried Grace and Lysi to the car.

12

"I can't believe it. A red VW Bug." Grace slid her hand across the shiny surface of the car's hood.

"Salsa red. The closest I could get to the old college burgundy." Amele pressed the keys into Grace's hand. "Stop gawking and get in. You may drive?"

"Oh no." Grace held up the keys with her thumb and index finger as if touching something slimy. "I've driven to Ikhaya before. Let's give Lysi that unforgettable experience." Grace winked at Amele.

Lysi pulled back in surprise. "Me? I don't think so. I don't even have an international license."

Grace nudged Lysi towards the open car door. "You got a photo on your California license. That's all you need."

"But I haven't driven on the left since Australia. Besides, I don't know the way."

"Stop with the excuses. Get behind that wheel, Lysi. Amele is a great navigator," Grace said.

"I—"

"In!" Grace pushed her into the driver's seat and dropped the keys into her lap.

Lysi glared at Grace then grabbed the steering wheel. She fingered the turn signal, light switch, windshield wiper knob. She fondled the stick shift. Not much different from the '67 VW she'd driven for eighteen years. She could do it. It might even be fun.

Grace folded her long legs into the back seat. Amele slid into the front passenger seat. Lysi shifted into gear and they started on the 35-kilometer drive to Ikhaya Township. "Be calm, Lysi," Amele said. "This will be easy."

"Uh huh," Grace said. "I'd rather drive Bolivia's Death Road without brakes." She hissed through clenched teeth feigning terror.

"Stop it, Grace," Amele said, a little tinge of laughter in her voice. "Ignore her, Lysi. Just listen to me. We will drive south on N2. When we pass the airport we will take the M44 Mew Way exit. Direction Ikhaya. Nice roads all the way to Ikhaya."

On Highway N2 Lysi squinted through the windshield at a horde of children playing soccer on the grassy verge along the freeway inches from the speeding traffic. She gasped then hit the brakes and slowed from 110-kilometers per hour to 60. She could have hit one of them? Her stomach went hollow when a soccer ball flew onto the road and several boys clamored over the median and dodged cars in pursuit of it. Sweat formed a little arc on her upper lip. "How much farther?"

"Not far." Amele seemed unconcerned about the dozens of kids playing alongside N2. Lysi figured it must be an everyday occurrence.

"At that speed we'll arrive sometime next week." Grace leaned over the seat back. "Come on Lysi. Get the pedal to the metal."

In Ikhaya, the VW followed narrow, unnamed streets past unnumbered shacks and shops constructed from whatever materials people could scavenge—tin, wood, cardboard, corrugated steel shipping containers. Paint in cheerful pastel pinks, blues, greens, and yellows covered the sad structures. Murals in bright primary colors decorated most of the tiny shops.

"Turn right at the first robots," Amele said.

"Robots?" Lysi switched her eyes around the scene ahead of her searching for a robot.

"Signal lights. Right there." Amele pointed to a single traffic signal. "Now! Turn!"

Lysi turned then swerved so hard she had to wrench the wheel to avoid hitting a fence on the right side of the street.

A man stood beside a sturdy wooden table that extended partially into the narrow street. In one hand he wielded a large knife. In the other hand he held a brown-haired sheep head over a rusty drum of steaming water.

"What was that?" Lysi smelled boiled meat.

"Smileys." Grace chortled from the back seat. "Hungry, Lysi. We'll come back here for lunch."

"Township residents use sheep heads as a free source of protein. Butchers just throw them out anyway," Amele said. "Turn right into that street in front of the CalTex Garage."

Lysi turned. "But why do they call them smileys?"

"Weird is it not? When the heads are cooked, the skin recedes from the sheep's teeth and they look like they are smiling." Amele stretched her lips back from her teeth. "At the first intersection, take a left. When you pass three roads—"

Lysi hit the brakes. "Hold it. Give me some street names, will you?"

Amele laughed. "Trade places. I will take over. I forgot you Americans like to know where you are going. Not all streets in Ikhaya have names, especially in the 'informal' imikhukhu or shack settlements. Newcomers build wherever they find a small piece of ground."

Two more turns and Amele stopped the car in front of a pink corrugated iron structure. Twelve-inch hand-painted blue letters on a plywood sign read, "Themba Educare Center." Smaller letters beneath it said, "Help children grow."

Clanging sounds caught Lysi's attention when she opened the car door. Across the street, under a clothesline sagging with laundry a goat had its head in an overflowing garbage bin. Cans toppled from the bin and rolled onto the street joining crushed Styrofoam containers, crumpled food wrappers and smashed soda cans. It reminded her of her old junior high cafeteria after lunch.

The exuberant voices of children rang from the interior of the one-story building. The three women passed through a fence made of slats from old wooden boxes. Just inside the fence a small garden of Thistle Sugarbush shrubs and some spindly annuals struggled to survive in the dry sandy soil. To the right of the front door the school had posted a hand painted mission statement. Lysi paused and read the statement aloud: "To prepare all our students to be lifelong learners through a challenging curriculum which nurtures students emotional and intellectual growth."

"Mandisa composed that mission statement and has always tried to follow it," Amele said with pride in her voice.

"It's a fine statement of goals." Lysi considered it just as well written as any she'd had to compose in the years she served as a school principal.

Amele stuck her head through the open door. "Mandisa…I'm here. I brought two friends to see your center."

No answer.

Lysi figured Mandisa couldn't hear Amele above all the boisterous kid chatter. After another try, Amele pushed open the door and they walked into a playroom full of romping, out-of-control children. Lindani didn't even look up from the chair where she sat staring off into space.

"Lindani," Amele said in a loud voice.

Lindani sprang up, eyes wide, mouth agape.

Several children paused at the sound of Amele's voice. They stumbled over and crowded around her. "Molo, Mama," they shouted as they pressed their little bodies against her. She patted their heads and shoulders, chucked their chins and returned their enthusiastic greetings. "Moloweni. Hello. Moloweni. Moloweni."

Children who couldn't squeeze close to Amele threw their arms around Lysi and Grace who joined Amele in her chorus of "Molos." With all the childish hugs, Lysi was back on the primary playground in the school where she'd spent several years as an administrator. In those days, all she had to do was visit the playground at recess and hordes of kids would rush up and throw their arms around her. The memory brought a smile to her face.

When the children returned to their games, Amele her face contorted in anger, looked at Lindani, "Where is Mandisa?"

"She is not here." Lindani scratched her head.

"I can see that. Where is she?"

"She said she would return?" Lindani's eyes clouded. "Do not be mad at me Mama Amele."

Amele sighed. "Okay, Lindani." She checked her watch. "Start cleanup. You should prepare the children for lunch."

Lysi smiled at a thin little girl with tight braids who tiptoed to Amele. She twisted the skirt hem of her uniform and remained quiet until Amele noticed her.

"Mama Amele. Mama Amele. My brother did not want to go to school today. The house of Qamata scared him very bad." Saba spoke so fast she had to interrupt her story to choke down some air. "I think Mama Mandisa had to take him to school or he would not go."

Amele's smile faded for an instant then reappeared. "Thank you, Saba." Amele stroked Saba's cheek with the back of her fingers. "Now let us clean up for lunch." She took Saba's hand, settled her in the group of children and returned to Lysi and Grace.

Amele's kid-friendly smile had disappeared from her lips. Lysi watched deep furrows darken her brow. "It is not like Mandisa to leave Lindani in charge. Something is not right."

At the sight of Amele's troubled expression, Lysi's smile turned to concern. "Does Qamata scare children?"

"Qamata tries to scare everyone." Amele spoke through clenched teeth. "He is a vindictive old charlatan who imagines himself a natural healer. He stole the name Qamata from the Xhosa Supreme Being. The blasphemous old quack is infamous for causing sickness not curing it. He..." Amele stopped.

Lysi studied Amele—stiff body, tight fists, grim mouth, troubled eyes. What did Amele fear? What did she leave out of the description of Qamata? Lysi leaned toward Amele. "What is it, Amele?"

Amele bit her bottom lip and took a long time to answer. "Qamata despises Mandisa. He has threatened her. I worry because she is not well. Qamata knows this. He would take the opportunity to hurt her if it presented itself. Also, I know Mandisa. If she thought Qamata frightened one of her children, she would go straightaway to confront him. She has done this before, when she had good health, strength and courage. Now she has only courage." Amele turned towards the door. "I must find her."

A quick glance between Lysi and Grace signaled agreement. "We'll go with you to look for her," Grace said stroking Amele's back.

A dark wave of worry slithered through Lysi's mind.

Chapter 5

Dr. Nambeko Nala could feel Mandisa's eyes following her every move as she leaned over Sipho's still body. She pressed two fingers against his wrist in search of a pulse then switched to his neck. She reached into her flat-bottomed, leather medical bag, pushed aside a blood pressure cuff, tourniquet and forceps; and pulled out a stethoscope. She moved the stethoscope around Sipho's cold chest and listened for a heartbeat. She knew it was useless, but still she went through the motions—for her stepmother.

Mandisa waited—fingers interlocked, hands clasped against her chest, brows knitted. Nambeko lifted sympathetic eyes to her stepmother and shook her head. Mandisa covered her face with trembling hands. Silent tears streamed down her cheeks.

Nambeko opened a damp sterile cotton pad and gently cleansed the chalky white substance from around her stepbrother's mouth. She stroked his cheek, positioned his arms across his chest then dragged an embroidered shawl from around her shoulders and draped it over his body. She rose with a deep sigh and wrapped both arms around Mandisa.

Time stood still as the two women waited for an ambulance in answer to their 112 emergency call. Nambeko understood the slow response. The understaffed and under-equipped Site B Community Health Clinic where she worked as staff doctor handled thousands of trauma patients per month. Picking up bodies got lowest priority.

Nambeko sniffed and recoiled at the nauseating odors in Qamata's hut—filthy bottles filled with bacteria-laden fluids, putrid animal parts drying on boards, multi-colored powders and herbs in old open vessels. How could anyone live in this squalor? As far as she was concerned, the old rhino was a plague on Xhosa folk medicine. Not a Sangoma. Not a practitioner of herbal medicine. Not a respected traditional healer. Nothing but a con artist. Over the years, Nambeko had had reasons to dislike the treacherous imposter. Now she despised him.

Nambeko was still a child when she first encountered Qamata. The old witch doctor had shouted to her one day when she passed his hut on the way home from school. He lured her inside, showed her his stash of disgusting witchcraft trash then running his foul fingers through her hair he told her she was destined to be a witch doctor and live with him. Terrified, she ran all the way home screaming. When her stepmother heard what happened, she grabbed a heavy shovel, marched straight to the witch doctor's hut and slammed him in the shins. When he collapsed in the dust, Mandisa warned, "This pain is nothing compared to what you will experience if you ever speak to any of my children again." After that, he gave Mandisa and her family a wide berth.

Years later, when Nambeko started medical school, Qamata began leaving dead rodents and reptiles on her family's doorstep with drawings of Nambeko lying dead in an open grave.

Nambeko didn't die. But now Sipho lay dead in Qamata's filth.

Mandisa's chest heaved with deep, suppressed sobs. Nambeko tightened her arms around her.

Chapter 6

A white truck, motor rumbling, blocked the doorway of the witch doctor's hut. Lysi read the yellow letters stenciled on the truck's door—Ambulance—and shot Grace a worried glance. An ambulance meant serious injury. Who was hurt? Mandisa?

Amele's words tumbled through Lysi's mind. Mandisa hates Qamata. Mandisa's health has deteriorated but her courage remains as strong as ever. This could be a dangerous combination. Maybe Mandisa confronted Qamata about the little boy. Maybe he attacked her.

Lysi bit her lip and tried to chase the questions from her mind. This was not her business. She was a tourist in South Africa. She should stay out of it.

Two black men jumped out of the ambulance, walked to the rear and opened the double doors. The short one pulled up his baggy trousers, nudged the other one's brawny arm and pointed toward the three women. Both men cast annoyed glances in their direction then reached into the truck.

Amele called to them. "Molweni."

"Molweni," the short one replied in a flat tone without looking at her.

The taller of the two men swept the air with his long arm. "Stand away." His base voice emanated from full lips framed by an angular jaw and sharp cheekbones. He dipped his shiny black forehead and lasered Amele with hard eyes.

Lysi thought he'd look right at home swinging a mace in a Roman arena. He had both the steel body and the icy eyes of a gladiator.

"What has happened?" Amele's words squeezed from her tight throat.

The two men unfurled a black plastic body bag and laid it on a stretcher. The tall one unzipped it and gestured with an open palm. "You can see we have come to pick up a body."

Amele choked and stumbled backwards. Lysi and Grace each grabbed one of her arms. They stood in the dust and watched the two men go into the hut. A few moments later they heard voices from inside.

"Which mortuary?" The bass voice of the tall ambulance attendant rumbled through the doorway.

A woman's voice. "No, not a mortuary. Go—"

"But it is a corpse." The deep voice sounded confrontational.

"Go to Site B Community Health Center." The woman sounded impatient.

Anger tinged the man's words. "But it is—"

"Thabo. Do as I say. Now." The woman's raised voice put an end to the discussion.

"That was Nambeko!" Amele's body lurched. "Oh no, Mandisa is dead."

Lysi and Grace tightened their hold on Amele's arms and pulled her back so the two men could pass with the long stretcher. A thin body lay zipped in the black bag.

Amele stared at the bag. Her eyes widened. Relief flooded her face. "That cannot be Mandisa." She broke loose and sprinted into the hut. Lysi and Grace followed.

In the half-light of the hut interior, Lysi saw a heavy-set woman seated on a chair squeezing and kneading her thick arms through the gauzy sleeves of a flowered print dress. A lanky young woman in green hospital scrubs stood behind the chair, arms wrapped around the older woman's hunched shoulders. Lysi guessed the medical practitioner to be Nambeko.

Amele rushed to the woman in the flower print dress. "Mandisa. Thank God you are safe."

The woman raised a tear-stained face to Amele. "Sipho is gone. I wish it was me and not my son."

"Sipho. How? Why?" Amele dropped to her knees beside Mandisa and tried to steady Mandisa's cold, shaking hands by cradling them in her own.

Nambeko wiped her eyes on the sleeve of her scrub smock and said, "We will not know any answers until after I have examined him."

"Qamata did this. I know," Mandisa said, her voice hoarse from crying. "Why did Sipho come to the old quack's hut? If he needed something, why didn't he come to you, Nambeko?" Mandisa dropped her chin to her chest. She seemed oblivious to the presence of Lysi and Grace who said nothing.

Lysi felt like an intruder on the women's grief. She understood the deep personal devastation of losing a loved one. Familiar sorrow over the sudden death of her younger sister stabbed at her chest. One moment the house door had closed on her vivacious sister laughing and calling, "Don't wait up for me." The next moment the door opened on two police officers saying, "We're so sorry for your loss."

Suddenly aware of the stifling heat and fetid stench of the hut, Lysi pulled her eyes away from Mandisa. Her unfocused gaze lit on an overturned table. A thick dirty-white mixture oozed from a bowl on the dirt floor next to its leg. Could someone have been angry enough to lift that heavy table and flip it on its side? And what's that whitish substance? Connections began to form in Lysi's mind. Could this be a homicide?

After a few moments, Lysi turned to Mandisa and asked in a soft voice, "Did you see Qamata attack your son?" The moment the question left her lips she wished she hadn't asked it. She should have waited for a better moment.

Mandisa raised her head. A surprised look in her eyes demanded to know the identity of her questioner.

"This is Lysi Weston," Amele said. "And Grace Wright. They are my American friends."

"We're so very sorry for your loss," Lysi said. The words sounded hollow but what more could she say?

As though she hadn't heard Lysi's words of condolence, Mandisa said, "No, I didn't see Qamata. I got here too late." She covered her face with her hands. "This is my fault. I should have come faster."

"Mama. Don't take blame. You could not have known." Nambeko pressed her cool, gaunt cheek against her mother's round hot one.

"Amele, you should call the police," Lysi whispered. "When a body's discovered with no witnesses to the death the authorities need to rule out homicide."

"No." Mandisa sprang to her feet. "In Ikhaya we take care of our own problems. No police. I will find out what Qamata did to Sipho. And when I do, I will humiliate that old devil. Expose him. Destroy him. See him thrown in prison." She clenched her fists. "I will see him dead."

"I'm sorry. I..." Lysi immediately regretted interfering and lowered her eyes. She gave herself a mental rebuke for ignoring her own advice to keep her nose out of this. What made her think a year of university criminal justice studies made her Sherlock Holmes?

"Where will they take Sipho?" Amele asked Nambeko.

"First to the Site B Community Health Center." Nambeko leaned over and helped Mandisa from the chair. "Then, after I examine him–the Amazizi Mortuary." She took her mother's arm. "Mother, you will ride with me."

"I know that health center," Amele said. "My car is at Themba. We'll pick it up and meet you there."

Amele parked in front of a makeshift corrugated steel shack painted white with big red letters that spelled out Serious Hair Saloon. The hair styling salon sat back from the street about a block from the Health Center. Lysi got out of the car and looked around. Informal settlement shacks constructed of scrap metal and boards lined the street. The area teemed with people—children shouting, running and playing; women doing laundry, sweeping and cooking; men leaning on fences, sitting on benches, talking and gawking. The scent of charred meat, detergent and cigarette smoke floated on the air.

Inside the center a strong antiseptic scent replaced the mélange of outside odors. A thin-faced, young black woman behind the information counter greeted the three women with a genuine smile. Lysi thought the woman looked out of place in her tailored pantsuit and stylish scarf. She belonged on the cover of Glamour Magazine with her shiny straightened hair, mascaraed eyelashes and bright-red painted lips. A nameplate with the name Lindle perched on the counter in front of her.

Amele glanced at the plate. "Molweni, Lindle. We seek Sipho Nala."

The young woman thumbed through some papers. "I'm sorry, we have no patient by that name registered." Lysi thought Lindle's English sounded very American. She had probably studied in the U.S.

Amele strained to keep her voice patient. "He must be here. The ambulance just brought him here. Please check again."

Lysi noticed Amele's mounting stress. She stepped forward and said in a voice just above a whisper, "Mr. Nala is not a patient. The ambulance brought him here for an autopsy."

"Oh." The young woman pulled a log from the file. Her glistening red fingernail moved down a long list of names.

"I am sure he would be listed under new arrivals," Amele said recovering her calm.

"Yes, yes. Here he is." Lindle slid her finger across the page to the location column. "Lab 2. Dr. Nala is preparing him for the autopsy." After a long pause, she looked up and asked in a tone mixed with curiosity and concern. "Is he…related to her?"

"Yes." Amele looked around. "Where is the Lab 2 waiting room?"

"Down that hall on the right." The dangly bracelets on Lindle's wrist clinked when she gestured in the direction of the hall.

"Enkosi." Amele thanked her and turned away before the woman could question her further.

When they arrived at the waiting room, they found Mandisa seated on a couch beneath a poster of Nelson Mandela. Nambeko, in clean green scrubs and a head covering, sat next to her. Both women hunched over a photo Nambeko held. Nambeko's head shot up when the three women approached.

Mandisa, still staring at the photo, nodded. "Of course I recognize this per—"

Nambeko squeezed her mother's thigh shushing her then reached under her smock and shoved the photo into her shirt pocket. "I will complete the examination this afternoon and will put a rush on the lab results. I will know by tomorrow. I can tell you the white froth on his mouth is Silene Capensis."

Lysi wanted to ask about Silene Capensis, but the pained shock on Mandisa's face jolted her into silence. She would store this question in her memory bank and return to it later.

"In the morning, the ambulance will take Sipho to Amazizi Mortuary," Nambeko said. "We will say goodbye to him there."

Mandisa swallowed hard, but her eyes remained dry.

"I have canceled all my appointments for today and tomorrow, but I have one patient I must see in the next hour." Nambeko stood and smoothed her smock. "I will take Mother home after my appointment."

"We could take her and stay with her until you arrive," Amele said.

Nambeko turned to Mandisa. "Mother?"

"Of course. Fine." Mandisa's words sounded detached as though she had buried her feelings and now was an impassive observer.

"Thank you, Mama Amele." Nambeko kissed her mother and left the room.

Lysi parked the VW close to the Themba Center fence. Mandisa led the three friends along a narrow, sandy path to a plywood lean-to attached to the back of the Themba Center. The door opened onto a sparsely furnished, studio-like room. Mandisa motioned the three women toward a sagging green sofa bed. She took a teakettle, filled it with water from an old porcelain bathroom sink, and set it on a double-burner hot plate. She pulled aside a print curtain covering two wide boards that served as cupboard shelves, took three cups, a bowl of teabags and a sugar jar, and set them on a low table near the sofa bed.

"Mandisa," Lysi said. "Please let us do that."

With a wave of her hand, Mandisa refused help.

Amele looked at Lysi. "Please sit. We are her guests."

"But—" Lysi didn't finish her thought. Her face reddened and she eased down on the sofa next to Grace. How many more faux pas would she make before she understood the South Africans? Lysi knew her habit of asking too many questions, involving herself in too many problems and offering too many suggestions tended to put people off. She had a genuine interest in helping people, but her efforts sometimes backfired. Would she ever manage to mind her own business?

The teakettle began a slow whistle on the red hot burner. Mandisa lifted the pot before the high-pitched sound shattered the somber silence in the room. All eyes followed Mandisa as she dropped teabags into the pot.

After a ragged breath, Amele turned to Lysi and Grace. "I will stay to help at the Themba Center tomorrow morning. You will take my car back to Cape Town. I will return by train tomorrow evening. Do you mind?"

"We stay with you," Grace said. She shot Lysi an eye question.

"Right, we stay with you," Lysi said.

"You two are crazy." Amele's words scolded but her smile conveyed gratitude.

"No, you're crazy if you think Lysi and I are going to drive that little bug of yours through the African jungle alone with all those lions and elephants and giant man-eating ants and—."

"There is no jungle here in Cape Town. No lions and elephants." Amele's eyes twinkled. "Maybe…a few giant man-eating ants but they have only a taste for Harlem sisters, so Lysi you need not fear."

"Very funny," Grace said.

Amele slapped Grace's shoulder. "And you need not fear. You are safer in a South African jungle than in the Harlem jungle. But I know how stubborn you can be. I will not try to dissuade you. You can stay at Sara's Bed and Breakfast down the street. I will arrange it."

With a sigh, Nambeko pulled the white fabric cover over her stepbrother's body that lay stretched out on the stainless steel autopsy table. Her shoulders drooped as she removed her latex gloves and cleansed her hands with antiseptic wipes. She hesitated before exiting the lab, hating to leave him alone in the cold stark autopsy room.

21

At her office desk, Nambeko's gaze lingered for several minutes on Sipho's graduation photograph. He hadn't changed much. She studied his youthful face and touched the long curled lashes that framed inquisitive eyes. As far back as she could remember Sipho's curiosity about everything made him an insatiable learner. With light fingers, she traced the smile lines on each side of his mouth, proof of his perpetual good humor. He laughed his way through life. She closed her eyes and thought about the joy his birth had brought Mandisa. Nambeko adored her younger brother. She never envied his blood ties to their mother because Mandisa showered both of them with love and attention. As children, Sipho and Nambeko were inseparable. They remained best friends into adulthood—until that day a year ago when Sipho changed. He turned secretive, withdrawn, depressed. Nambeko wondered if anyone else noticed how much he had changed.

Performing the autopsy had worn her out both physically and emotionally. When Sipho's body arrived at the hospital, the other staff doctor had recognized Nambeko's stepbrother and offered to perform the autopsy saying the emotional strain of working on a loved one would be too great. Nambeko refused the offer. She insisted she could do it. She said she needed to do it because it would bring closure. She didn't want an indifferent stranger touching him. The doctor consented but his face told her he had yielded against his better judgment.

Nambeko rubbed her eyes, blurry from working under the glare of fluorescent lights. She picked up an autopsy report form and studied it. She started to record the cause of death then paused. Two possible causes of death—one obvious but not the true cause, the other not so obvious but clearly what killed Sipho. She would record only one. The obvious one. The one that would lead immediately to that bumbling witch doctor Qamata. She would not even mention the other possible cause? Why complicate things? The Hippocratic oath cautioned her to abstain from doing harm. The uncertainty of two possible causes of death would do harm—harm to everyone. Harm to her mother. She leaned over the photo and kissed Sipho's high forehead. She would miss him.

Sara's Bed and Breakfast reminded Lysi of a hotel she'd built out of cereal boxes for a social studies project as a fourth grader. Constructed of tree trunks, corrugated iron and hardboard, it looked like two cardboard cartons stacked and glued together then painted with salmon-colored tempera. She trailed Amele and Grace through a purple gate and entered the inn under a pink sign. Twelve inch, hand-painted letters in rainbow colors spelled out Sara's B&B. An old camper shell dangling from the second story deck added to the piecemeal scene.

Sara, the plump-faced innkeeper greeted them at the door with a broad grin that made her eyes disappear into her round, dimpled cheeks. Her brown skin matched the traditional African turban she wore. The hem of her bright multi-colored cotton skirt brushed against the dusty yellow flip-flops she wore.

"Sara, please meet my two American friends, Grace and Lysi. They will stay here tonight. I will stay with Mandisa."

Sara curtsied to Lysi and Grace. "Welcome to Sara's B&B. I will make you very comfortable."

Amele backed out the door. "Then I leave them in your hands until tomorrow."

Sara led them through a living room up rickety stairs to a turquoise bedroom furnished in early goodwill—clean and functional. A double bed covered with a white chenille bedspread took up most of the room. A narrow full-length mirror hung on the bathroom door. Lysi could smell a delicate potpourri scent.

The view from a small window revealed a sea of corrugated iron roofs and clothes hanging from dozens of lines.

"The bathroom is through that door. I serve breakfast between 8:00 and 9:30." Sara measured Lysi and Grace with a critical eye. "Do not skip breakfast. You both look like you need to eat a lot more than you do." She chuckled and left the room.

The moment Sara closed the door, Lysi lanced the question she'd held off asking, "Didn't you find it a little strange the way Nambeko stashed that photo when we walked into the waiting room?"

Chapter 7

"Cream of wheat?" Lysi asked after her second spoonful of the hot mush innkeeper Sara had set out for breakfast.

"Nope... Pap." Grace spooned some peach slices on her bowl of pap. "It's a staple around here. Made of ground maize. It's good. Reminds me of my grandma's Mississippi grits."

"Really," Lysi said, her mind flashing on the stories Grace had told about eating through summers on the Mississippi Delta with her Grandmother Grace. She loved her grandmother's cooking—catfish, collards, cornbread and crawfish pie.

Sara shuffled in. The slap of her flip-flops sounded like an old-fashioned toy gun setting off a round of caps. She placed a bowl of yogurt on the oilcloth-covered table then wiped her hands on the bib of her African print apron. "Try this with the peaches. A Sara's B & B specialty. Very good for you."

Lysi nodded at Sara then filled a small bowl with yogurt, spooned on some peaches and tasted it. "Delicious."

"Now you will have a slice of umbhako." Sara cut two thick slices from a round loaf and set them on the table. "Xhosa corn bread. Try some. It will make you fat like me." Sara patted her big, round belly and sat down at the table with Lysi and Grace.

Lysi held up her hand and opened her mouth to protest that she was stuffed.

"You do not like umbhako?" Sara looked incredulous.

"No, no. That's not it. I just—" Lysi didn't want to risk offending another person so she reached for a slice.

"Butter or jam?"

"Jam," Lysi said with resignation.

"Now, what would you like to know about Ikhaya?" Sara folded her arms and leaned back in the chair.

Lysi couldn't pass up the invitation to ask questions about the murder victim. "Did you know Sipho well?"

"That boy was like my own son." Sara's lips broadened into a smile. "He and Thabo with little Lindani used to sit right there and snack on my homemade cookies." She pointed to a braided rug in front of the sink.

"Thabo. The ambulance driver?" Lysi remembered hearing Nambeko shout his name from inside Qamata's hut.

Sara nodded. "Seemed like all the kids in the township used to show up here for snacks. Even Uuka and his two brothers came for awhile." Sara took a big bite of umbhako and shook her head while chewing.

"Uuka?" Lysi noticed Sara specifically named Uuka and wondered why.

"You have not yet heard about Uuka?" Sara dabbed her mouth with a paper napkin. "I am surprised Amele has not mentioned Uuka to you. He and his brothers have vandalized her car more than once while she volunteered at the Themba Center."

Lysi cast a questioning glance at Grace. Strange Amele hadn't said anything about repeated vandalism of her car. Maybe she didn't want to risk telling them for fear they wouldn't come to Ikhaya to meet Mandisa.

24

"Mean kids those Dlomo boys. Uuka was the worst." Sara spread more butter on her umbhako. "Not surprising. Those poor boys had to fend for themselves most of their lives. Uuka's mother gave birth to him when she had just turned fourteen. It upset Uuka's grandmother so much she turned both mother and baby out into the street."

"How could she do such a thing to her own daughter—and a baby?" Lysi said, her tone irate.

"They had to rely on charity to survive. So sad." Sara's eyes looked thoughtful. "During most of their childhoods, Uuka and his brothers ran the streets begging."

"What about Child Protective Services?" Lysi asked.

"Nothing could keep the boys from the streets. I tried but they caused me so much trouble. They picked and picked at Sipho and Lindani. This angered Thabo and he used to stop them with his fists. I could not have fighting in my home. I had to give up on the Dlomo boys."

"What happened to them?" Lysi asked.

"When Uuka's mother died—I guess he was about fifteen or sixteen—he went wild. He and his brothers started stealing, intimidating, beating and extorting money whenever they could. Even now everyone's afraid to report them to the police. Thabo is the only person who stands up to them."

Sara cupped her chin in her hand and gazed into space. "I could never figure out how four siblings could be so different."

"Four?" Lysi thought she'd missed something. "Didn't you say Uuka had only two brothers?"

"And one sister. Nambeko."

Outside the inn, Lysi turned a serious face to Grace and broached the subject of the hidden photo. "About that picture Nambeko shoved into her pocket. Didn't that seem a little strange to you?"

"Maybe a little," Grace said. "But why do you care?"

"It seemed odd, that's all," Lysi said as they walked slowly toward the Themba Center. "Like there's something she didn't want us to know."

"Lysi, there's nothing we *need* to know. We're on vacation, remember?"

"And another thing," Lysi said, ignoring Grace's comment. "What is Silene Capensis?"

A rubber ball bounced out into the road. Grace picked it up and tossed it back to a little girl standing in a doorway. The girl caught it and rewarded Grace with a squeal of delight and a big toothy grin. The girl's mother looked up from the clothes she was washing in a tub outside the door and managed a weary smile.

"I guess you didn't learn anything from your college African Studies courses," Grace said slapping the dust off her hands. "It's a root witch doctors use to communicate with ancestors through dreams. Too much of it can cause serious vomiting."

"Right." Lysi remembered African Anthropology 1A. South African witch doctors use herbal purgatives to cleanse the body of physical and mental ailments. What kind of ailment afflicted Sipho?

Grace snapped her fingers and broke into Lysi's thoughts. "Earth to Lysi. Where are you? Oh right, you're on vacation."

"Grace." Lysi bit into her bottom lip. "I think—"

"Why do I get the feeling I won't like what you're about to say, Lysi?"

"I'm going back to that hut this morning and have a quick look before we go to the mortuary." Lysi's words tumbled from her mouth. "I've got a gut feeling there's a connection between the photo and the murder."

Grace rolled her eyes and blew air through her lips. "Oh please. You don't even know what you're looking for. Besides, we'll be late for the memorial."

"Don't get your knickers in a knot, Grace. As you always say." Lysi checked her watch. "We've got plenty of time. I'm just going to take a quick peek."

"A quick peek?" Grace shook her head. "Listen, girl. You've got to stop playing detective. Your private dick uncle sure planted those investigation seeds deep in your hippocampus. Why'd you even bother changing your major from police science to education?"

Lysi didn't answer. She'd been around that block with Grace before. No time to belabor it today.

Grace asked in an offhand tone, "What about your Aussie sheep farmer cop?"

Lysi felt a hot flush start at her neckline and swirl around in her cheeks. "*Detective* Maynard Christie is a grazier, and this has nothing to do with him. He doesn't even arrive until tomorrow."

"Nothing to do with him now, but I'll bet he's going to find himself in this mess up to his tight little buns if you keep nosing around."

"Grace, you don't have to come." Lysi started walking towards the trail to Qamata's hut.

"Yeah. Like that's going to happen." Grace trotted up and marched along side Lysi. "You think I'll just stay here and let you go into the jungle alone and visit some witch doctor who'll probably turn you into a toadstool and toss you into his brew."

"Don't be ridiculous. You heard Amele. Harlem's ten times more dangerous than South Africa. And witch doctors are nothing more than herb-pushing con men." Lysi increased her gait and moved ahead of Grace.

Grace jutted her lower jaw and glared at Lysi. "Grrr! I said I'm going with you."

A tinge of guilt swept through Lysi. Maybe she shouldn't drag Grace back to that hut. Maybe she should drop the whole idea. Maybe she shouldn't stick her nose into someone else's problem, even a murder.

She yanked Grace's arm. "Okay, come. But keep up."

The twenty-minute walk along the path to Qamata's hut left Lysi and Grace's sandals and pant legs coated with a powdery tan dust. They paused on the mossy ground under a huge yellowwood tree and stomped their feet to remove the dust. Lysi swiped at her Chloe sandals with a tissue. "After this, it's Birkenstocks for me."

Grace said, "Shhh. Did you hear that?"

"What?"

"I don't know." Grace's eyes shifted left and right. "It sounded like a twig snapped or something?"

"It's your imagination. I didn't hear anything." Lysi gave Grace's arm a little punch. "Come on, Big Bad Ghetto Girl."

Lysi pixie-stepped toward the hut. She noticed its door ajar and flashed Grace a mischievous grin. She combined a loud knock with a little push and it swung open. She wiggled her eyebrows at Grace. "The door's open. We may as well take a look inside."

"Real cute," Grace said.

Inside the hut everything was as it had been before. They smelled the same stench of dried rodents and moldy animal pelts. They saw the same table and spilled gunk. They heard the same soft clicking of strings of weightless animal bones stirred by the light breeze that whisked through the open door.

Grace covered her nose. "This place wreaks worse than a Mississippi privy."

"Try breathing through your mouth, you won't smell it."

"I don't want to taste it either." Grace made a gagging sound.

Lysi's gaze roamed the hut. "Clearly, Qamata doesn't live here—no bed, no dishes, no food, nothing that says home."

She edged along the shelves.

"What are you looking for, Lysi?"

"I don't know."

Lysi scrutinized the ground around the table. She started to examine the bowl when a hoarse intake of breath pulled her eyes to the door.

Lysi heard Grace gasp, or maybe it was her own gasp she heard.

A short stick of a man stood frozen in the doorway. His feathered headdress sitting atop heavily greased bright red hair, made him look like a hat rack in a women's expensive but tasteless chapeau salon. The type of shop that catered to the nouveau riche. He carried a bag bulging with whatever witch doctors carry these days. He lifted his animal skin cloak and stepped over the raised threshold. His slitted eyes glued to Lysi, he said something in Xhosa she didn't understand. Taking another step forward he spoke in broken English, "Who are you? What are you doing in here?"

Lysi's heart pounded in her throat. Must be Qamata.

Qamata flailed his arms and tried to look intimidating. Instead, he looked constipated. "Get out. Get out before I—"

A loud guffaw from Grace jolted Lysi and drew a venomous scowl from Qamata. She stepped from behind Lysi, rose to her full height and positioned herself about twelve inches from the witch doctor. At that well-practiced vantage point, she looked down on him from over a foot above. "Well now. What have we here bro? You in a heavy metal band or something?"

Qamata, forced to tilt his head back in an undignified position to meet Grace's amused eyes said, "How did you get in here?"

"The door was open," Lysi said. "We thought we found a store. You don't carry Pepsi and chips, do you?"

Qamata rocked back on his heels and looked like he'd just encountered two escapees from the Maximum Security Unit of the local psychiatric hospital.

He didn't speak but flicked beady eyes first to Lysi then Grace then back to Lysi. He backed toward the door in slow motion. When he reached the threshold he spun around like a whirligig and quick-stepped up the path, his feathers fluttering in the breeze. Lysi and Grace watched until he disappeared then high fived each other.

"He didn't even take the time to pull out his fancy poison dart blowgun," Grace said.

"You're thinking of the Pygmies in the Congo," Lysi said. "Remember African Anthropology 1A."

"I thought he *was* a Pygmy." Grace's raucous laugh seemed to bounce around the hut.

"Next to you, I think *he* thought he was a Pygmy. The poor guy looked terrified like he'd encountered a giant Watusi."

Lysi pointed to the upper row of cluttered shelves that lined the room. "How about checking out those top shelves, Watusi princess."

"Sure. I'm glad my statuesque height is good for something besides noble elegance and queenly beauty."

Lysi shook her head. "Please, not another ode to your ego." She did admire the dark beauty Grace had inherited from her tall, firm-bodied African American father and curvaceous, raven-haired Puerto Rican mother. Lysi almost matched Grace in height, but her fair skin and perennially rosy cheeks contrasted sharply with Grace's dark honey complexion.

Lysi stooped to examine the area around the table and the bowl of viscous white goop. Near the bowl a tiny red stone caught her eye. She pulled an emery board from her purse and started digging the sand out around the stone. The emery board caught on the broken link of a silver bracelet decorated with multi-colored ceramic beads. She took a tissue, picked up the bracelet and showed it to Grace.

Grace dipped her chin and blinked twice. "Now, will you look at that?"

Lysi wrapped the bracelet in the tissue and placed it in her pocket. Could this belong to Sipho's killer?

Chapter 8

Lysi and Grace stood in the hot sun outside the Amazizi Mortuary next to a small garden of red fynbos and waited for Amele to come out. Lysi raised a damp face to catch the whisper of breeze that seemed to come from nowhere and disappear in an instant. She glanced at the mortuary door for the hundredth time and willed Amele to appear. What could she be doing that was taking so long?

The mortuary door whipped open and a little girl Lysi recognized from the Themba Center skipped up and skidded to a stop less than two feet from Lysi. "Do you remember me? I am Saba. I miss Sipho."

Lysi stooped and took Saba's hands in hers. "Of course I remember you. I didn't know Sipho, but everyone says he really loved the Themba children."

"He did," Saba said in the voice of authority. "But not everyone liked Sipho."

Lysi's brain snapped to attention and a concerned frown replaced her smile. "Not everyone liked Sipho?"

Saba smoothed her fluffy skirt and thrust out a lower lip. "No. Once someone even hit him. A big man. Very strong."

"You saw someone hit Sipho?"

Saba shifted her weight from one foot to the other dancing to the private little rhythm all kids carry around in their heads. "No. Not me. You know my brother, Philani? He did. But do not tell him I told you."

"Oh no. Of course I won't tell him." She crossed her heart. "Did Philani tell you who—"

"Saba! Time to go." At the sound of her mother's tired call, Saba scampered off, her yellow polyester skirt flying in her own light breeze. Lysi, eyes glued to Saba and her mother, mumbled the rest of the question, "—hit Sipho?"

Amele said goodbye to Mandisa and Nambeko under the mortuary sign then joined Lysi and Grace. "We can go now. Nambeko will watch over her mother. I will check on her next week." Amele inhaled and bit her lip. "Sipho's remains will rest in the cemetery, his grave covered with thorn tree branches in the Xhosa tradition."

Lysi's brow creased in question. "The Xhosa tradition?"

"Yes, many Ikhaya burials combine both Christian and Xhosa rituals. The Xhosa place thorn tree branches on a new grave to protect the deceased's spirit from sorcerers who might dig up his body and change it into an Evil Familiar."

"Evil Familiar?" Lysi's face revealed her intense fascination about this aspect of the Xhosa culture. Nothing about this had come up in African Anthropology 1A.

"An Evil familiar is a resurrected dead body that a witch doctor can use to cause misfortune and death." Amele shook her head. "Enough of this superstitious talk. The point is we can go now."

Grace put her arm around Amele's shoulders. "Come on, honey. You've been a great support to Mandisa. It's time you got a little respite." Grace licked her lips. "How about a swig of sorghum suds?" She pointed to a bar a few doors down the street. "Let's hit that shebeen before heading home?"

Inside the cream colored corrugated-steel shebeen the walls gleamed bright red under a bare incandescent bulb. Soccer posters and beer ads provided relief from the red glare. The musky scent of stale beer left no doubt as to the shebeen's specialty.

Lysi and Grace dropped onto folding chairs at a table covered by shiny red oilcloth, and decorated with hand-made aluminum daisies in old coca cola can vases. Amele picked up three mugs of beer at the counter and set them on the table.

Lysi took a big gulp of the pinkish-brown liquid then swallowed fast. With great effort, she stifled a cough and managed not to scrunch up her face. "That has a very unusual taste."

Grace quaffed down half the glass. "The sour taste of sorghum beer takes a lot of getting used to. A health nut like you should love it though. It's actually good for you. Loaded with protein."

Amele looked concerned. "Would you prefer an American beer?"

"No, no. I can drink American beer at home. I travel for new experiences," Lysi said and she meant it.

Grace slapped Lysi on the shoulder. "That's my girl. Drink up and we'll order another round."

Lysi scowled then turned to Amele. "How'd Luvo handle our little overnight?"

"Not very well. He considers Ikhaya unsafe for men and terrifying for women. He grumbled and made me promise to stay in after sunset. Then he threatened to quit cooking for us if I did not get home early today."

Grace raised her glass. "To Luvo. God love him. I want a man just like him. He's a total fox. He worships you. And he cooks." She turned hopeful eyes to Amele. "Does he have a twin brother somewhere?"

This time, Lysi took a much more cautious sip of beer and swallowed with care. "Amele, did Nambeko show you a photo?"

"A photo? No. Why?"

"Well when we walked into the Lab 2 waiting room, she and Mandisa were looking at a photo. When Nambeko saw us, she took it out of Mandisa's hand and shoved it in a pocket."

"To tell the truth, Lysi, I was so worried about Mandisa that I did not notice a photo. Why do you ask?"

"I have a nagging feeling it relates to Sipho's death. And another thing, Grace and I found a bracelet in—" At the sight of Nambeko framed by the door, Lysi stopped short. This was not the right time to bring up the topic of homicide. She'd save questions about the photo, the bracelet and the person Philani saw strike Sipho. What Nambeko needed now was sympathetic support.

Nambeko didn't enter immediately. She paused to speak to a man whose face Lysi couldn't see. Nambeko's voice carried into the Shebeen. "What are you doing here, Paki? Leave. Now." The man said something Lysi didn't hear then turned and seemed to fade away. Nambeko stared after him for a few seconds, her face irate.

Nambeko pulled a chair from another table and crowded next to Amele. She still smelled of hospital antiseptic. Nambeko turned to the bartender and pointed at Grace's glass. "One of those."

Amele smoothed a bit of hair back from her goddaughter's face. "How is Mandisa?"

"She is good. She wanted to go back to Themba. A close friend will drive her."

More people began to dribble into the shebeen. Lysi recognized several from the funeral—two young women in colorful native dresses with matching headdresses who had led songs in Xhosa, several twenty-something men and women red-eyed from crying and two older couples who had sat near the coffin. Lysi thought they might be Sipho's grandparents.

As soon as the young server placed the sorghum beer in front of Nambeko, she opened her woven bag and reached for her coin purse. Lysi glanced into the open bag and her eyes widened. Right next to the wallet she saw a photograph of a young man with fawn eyes, a firm jaw and an engaging smile. Could it be the photo Nambeko stashed in her pocket in the waiting room? Dare she ask the name of the man in the photo? No. This is not the right time.

Nambeko took a sip of sorghum beer then held the cold glass against her cheek and stared into some empty realm. "I did the autopsy on Sipho myself."

Amele patted Nambeko's shoulder. "It must have been so difficult for you. I am so glad it is over. I wish it would all end now."

Lysi turned to Nambeko. "You know your mother will not rest until she knows what happened to Sipho. Were you able to determine the cause of death?"

"I am almost certain it was an overdose of Silene Capensis. Proof Qamata murdered my brother."

Lysi started to say something when a cold shiver snaked down the back of her neck. She lifted her eyes from the beer and caught a tall man staring at her. She had seen him somewhere before but couldn't quite place where. Her mind raced through the events of the last couple of days trying to connect the man to one of them. The fog began to lift. Qamata's hut. Sipho's body. The ambulance. The tall attendant.

He didn't avert his eyes when she looked up but openly glared with the same hard-as-steel expression Lysi remembered at the hut. The set of his jaw spoke of a dangerous man not to be crossed.

His short partner ambled up to him, flashed a few rand and slapped the big attendant on the back. "What will you have?"

His eyes still lasered on Lysi, the attendant said, "A Castle."

Lysi leaned towards Nambeko. "That tall man. By the bar. Who is he?"

Nambeko switched her eyes to the bar. "Thabo Deyi. He is an ambulance attendant."

Thabo, Lysi thought. The person Sara, the innkeeper, mentioned.

Amele nodded. "I remember him. He and his friend came to Qamata's hut to pick up Sipho's body. Not exactly Mr. Congeniality."

Nambeko studied Thabo for a few seconds. "Thabo is a good worker. Very intelligent. He could succeed in university. On the other hand, he is impulsive. He has not learned to harness his temper. He resents authority—especially in women."

"He keeps staring at me. Why would he do that?" Lysi said.

"Probably because you are the only white woman here. Look around," Nambeko said.

Lysi surveyed the shebeen patrons. Couples at tables. Men at the bar. Women leaning against the walls. All shades of brown.

Amele picked up her cell phone and checked a new text message. "Luvo." She patted Nambeko's hand. "We have to go. You know Luvo. He will start to pace."

Nambeko squeezed Amele's arm. "Of course, Mama Amele. I understand. Thank you for your help."

The three women stood. As they walked to the door, Lysi still felt the stabbing stare. She turned and locked eyes with Thabo. She pulled her eyes away. Of course, he would stare at her because of her skin color. Why else?

Chapter 9

Lysi zigzagged around the throng of harried people darting in all directions through the ultra modern glass and tile Cape Town International Airport. She glanced at shop windows displaying everything from designer originals to African specialties as she followed the arrows to Maynard Christie's arrival gate. The plane was on time. Lysi was early. She'd planned it that way. She needed to calm the butterflies fluttering in her stomach.

In the ladies lounge she combed her hair and fussed with the makeup Grace had insisted she wear—mascara, blush, eye and lip liner. She looked good, but the taut face in the mirror reflected back her anxious mood. A year had flown by since that last spectacular night with Maynard in Sydney. The midnight stroll along the quay, the dark little dance floor in the half-empty bar where they slow-danced past closing time, the lingering goodnight at her hotel door. What would it be like to see him again? Would he feel the same way about her? How would she feel about him now that her Montana romance had crashed?

Lysi checked her watch for the tenth time in ten minutes. Fifteen minutes to touch down. She smoothed her fuchsia-colored silk blouse over her tailored white summer wool pants, swallowed from her water bottle, and hurried to the gate. Weary passengers trudged from the air bridge into the waiting area, eyes searching. Lysi scanned the mélange of multi-racial faces. When she spotted his tall, lanky figure sauntering behind a short Indian woman in an orange and red sari, her heart dropped to her stomach. He hadn't changed.

A light colored shirt hugged his broad chest and slim waist. The shirt's open collar and rolled up sleeves revealed the permanent ruddy tan of his skin. His pants slung low on his narrow hips. Lysi's pulse rate increased as she watched him. He removed an Australian bush hat, brushed his unruly brown hair off his forehead and looked around. When he recognized her, he grinned. She had an urge to run to him, throw her arms around him. Instead she smiled and waited until he approached her then took his hand in both of hers. "Maynard, it's great to see you."

Was that disappointment she saw in his eyes? She gave herself a mental punch. How stupid was that? "Did you have a good trip?" she said, her voice way too formal. Oh, God. Why don't I just shut up?

A man in a plaid sport coat sprinted up to a woman who stood a few feet away. He dropped his briefcase, encircled the woman in his arms, and planted a long kiss on her lips.

Maynard glanced at the couple then back at Lysi. "Let's try this again."

He strolled back to the gate, flashed a warm smile, sprinted on long legs over to her and replayed the scene just acted out by the couple next to them.

Lysi caught her breath. Her heart hammered in her chest. Her knees almost buckled. She swallowed and tried to stabilize her rampant emotions.

Maynard, his arms still wrapped snugly around her, looked down into her face. "Now, isn't that better?"

Lysi sucked air. He smelled so...so... "Uh huh."

Maynard picked up his bag, took her hand and they exited through the baggage section to the sidewalk just as Luvo on his third round of the airport road swerved to the curb. Maynard opened the passenger door and extended his hand. "Maynard Christie."

"Luvo Butshingi. Good to meet you." He jumped from the car, took Maynard's carryall and shoved it into the boot.

Luvo grinned when Lysi got into the back seat, her face still flushed. He put his arm on the back of the seat and turned to Maynard who'd settled in next to her. "It looks like she is happy to see you."

Lysi squirmed and her face burned. Maynard laughed. "I hope so."

On the way home, Luvo asked endless questions about Australia, sheep stations and the Outback. Maynard answered without taking his eyes off Lysi. She was acutely aware of his nearness. When he whispered in her ear that he'd missed her, she felt lightheaded and had to take a sharp breath to get enough oxygen. Everything about Maynard sent surges of emotion ricocheting through her body—his fingers stroking her hand, his hard muscular thigh against her leg, his light minty breath on her cheek. His earthy masculine scent ignited her senses. She struggled to recover her equilibrium. They turned onto Rugby Road and Lysi had to steady her out-of-control sensations before they reached the house. She pulled her hand from Maynard's, moved to the opposite window and peered out as though some exciting event had occurred. "Well, there's the house."

"Right," Maynard said.

Lysi felt like slapping herself. Nothing like stating the obvious. I can't wait to hear what inane thing my undisciplined mouth will blather next.

Luvo pulled to the curb in front of his garage and Lysi bounded out of the car, relieved to have escaped Maynard's mesmerism. She started around to the trunk. "I'll help with the luggage."

Maynard unfolded from the backseat. "I only have one small piece."

"Oh." Lysi couldn't hide the frustration she felt at her inability to relax with Maynard. She hoped he hadn't notice, but she knew he did.

Luvo studied Maynard then Lysi, a grin crinkling the corners of his eyes. After a few seconds of uncomfortable silence, Luvo said, "A…You must be very hungry. These days food is scarce on air flights. While you freshen up, I will get the wood started for the Braai."

Lysi's eyes widened in question.

Maynard put his arm around her, quick starting her pulse again. "Braai means cook on the barbie or as you Americans call it—barbecue." He drew her a bit closer and looked into her eyes. "You haven't forgotten our braais at the sheep station, have you?"

A quick glance at Luvo told Lysi he hadn't missed the little amorous scene.

"A…a…Yes, yes. Barbecue." Luvo said. "That is correct." He averted his eyes and cleared his throat. "You seem to know a bit about the Braai, Maynard."

"My son in Namibia introduced me to the African version of Australia's national pastime." Maynard pulled his jacket out of the backseat.

"I hear the braai is very popular in Australia." Luvo opened the boot and got the carryall. "Here in South Africa it's so popular we even have Braai Day on September 24th which happens to be South Africa's National Heritage Day—a celebration of our countries diverse population."

Lysi looked around for Amele's car. "Where are Amele and Grace?"

A shadow clouded Luvo's face. "They have gone again to Ikhaya to stay with Mandisa Nala."

Lysi hid a surge of disappointment that Amele wasn't here to greet Maynard. "Will they be back tonight?"

"I cannot say for sure. Mandisa's daughter, Nambeko, has to work at the health center tonight and is afraid to leave Mandisa alone." Luvo closed the trunk and picked up the carryall. "Nambeko worships her mother—but I think she may worship success more. All her life she has struggled to prove herself number one in everything she attempted."

"She certainly seems like an excellent physician," Lysi said.

"She is. She is. I just think she places too much importance on success." Luvo flashed a forced smile. "Please forget what I said. Amele would not agree with me." Luvo locked the car and led the way up the steps to the living room.

"Forgotten." Lysi didn't question further. "Shall I show Maynard to the guest room?"

"Please," Luvo said. "I will go to the garden and the braai."

Lysi opened the door to the guest room but didn't follow Maynard inside. She stood on the threshold keeping a safe distance from him. She wanted to brief him on Sipho's death; that required a clear head.

"A young man in Ikhaya died. His mother thinks a witch doctor killed him because a little boy discovered the body in Qamata's hut. Qamata is the witch doctor. Ikhayan's think he can cast spells. I'm not sure, I think—"

Maynard stiffened. "Lysi, wait. *You're* not sure? What do *you* have to do with witch doctors, spells, murder? "

"Nothing. I just—"

"I hope you're not involving yourself in another homocide." After a deep sigh, Maynard shook his head. "And you don't need a witch doctor. Murder casts a spell on you."

Lysi figured Maynard still smarted from her poking around in his Sydney homicide case when she visited Australia, even though she did lead him to the killer. She decided not to tell him about her trip to Qamata's hut or her other little investigation activities. Why bother him with trivialities.

"No," she assured him. "I'm not getting involved. I just want to tell you about it and maybe you might share some of your expertise."

"Don't try to involve me either." Maynard sounded adamant and frustrated at the same time. "You know I'm off duty. You know I'm out of my jurisdiction. You know I didn't come over 1200 kilometers to stick my nose into a murder case." He walked to the door, pulled her inside and tipped up her chin with two fingers. "You must know I came just to see you."

Lysi sighed and lowered her eyes. "I won't involve you."

"Thank you."

His kiss had made her forget the homicide until he said, "Here's my expertise. Tell the kid's mother to report her suspicions to the police."

"Well that's just it. His mother—"

"Lysi!"

"Won't you at least listen to me?" She saw a vein throbbing in his temple.

He pressed his thumb and finger to his eyelids. "All right. I'll listen, but that's all."

He put his carryall down and sat on the bed. Lysi sat next to him. Whoops. Lysi's brain sent out a warning signal. Dangerous territory. Stay on topic. With superhuman effort she focused on the murder in Ikhaya not the magnetic male sitting too close to her.

"The mother claims the Ikhayans never involve the police. They handle their own problems."

Lysi reached into her purse and pulled out the multi-colored stone bracelet. "I found this half buried in the dust when Grace and I checked out Qamata's hut." As soon as the words left her mouth she knew she'd made her first mistake. So much for not telling him about going to Qamata's hut.

Maynard's mouth dropped open. "You what? Cri-key! Trespassing. Unauthorized intrusion on a crime scene. Tampering with evidence. I'm surprised you're not in jail."

"There's no cordoned off crime scene. I told you, the police are not involved."

Maynard threw up his hands in exasperation.

Lysi thrust the bracelet into his open palm. "Do you know what this is?"

Another frustrated sigh. Maynard turned the bracelet over in his palms. "A bunch of colored rocks." Then his eyes widened in obvious recognition.

"That's right, Detective. A Rainbow Pride bracelet. The kind that originated in San Francisco in memory of the '76 Gay Pride Parade. The symbol of the Gay Rights Movement."

"All right, so I recognize it. So what?" Maynard stood. He unzipped his carryall, took out a tweed sports jacket and draped it on a hanger.

"So, most Ikhayans don't accept homosexuals." Lysi took the hanger from him, straightened the jacket and hung it in the closet. "Many think witchcraft spells cause homosexuality. They blame homosexuals for AIDS."

Lysi thought about the International Conference on Sexual Harassment of Homosexuals she'd attended in Sydney and wondered why Maynard didn't show more sympathy for her crusade to stop all harassment of both men and women.

She looked hard at Maynard. "In Ikhaya , extremists murder homosexuals."

Just as Lysi and Maynard stepped onto the deck, Luvo flipped a coiled foot-long boerewors on the braai and the sausage sizzled. The flames sparked and the scent of coriander and nutmeg mingled with the garlicky scent of herbal pot bread. Lysi inhaled. "That smells like ambrosia of the gods."

Luvo chuckled. "Farmer's sausage is a South African braai tradition." He cut a small piece off the cooked end of the sausage. "Here, a taste for you."

The spicy meat stimulated Lysi's taste buds and her stomach growled. She realized she hadn't eaten since morning. At least her hormones had relaxed enough so she could eat while still near Maynard

"Please help yourself to a beer and take a seat at the table. The 'boerie' will finish cooking in about ten more minutes."

Maynard opened a beer, took a big swig, and slid into a chair next to Lysi. He stretched a long arm across the back of Lysi's chair, cast her a resigned glance, and turned to Luvo. "Lysi tells me Amele volunteers in a preschool in Ikhaya Township. My son volunteers in a school in Namibia. I'd be very interested in seeing your wife's school."

Chapter 10

Lysi slid from the car almost before Luvo stopped in front of the Themba preschool. Maynard followed close behind. She yanked the bell pull cord then opened the door. Questions about the murder had bounced around in her brain throughout the night. She needed answers if she expected any help from Maynard, and she had a good idea where to find those answers.

The chatter of high-pitched voices drew Lysi into a small room where children, seated in a circle, munched crackers. Grace had her back to the door, a child on her lap, his head draped over her shoulder. He yanked a strand of Grace's hair and pointed a pudgy finger toward the door. "Mama!"

Grace glanced over her shoulder. "Hey, Lys." Her brown eyes snapped when she spotted Maynard. "Well look who's here." She set the child on the circle, sashayed over to Maynard, gave him a warm hug then stepped back and fanned her face with her hand. "Whew." She fluttered thick doe-like lashes at him and said to Lysi, "Hey girl, this man is so…a…fit."

Maynard's annoying broad beam told Lysi how much he enjoyed Grace fawning over him. She tried not to react, but sometimes Grace overstepped her boundaries.

"Chill, Grace," Lysi said.

Grace fanned her face again. "I'll try, but I got to tell you, it won't be easy."

Amele entered through a door in the rear of the room carrying a tray of open half pint milk cartons. She set the tray on the rug in the middle of the circle and instructed a little girl to distribute one carton to each child. Then she stood and wiped her hands on her apron. "Lysi, so nice to see you here. And this must be your Australian."

"Amele Butshingi meet Maynard Christie, my friend from Australia."

Amele looked Maynard up and down, bobbed her eyebrows and smiled. "Friend? Umm, humm. You better rethink that, Sister."

Lysi's eyes widened at Amele's unexpected comment. "How will I survive a vacation with the two of you needling me?"

Maynard flashed an eyebrow-wriggling grin. "I can't speak for you, but I'm enjoying this vacation more every minute." He shook hands with Amele.

Luvo who had just come in from locking up the car stifled a laugh and changed the subject. "Maynard's son volunteers in a Namibian village school. He has an interest in seeing how South African township schools compare with those in Namibia and in the Australian Outback villages. Would Mandisa mind if I took him for a brief tour of the school while the children finish their snacks?" He looked around. "Where is Mandisa?"

"She will return shortly," Amele said. "She needed to buy some crackers and apples."

Luvo glanced at Lysi. "I understand you wish to show Maynard Qamata's hut as well."

Before Lysi could answer, Grace exploded in laughter. "Some vacation, eh Detective Christie? Don't think for a minute Lysi's going to let you get away with just visiting the old boy's hut."

Dark eyes followed Luvo, Lysi and Maynard as they strolled down the dusty street toward Qamata's hut. Young men lounged on boxes and leaned on fence posts muttering to each other, curious women raised their heads from laundry tubs and clotheslines. A gaggle of chattering children trailed behind the trio. A girl, no more than six or seven, grabbed Lysi's hand and skipped along beside her. Lysi swung her hand back and forth and the two of them did a giggle duet for a couple of blocks. Then the girl waved goodbye and galloped off.

When they drew near Qamata's hut, Lysi told Maynard about Mandisa's long time disdain for the witch doctor. "She's never forgiven him for frightening her daughter, Nambeko."

"It is a pity so many Ikhayans still believe witch doctors have supernatural powers," Luvo said. "I think it is because many of the people here are poorly educated."

At the hut, Maynard took a pen and small notepad from his pocket. He told Lysi and Luvo to wait by the large tree and not to follow him to the hut because he wanted to preserve what was left of the already-contaminated crime scene. "I need to get the general layout of the site," he said. Lysi and Luvo watched Maynard's methodical examination of the scene. Before entering the hut, Maynard circled its exterior. At each step he studied the ground. He paused behind the hut to examine a grassy area then continued around to the front of the hut picking up objects and dropping them into his handkerchief. Maynard stopped just outside the hut door and continued his systematic inspection of the crime scene before entering. "The point of entry and of exit are the same," he said. "Only one way in and one way out. The victim may have seen his killer enter. He may have known him."

Maynard's eyes slid over the walls, corners and ceiling of the hut. He paused now and then, focusing on something then scribbling on his notepad. Once inside the hovel, Maynard scrutinized every bottle, jar and basket. He surveyed the animal skins hanging from the ceiling. He stooped, pointed to a section of the dirt floor and raised his head to Lysi and Luvo who now stood just outside the door. "This is where they found the body?"

"I don't know," Lysi said. "Grace and I waited outside while the ambulance attendants removed him."

Maynard continued to study the floor near the table. "The table had toppled. Maybe due to a struggle. Someone set it back up."

He squatted and sifted the dirt on the floor like a farmer testing the richness of the soil. He held back a sneeze in the dry dusty air and wiped sweat from his forehead. Holding his hand out to Lysi he said, "Got a tissue?"

When Lysi stepped inside and handed him a pocket-sized Kleenex packet, he scooped up a small amount of light colored soil and placed it on a tissue. "See the difference between this soil and the surrounding soil?"

Lysi squinted at the sample. "It looks more yellowish."

"That soil is not typical of the soil in this area," Luvo said. "In fact, I have never seen soil that color."

Maynard twisted the tissue around the sample and handed it to Lysi. He picked up a small white cap and studied it. "See the yellow stain on this lid."

Lysi nodded.

Maynard wrapped the lid in another tissue then asked, "Where did you find the bracelet?"

"There, next to the table leg."

Maynard scratched the soil near the table leg and found the bracelet latch—broken. "Someone ripped this off the victim's wrist."

"Very interesting," Luvo said from outside the open door observing Maynard with curious eyes. "I've never watched the investigative process. I see why it is so important to preserve the crime scene."

Maynard scanned the room once more. "It smells like hell in here." He stepped out over the raised threshold and blew out a lung full of air. "Too many footprints. Too many changes to the original scene. Too little to go on."

When they returned to Themba, Luvo told Maynard he wanted to show him some of the sites around Cape Town. Lysi decided to stay and help at the preschool then ride home with Amele and Grace.

After the last parent picked up her child, Mandisa locked the preschool and led the three women into the kitchen of her lean-to. Grace and Lysi sat on a bench on one side of a small table and Amele sat on a chair on the other side. They waited in silence while Mandisa prepared tea.

Over hot rooibos, Lysi asked the question she'd wanted to ask since little Saba had told her someone hurt Sipho. "Mandisa, did Sipho ever mention someone who bullied him?"

Mandisa pointed her chin toward Lysi. "Why do you ask such a question?"

Surprised at the curt response, Lysi wasn't sure how to answer. Did Mandisa resent the question? Did she consider the question an insult to her son? Should I apologize? "I'm sorry. I didn't mean to offend you."

"You had a reason for asking the question." A small worry line creased Mandisa's brows. "Please tell me what it is."

Lysi hesitated a moment. "The reason I asked is because of something one of the children told me in confidence. She said that a man hurt Sipho."

"Who told you this? I know nothing of this?" Mandisa's pupils darkened. Was she angry, fearful, hurt?

Amele and Grace stared at Lysi making her wish she could disappear. When would she ever learn to control her insatiable need to uncover facts. She hadn't intended to annoy or worse, hurt. Again she wished she hadn't asked the question. Should she reveal the name of the child? What about her promise? Would Mandisa accept Saba's credibility?

"It was probably childish patter. Please forget I asked," Lysi said.

"No. Children speak about things they have seen," Mandisa said. "They may misinterpret, but usually their comments are honest based on facts as they see them. Who was the child?"

Now Lysi had no choice. "Saba. She said her brother Philani told her he saw a man strike Sipho."

"I will talk to Philani." The furrow between Mandisa's eyebrows deepened.

Lysi paused for a moment. Mandisa had accepted her first question maybe she could venture just one more. "Mandisa, do you know Thabo Deyi?"

"Thabo? Yes. He is Lindani's brother. You remember Lindani, my playroom assistant." Mandisa blew her hot tea then took a cautious sip. "How do you know him?"

"I don't really. I saw him at the Shebeen. Nambeko told me his name."

Mandisa's face hardened. "Thabo is a difficult personality. Not well liked. He has had a hard life. His mother died when he was 16. Lindani was only 5. The father abandoned the children right after their mother died. Thabo raised Lindani."

"How did he manage at such a young age?" Lysi said.

"He quit school and worked odd jobs to support her. He has always taken good care of her. Lindani is 22 years old, but she has the mind of a nine year old. Thabo has always protected her."

Lysi remembered Sara telling her about Thabo and Lindani munching cookies on the kitchen floor, and Thabo beating up kids who made fun of Lindani. No wonder Thabo has such a jaded attitude. He's spent his whole life caring for Lindani.

Amele patted Mandisa's hand. "Was Lindani here this morning?"

"No, unfortunately not. Sipho's death dealt her a terrible blow. Her continual crying upset the children so I told her to take a day off. She will return tomorrow. She is such a silly girl. I'm almost better off without her."

"How so?" Lysi said.

"Lindani tries, but she doesn't notice what is going on around her. It is as though she has her head in a different world. I have always wondered if—"

The doorbell jangled. Everyone's head turned toward the hall that led to the school entrance. "No more children waiting for pickup." Mandisa looked concerned and started to push herself up from the table. "Who could that be?"

A deep voice pierced the silence. "Mandisa." Heavy footsteps drew closer. A moment later, Thabo Deyi stood in the doorway. His eyes galloped around the room. For a microsecond his disapproving gaze lighted on Lysi. Then switched to Grace and back to Mandisa.

"What is it, Thabo?" Mandisa said.

Thabo answered in the Xhosa language.

Mandisa frowned. "Repeat that in English. We have guests."

Thabo thrust a wilting look at Lysi and repeated what he had just said. "Lindani does not feel good and will not come to work tomorrow." He continued in English. "Why did you allow Paki at the funeral?"

Mandisa ignored the question. "Is that all, Thabo?"

Chapter 11

The petite African jazz musician caressed the microphone as she ended her song in a deep, sensual voice that seemed too full to come from her slender body. Her red satin gown shimmered in the spotlight. She dropped small hands to her waist, slid them down her hips and ended in a deep bow. The audience at Marco's African Place sprang to its feet and applauded. She started to leave the stage, and every voice began chanting, "Gotyana…Gotyana…Gotyana."

Lysi and Grace rose and clapped until their hands hurt. They joined in the chant. "Gotyana…Gotyana."

When Gotyana glided back to center stage the audience cheered and returned to high back wooden chairs at tables draped in leopard cloth. Tangerine colored candle centerpieces tinted sparkling liqueur glasses orange.

"She's wonderful," Lysi said.

Amele's eyes lit up. "Of course. She is Xhosa and comes from Ikhaya Township."

Luvo nudged Maynard. "Amele thinks Gotyana is Xhosa, but she is Zulu."

"Whatever she is," Maynard said, his eyes glued to the singer, "she has a voice as voluptuous as black velvet."

Luvo slapped him on the back. "Well said, Maynard. Well said."

Gotyana's encore number was dark and breathy. She slow danced in rhythm to the sultry saxophone that accompanied her. The audience seemed spellbound.

Lysi felt a charge of electricity and her breathing quickened when Maynard's hand slid over hers under the table. Adrift in a sea of intense feeling she couldn't think beyond his touch. When the song ended he gave her hand a squeeze that brought her back to the real world like a hypnotist's snap awakening someone from a hypnotic trance.

Maynard held up his glass of Amarula and looked at Lysi. "That song was as intoxicating as this liqueur."

Grace nodded agreement. "She has the kind of African voice you find in southern Black women in the U.S. I heard lots of them in Mississippi. Not just in clubs, but on front porches at sunset."

Amele slapped the table. "Yes. It is the same in Ikhaya. In the evening you can hear these cavernous female voices crooning to children. They sing in shebeens, at celebrations and music festivals. Mandisa has a voice like that. She used to sing to Sipho and Nambeko when they were little. Now she sings to the Themba preschool children." Amele's voice softened. "I hope the death of Sipho does not silence her. So sad. So sad."

At mention of Mandisa's name Lysi thought about eight-year-old Philani. Had Mandisa talked to him about the man he saw hit Sipho? Thabo Deyi's face flashed into her mind. Could he be the man who struck Sipho? Lysi gave herself her usual mental kick. She had no reason to suspect Thabo.

What about Thabo's visit to Themba preschool and the icy look in his eyes when he saw her at the table with Amele and Mandisa? What could she have done to deserve such disdain? Maybe he hates white women. Or all women—he glared at Grace, too. Or maybe he hates foreigners. Or Americans. Just because he was rude to her doesn't mean he bullied Sipho. Lysi bit her lower lip. Something about Thabo frightened her.

A warm night breeze whispered through the leaves of an old oak tree in the side yard of the Butshingi house. Lysi sat next to Maynard on the patio porch swing. They rocked slowly back and forth.

Everyone else had retired, sleepy and contented after an excellent meal, good wine and fine entertainment at Marco's African Place.

Maynard slipped his arm around Lysi's shoulders and gazed at the red-orange blaze of color that trailed the sun as it sank beneath the dark waves of the Atlantic. She felt a leap in her pulse accompanied by an out-of-control surge in desire. She wanted him to press her close and hold her tight.

Too fast, she thought. Slow down.

Still, she wanted to lay her head on his chest and bask in the warmth of his affection—to trust him, to abandon her fears, to take a chance on this man who had come 1200 kilometers just to see her. She wanted to, but…she couldn't. The same thing happened every time she felt something for a man. Fear robbed her of even considering a relationship. One disastrous marriage was enough. How could she risk another one?

She swallowed her growing feelings and broke the silence. "About Sipho—"

Maynard moved closer to Lysi. "Do we need to talk about this now?"

Lysi looked straight ahead. "I don't want to talk about it. I just wanted to tell you one thing. People say everyone liked Sipho."

"Uh huh. That's nice." Maynard's lips cruised over her cheek leaving a tingly trail to her ear.

Now she really didn't want to talk about Sipho. She would just finish her thought then drop the subject. "But it seems he did have one enemy. A child at Themba saw someone punch him."

Maynard took his arm from around Lysi's shoulders. He looked resigned. The moment was lost. "How do you know this?"

"The child's five-year-old sister told me."

"A five-year-old? Cri-key, Lysi."

Lysi's eyes sparked. There's that superior tone again. Why does he get his hackles up every time she mentions anything about the homicide as though she didn't have enough common sense to even approach the topic? "Of course I wouldn't just rely on the word of a five-year-old. Mandisa is going to talk to the kid's older brother."

"Older?"

"He's eight."

"Eight." Maynard stood and his jaw tightened. His brown eyes snapped. "Lysi, I'm tired. I'm going to bed."

"Maynard, wait."

"We'll talk tomorrow. Good night." Maynard's tone was cold and dismissive.

Lysi swallowed an angry lump in her throat. How dare he talk down to her. Treat her like a child. Why waste her breath? She wouldn't ask for his help again.

Chapter 12

Lysi woke to the grinding sound of a garage door opening and a car engine starting. She rolled over and checked the bedside clock. Eight o'clock. Overslept. A huge yawn didn't clear her ten-ton head. Still groggy after a restless night spent replaying Maynard's condescending behavior over and over again, she still didn't have an answer to one nagging question. Why had he turned cold? He seemed so content just to sit next to her, arm around her shoulders. Why suddenly the big chill?

Lysi dragged herself out of bed, walked to the bathroom sink and splashed warm water on her face. Tired eyes stared back at her from the mirror. "Stop kidding yourself," they chided. "You know exactly why he chilled."

Deep inside, she did know the reason. Bad timing. Of course he didn't want to discuss the Sipho case at that moment. He wanted to bask in the warmth of the private moments they had together. She dried her face. How could she have been so unaware? So insensitive?

Pulling on white Capri pants and a yellow striped sleeveless top, she determined to make it up to Maynard that very morning. She'd suggest they spend the day doing some touring. Just the two of them. Maybe a scenic drive along the coast and later an intimate dinner in a small romantic restaurant overlooking the sea. She'd wear the cleavage revealing, frilly dress she'd worn on their first real date in Alice Springs. She pulled the dress out of the closet and examined it. A bit racy for her, but Maynard couldn't take his eyes off her when she'd worn it the last evening they spent together in Sydney.

She would go and find Maynard right away. She dabbed on a little eye makeup, a touch of rose lipstick and felt confident about her decision. A few seconds later, Lysi jolted to a stop in the living room doorway and her eyebrows lifted in a questioning arc at the scene before her.

Amele swayed unsteadily. A cell phone fell from her hand and clunked on the hardwood floor. Grace sprang from the couch and grabbed for Amele.

"Qamata is dead," Amele said in an almost inaudible voice. "They found him in the bushes near his hut. His skull crushed with a rock. The police have arrested Mandisa."

Lysi reached Amele just as her knees started to buckle and helped Grace lug her to the couch. Grace dropped next to her. Lysi sat on the other side and put her arm around Amele's trembling shoulders. "I'm sure there's some mistake."

"I have to go to her," Amele said, her voice shaky.

"Of course," Grace said. "We'll go with you." She stood. "I'll get Luvo."

"Luvo is not here. He took Maynard to see the Cape of Good Hope. They will not return until this afternoon." Amele reached for her purse on the coffee table where she'd dropped it the night before. "I will drive."

A pang struck Lysi's midsection. Maynard must have known last night he would tour Cape of Good Hope today. Why didn't he invite her to go? She knew why. You don't trample on someone's affection and expect him to bounce back for more punishment. He didn't want an encore of last night. A voice inside whispered, "Have I destroyed any feelings he might have had for me?"

The three women drove in silence along the N2 freeway, each caught up in her private thoughts. Lysi tried with little success to put the argument with Maynard out of her mind and to focus on Mandisa's plight. They turned on Bonga Drive in Ikhaya Site B and followed it to the one-story police station. They parked behind a white car with POLICE printed on six-inch blue stripes that ran along its front door.

Inside the building, a woman whose white blouse and blue skirt matched the police car stepped out from behind a precarious stack of files sitting on a low desk. She shoved thick reading glasses up into her hair, glanced at Lysi and Grace then addressed Amele. "What can I do for you?"

Amele started to speak but choked on the words. The woman waited. Lysi knew the emotional stress Amele must be feeling at Mandisa sitting in a cell somewhere in a police station. It brought home the reality of Mandisa's arrest. Lysi stepped next to Amele and took her arm. "Let me help." Amele turned teary eyes to Lysi and nodded. Grace put her arm around Amele's shoulders.

"We're looking for Mandisa Nala," Lysi said.

"Your name and relationship to Mrs. Nala?" The desk clerk spoke in a clipped business-like tone and cast a curious eye at the white woman before her. Lysi figured Caucasians were a rarity in the Ikhaya police station, and a Caucasian woman even more rare. She described her relationship to Amele Butshingi, and explained that Amele was searching for her close friend, Mandisa Nala who had been arrested early this morning.

The desk clerk lowered her glasses and picked up a pencil ready to log-in critical data. She hesitated before recording the information on a standard form, and looked at Amele for confirmation.

After completing the form, she asked Amele to sign. Amele signed and looked at the woman. "Where is Mrs. Nala?"

The clerk pointed to a wooden bench under a big, round clock at the rear of the room. Mandisa slumped on the bench, her head drooped on her chest. The three women hurried over and sat close to her.

"Oh Mandisa. What happened?" Amele stroked Mandisa's cheek with the back of her hand.

"They accuse me of killing," she said in a flat, monotone.

Lysi took Mandisa's hand. "How could they?"

Mandisa fired her eyes at Lysi. "Everyone knows he almost destroyed my daughter. Everyone knows he killed my son. Everyone knows I hated him. Why wouldn't I want him dead?" Mandisa's voice rose in pitch and volume. Tears carved rivulets down her cheeks. "What does it matter whether I did it or not? A death for a death."

"It matters," Lysi said.

"I did not kill him. I almost wish I had." She stared at her lap and shook her head several times. "I could never take the life of a human being."

"Do you have a lawyer?" Lysi immediately regretted the ludicrous question. Had she already forgotten the Township culture?

Mandisa didn't reply. She just raised her head and looked at Lysi as though she had less sense than one of her Themba Center two-year-olds.

Amele broke the heavy silence. "Have they questioned you, yet?"

"Yes. I wait now for them to finish processing me, whatever that means."

"That could take hours." Amele's eyes sparked. She took out her wallet and marched to the desk. "How much for bail?"

The irritated clerk shuffled some papers then handed Amele a half sheet. Amele glanced at it, passed the woman a handful of rands and started back to Mandisa.

When a commanding male voice said something in Xhosa, Amele stopped short and turned towards the voice. "Are you talking to me?" She spoke in English.

"Yes. I apologize if I startled you, Mrs. Butshingi." A man in a blue and white uniform stepped in front of Amele and extended a big hand. "I'm Officer Billy Joe Mbeki, lead investigator on the Qamata murder case. I am a friend of your husband."

"I know who you are. What can I do for you Officer Mbeki?" Amele's voice would have frozen a welder's torch.

Lysi and Grace exchanged glances, blinked and did a couple of is-that-for-real head jerks.

"Billy Joe?" Grace said in a loud whisper.

"You heard right. That's his name." Lysi said.

They stared at the tall broad-shouldered officer. He had a narrow waist, but his buttons strained to hold his shirt closed over his muscular chest. Charcoal curls capped his mocha colored face and his lips curved in a perennial smile.

Officer Billy Joe Mbeki continued in English. "I hope you understand Mrs. Nala is a person of interest in this case. She must remain in Ikhaya until further notice from us. Since you paid her fees, you are responsible for ensuring she doesn't jump bail."

Lysi leaned over to Grace. "Either my imagination is working overtime or that guy's got a southern drawl."

Grace snickered "Yeah." She said the word in two syllables. "Straight out of the Mississippi Delta." She tipped her head toward Lysi. "No wedding ring. I'll take him."

"I understand, Officer Mbeki." Amele gave a curt nod and turned away. "Good day."

Officer Billy Joe Mbeki's eyes trailed over to the three women seated on the bench. They paused at Grace and he flashed an appreciative smile. Grace lowered her eyes and he turned his attention back to Amele.

"Mrs. Butshingi? One more thing." The word *thing* sounded like *thang*.

"Thang?" Grace elbowed Lysi. "I'll bet you a hundred rands that boy's spent time in Mississippi."

"What is it now, Officer Mbeki?" Amele's voice turned as prickly as a porcupine.

"You need to understand we know Sipho Nala is dead. We know Mrs. Nala didn't report his death to the police despite indications that he did not die of natural causes. We know she believes Qamata killed her son." Officer Mbeki spoke in a cold, matter-of-fact tone.

Amele looked like someone had just slapped her. She swallowed hard. "I understand."

"I'm sure you see why Mrs. Nala remains a person of interest. She has a compelling motive."

Amele nodded and returned to her seat next to Mandisa.

Grace leaned toward Amele. "Officer Mbeki doesn't seem like your regular everyday Ikhaya cop?"

"He's from Cape Town." Amele showed no interest is discussing Billy Joe Mbeki, but Grace persisted.

"Honey, let's put it this way, he doesn't seem like your everyday *African* cop. Where'd he get that Mississippi drawl?"

"I'll tell you his story later. Let's get Mandisa home." Amele patted Mandisa's arm. "Let's go."

As Mandisa leaned forward, hands on knees to push up, her eyes jerked to the door and sparked. Lysi followed her stare to where a man stood on the threshold. His knit shirt stretched across the ripples of his chest. Tight jeans emphasized narrow hips and slim legs. Lysi thought he looked like he'd just stepped out of *Gentleman's Quarterly*. Where had she seen him before? Lysi sifted through her memory bank. The photograph in Nambeko's purse. Yes. Same fawn eyes, sculpted jaws, straightened hair.

"Why are you here, Paki?" Mandisa said.

Paki spoke in a pleading tone. "I must talk to you."

"There is nothing to talk about." With a strong push, Mandisa got to her feet.

"Please. I came to help you. You were kind to me when everyone else shunned me. I owe—"

"You owe me nothing. I did only what was right."

"Mandisa, please. I know you are innocent of this crime."

"You don't know anything. Leave Paki."

His eyes clouded, but Paki stood his ground. "Listen to me. I saw something." He leaned toward her. "I just want to talk to you." He lowered his voice. "Alone."

"These are my sisters. You may speak in their presence."

Paki looked at Amele and Grace then cast a puzzled glance at Lysi. "Sisters?"

Lysi couldn't suppress a grin at Paki's comical expression. What went through his mind when Mandisa referred to a white woman as her sister?

"Speak, Paki. Then go," Mandisa said.

"I saw someone outside Qamata's hut the night of his murder. The same man I saw on the night Sipho died."

Lysi's brain leapt into high gear. Whom did he see? What was he doing outside Qamata's hut? Who *is* this Paki? Why does Mandisa dislike him so much? Why did his presence at Sipho's memorial anger Thabo Deyi? Why did Nambeko hide his photo?

Mandisa cast a skeptical eye at Paki. "Whom did you see?"

"Thabo. When I saw him, I hid behind the hut near a bush and waited," Paki said.

Lysi caught her breath. Did Thabo Deyi murder Sipho and then Qamata? Why?

"Do you have more to say?" Mandisa asked.

Paki dropped his eyes to his feet. "No. I did not stay." He turned and shuffled away.

Grace's admiring eyes followed Paki out the door. "My favorite African products are its beer and its men."

She looked back into Amele's amused face. "Stop panting, Grace. He does not go with women. That is why he was ostracized and sent away from Ikhaya."

Chapter 13

The VW spluttered to a stop in front of the Themba Center. Lysi pushed open the car door and stuck one leg out but jerked it back just before a hot dry gust of wind slammed the door. She grabbed Grace's arm. "What the...?"

"You okay?" Grace's head nearly hit the car roof.

Lysi moved away from the door. "I think I'm hallucinating. Ten minutes ago we strolled to the car accompanied by a delicate little breeze that barely rippled our hair." Lysi squinted in question. "Is it my imagination or did a rhino wind just crash into that door and almost sever my leg?"

Amele behind the wheel spoke to Lysi's image in the rearview mirror. "Allow me to introduce our Cape Doctor, a strong south-eastern wind that blows off False Bay and hits the Flats with a vengeance."

"Cape Doctor? I guess that name works since it amputates limbs." Lysi rubbed her leg as if checking to see if she still had one.

Mandisa leaned her elbow on the back of the seat and faced Lysi. "We call it our Cape Doctor because it races around Cape Town cleaning up the 'smogwebs.' Just look at that cloudless sky."

Lysi looked through the windshield at the unending expanse of cornflower blue. "From balmy breeze to roaring gale in ten minutes? Crazy."

Amele rolled down the window. Wind rushed through it allowing her to push open the car door. "Capetonians say the Cape has four seasons–sometimes all in the same day."

Pushing her way out the other side of the car, Grace yelled above the wind. "Come on Lysi. Man up. Don't let a little puff of air get the best of you."

Lysi brought up the rear of the wind-blown gaggle of women that struggled to the daycare center door. Her skirt flapped around her legs and sandy grit stung her face.

Mandisa unlocked the door and slammed it after everyone was inside. She looked around the room, exhaled a lung full of air and headed for a desk cluttered with sheets of binder paper, envelopes, loose cash and assorted notes. Lysi figured half a day lost at the police station had put a crimp in Mandisa's schedule and now she needed to get busy with preparations for the Friday onslaught of kids. Noticing how Mandisa seemed to let go of all extraneous concerns and focus on what she had to do Lysi shifted into high gear. "How can we help?"

Mandisa ticked off on her fingers what needed to be done. "Prepare snack and lunch supplies, fold fresh rest-time towels, sweep floors and wipe down furniture, set out puzzles, games and books—" She paused on her thumb. "Oh, and I need to visit Lindani and see if she has recovered." Mandisa brought shaky fingers to her forehead and closed her eyes. "So much to do." She nodded several times. "Yes. I could use some help."

Grace picked up a fresh towel from a large laundry basket and started folding it. "I'll take care of these towels." She sniffed the towel. "Mmm. Fresh."

Amele put a hand on Mandisa's shoulder. "Listen. Lysi and I can check on Lindani."

Amele parked on the roadside about a block from Lindani's house. She led Lysi a short distance to a dirt pedestrian road too narrow for even a Volkswagen. The path crawled through improvised wood and tin shacks, outside toilets and wind-tossed laundry struggling to stay on clotheslines. Lysi's throat felt like sandpaper by the time Amele knocked on Lindani's fire engine red door. A quiet voice answered from inside the tan corrugated steel hut. "Who is it?"

"It is Amele, honey. Lysi is with me. We came to see if you are feeling better. May we come in?"

"Come."

Lysi and Amele stomped the road dust from their feet, pushed the door open and closed it against the wind. Lindani sat on a cot her back against a pillow, feet under crisp white sheets. "You can tell Mandisa I am better. I will come tomorrow."

"Good," Amele said.

The floral scent of rooibos tea mixed with the clean scent of sweet corn bread wafted from the table. The well-maintained condition of the one-room hovel surprised Lysi—spotless floor, clothes hung neatly on a corner crossbar, covers on two small cots tidily folded. Thabo and Lindani have created a home out of so little.

"Please sit," Lindani said sliding off the cot. "I will pour you some cool rooibos."

Lysi opened her mouth to offer to get the tea but stopped short remembering her last painful cultural lesson when Amele had had to explain that no matter how sad Mandisa felt, custom demanded *she* serve guests in her home.

Lindani gestured Lysi and Amele toward two folding chairs at a card table and pulled up a blue lacquered wood crate for herself. A white cloth embroidered with yellow roses covered the table. Lysi ran her fingers over the finely embroidered flowers. "What lovely work."

"My mother sewed them. Lindani's eyes brightened at the compliment. "She knew how to make lots of pretty things. Want to see?"

Lindani pulled a cardboard box from under the cot and set it on the bed. Using both hands, she lifted out crocheted doilies, embroidered pillowcases, baby clothes, and knitted booties. "Aren't they beautiful?"

"Her mother was an artisan," Amele said.

Lindani started to return the pieces to the box. She smoothed one of the soft baby booties against her cheek. "These were mine." Setting them in the box she added, "Mother is dead, you know. She died when I was little, but I still remember her. I still miss her."

The face of her own mother flashed through Lysi's mind. Her chest tightened. She still missed her. How lucky to have had her for so many years. Poor Lindani to lose her mother at such a tender age. And Mandisa to lose her son. "We always miss a loved one who's taken from us. I miss my mother. Mandisa misses Sipho."

Lindani's clenched fist flew to her mouth. "I miss him too. I...I..."

"What is it, Lindani?" Lysi leaned closer.

"I don't know if I should tell you. My brother might not like it." Her eyes grew big and round like a worried child's. "Can it be our secret?"

"Thabo will not know unless you tell him," Amele said.

Lysi nodded.

Lindani wedged her knuckles under her chin. "Can I tell it in Xhosa?"

"Of course. I'll translate for Lysi later."

As Amele listened to Lindani, her body stiffened, her mouth slowly opened and deep furrows plowed her brow. She didn't interrupt with questions but sat perfectly still until Lindani finished.

Much to Lysi's disappointment, Amele did not translate but took a couple of sips of her now tepid tea, said a few words in Xhosa to Lindani, and walked to the door.

In the car Amele didn't start the motor but sat looking straight ahead for a few long seconds. Lysi wanted to know what Lindani had said, but hesitated to ask. She would give Amele time to digest Lindani's words. Without comment, Amele started the engine and drove back to Themba.

Mandisa looked up from sweeping when they walked in. "So, how is Lindani?"

Without meeting Mandisa's eyes, Amele said, "She is well. She will come to work tomorrow."

Grace looked up with a loud guffaw. "You two literally blew in. Your wild hair makes you look like pups peeking out from under haystacks."

A smile stretched across Mandisa's lips for the first time since Sipho's death. She dropped the broom. "Come along, we all need a break. Let us blow over to the Shebeen and have a drink."

Mandisa's little joke brought grins of relief to all three women. Mandisa would move on with her life.

Pulling a towel from the last basket Grace said, "I'll put these towels and baby mats away first."

"Let me do it," Lysi said. "I wouldn't want you to miss one of those sorghum beers you love so much. I'll join you in a few minutes."

"Thanks, pal." Grace got up and feigned an eager gallop to the door.

"Wait." Lysi patted the stacked towels. "Where do they go?"

On the way out the door Mandisa pointed to a curtain that divided Sipho's bedroom from the kitchen. "There's a shelf in Sipho's room next to the window."

After folding the last towel, Lysi carried the basket into Sipho's room, placed it on a cot covered with a thin sheet and started to unload. She paused as her eyes wandered over the walls decorated with crayon pictures drawn by childish hands, posters of musicians, two African prints and a light blue University of Cape Town pennant. The towel shelf stood next to a small window. The two top shelves held towels and baby pads. The two bottom shelves held books— biographies of famous Africans, contemporary novels and an assortment of self-improvement titles. A guitar leaned in a corner near the shelf.

Lysi dropped down on the cot next to the towel basket. A whiff of male cologne emanated from the pillow. She tried to imagine the story this room could tell about Sipho. A gentle young man who cared about children, loved music, planned to attend university, proud of his heritage. She blinked and scanned the room again. No posters of hot cars or athletes. No photos of himself with buddies. No sports equipment, not even a soccer ball. Could what was missing from the room also tell a story?

The road toward Cape Town seemed almost empty of cars while heavy traffic whizzed by in the direction of Ikhaya. A steady stream of buses roared past bloated with passengers heading back to Ikhaya from their jobs in Cape Town. The passage of the heavy vehicles rocked the Volkswagen forcing Amele to grip the wheel to keep the car steady on the road.

"I'd almost forgotten the thrill of trying to keep a VW right side up," Lysi said.

Amele dipped her chin but kept her eyes on the road, squinting at the continual flash of headlights.

"Amele could drive this route blindfolded," Grace said. "She knows how to avoid cops, too. Which brings me to the topic of Officer Billy Joe Mbeki. Tell me all."

Amele frowned. Lysi figured Amele still smarted from Mbeki's overbearing attitude back at Ikhaya police headquarters.

"Mbeki was born in South Africa, but his family emigrated to the U.S. when he was still a young child," Amele said. "He grew up in Mississippi." She merged onto De Waal Drive and slowed her speed.

Grace snapped her fingers. "I knew it. I'd recognize that Mississippi drawl if a dog barked it."

"He met a Stellenbosch exchange student at the University of Mississippi and followed her back to Cape Town, married her and settled here. Unfortunately the marriage failed."

"How'd he end up in Ikhaya?" Lysi asked.

"He found a position in Cape Town Metropolitan Police Department then took over as head of Ikhaya's department. He is well-liked in Ikhaya and has a good reputation." Amele sounded like she couldn't understand how anyone could possibly like him.

Lysi decided this would be a good time to ask Amele what Lindani had revealed. She thought about the best way to ask. On the one hand, her gut told her the information might relate to Sipho's death. Maybe even to his killer. On the other hand, she needed to respect the traditions and rituals of African culture. Difficult as it felt, she needed to—No, wanted—to learn the lesson of patience from these people.

Chapter 14

The sea breeze from the open car window rippled Maynard's shaggy hair as Luvo steered his conservative dark gray Toyota along the coastline toward Cape Town. The quiet, steady hum of the engine and the herbaceous aroma of the roadside fynbos plants had settled the two men into a comfortable silence after the long day tour of the Cape of Good Hope and the rigorous hike up the peak to the historic lighthouse at Cape Point.

Maynard tried to focus on all the intriguing information he'd learned about the two famous capes— the wreck of the Lusitania liner, legend of the Flying Dutchman phantom ship and the unpredictable False Bay where the cold Atlantic current collides with the warm Agulhas of the Indian Ocean. He tried, but Lysi's face clouded his mental screen. His anger with her had subsided, replaced by resentment. He'd had so many things he wanted to tell her. He thought she'd share his excitement over the progress toward converting his family sheep station into a tourist attraction, his son's work in Namibia and ideas about his future. Their future. Against his better judgment he'd even consented to get involved in her daft attempt to investigate that township homicide.

No way now.

How could he have forgotten how persistent she could be? Her ear-bashing chatter about the murder of that young bloke seemed endless. The woman had to have kangaroos loose in the top paddock to think she could or even should solve that homicide. He figured it'd be even worse now that they'd taken Mandisa Nala in for questioning as a person of interest in the murder of the witch doctor.

The call about the Nala woman's arrest in the murder of that witch doctor had come just as Luvo finished explaining the history of the Cape Point lighthouse. When Amele told Luvo she had to go to Ikhaya, he'd started to protest then just shook his head. "I will see you when we return." After telling Maynard about the arrest, Luvo dropped the subject, turned toward the mountain and said, "Let's go." They trudged up to the lighthouse at the top of Cape Point and hadn't spoken about Amele or Ikhaya again.

Maynard blinked at the luminous almost blinding crystals of sunlight randomly dimpling the surface of the azure bay below Chapman's Peak Drive. The sheer drop from the narrow road to the sea below and the towering mountains rising above momentarily diminished Maynard's problems until Lysi's eager face invaded his thoughts again. Sure, her intentions are good, but why does she have to be so…so…*compulsive?* Where do I fit in her world? Maybe I don't. Maybe it was a bad idea to come here. Maybe…Maynard pressed two fingers to his temple and exhaled hard.

"You know, I almost did not marry Amele." Luvo's sonorous voice broke into Maynard's thoughts and he wrenched his eyes to the big square-jawed man behind the wheel.

"My dear Amele." Luvo stared straight ahead, the sun radiating light off his glossy coffee-colored skin. His voice seemed to come from somewhere in a distant past. "I found her too…too opinionated. Obstinate. Determined." Luvo groped for the right word. "Compulsive."

Maynard furrowed his brow and continued to stare at Luvo. Compulsive. Cri-key. That's exactly how he felt about Lysi.

Luvo continued to speak to the road ahead. "That woman. Once she set her mind to something, she clamped her jaws down like a crocodile and nothing could dislodge her from it."

"Why did you?" Maynard's voice tightened. "Marry her I mean?"

A smile tickled the corner of Luvo's mouth and he glanced Maynard's way. "Why? Because I loved her."

Maynard stiffened. He didn't know what response he'd expected, but this one hadn't satisfied him. "That simple, huh." He turned his gaze back to the window.

An anxious driver behind them beeped his horn to signal he planned to pass. Luvo pulled onto the road shoulder to give the driver room. He stared after the speeding car. "Why must people always race through life?"

Maynard didn't comment. He waited for Luvo to say more about his decision to marry Amele despite her exasperating personality.

"I did not say it was simple," Luvo said pulling back onto the road. "Amele kept me on a wild rollercoaster ride with her impulsive and often reckless behavior."

"You may not have noticed, but that's Lysi," Maynard said. "She's the most pigheaded woman I've ever met." He ended on note of resignation and sadness. "Unlike Amele, she'll never change."

"Oh, Amele has not changed. Look where she Volunteers for example. Ikhaya, one of the most dangerous townships in South Africa." Luvo shifted down to negotiate the steep grade. "Do you think I would allow her to go to Ikhaya if I had any say in the matter?"

"Then how much did you have to change?" Maynard spoke in a challenging tone.

"I have not changed. We have lived together for over twenty-five years. Amele remains exactly the same as the first day I saw her carrying a placard and marching behind Desmond Tutu in the great anti-apartheid demonstration." Luvo's face turned dreamy. "God she was beautiful."

Maynard's mind flashed on Lysi's face and his heart skipped a beat.

"I soon realized her reckless impulsiveness was one of the reasons I fell in love with her," Luvo continued. "My heart not my ego made the right decision. We are happy."

The almost silly twinkle in Luvo's eyes brought a grin to Maynard's lips. Hard to believe this giant man, this Zulu warrior could dissolve into such adolescent sentiment. "Amele is special."

"So is Lysi, Maynard. So is Lysi."

Chapter 15

Tired from the long day in Ikhaya, Lysi and Grace chatted with Amele as she warmed a simple vegetable and kidney bean soup and served it with deep-fried vetkoek bread at the informal kitchen table. Maynard and Luvo had eaten dinner in a restaurant on the way back from the Cape and decided to pass on Amele's light supper. They just wanted to relax after the rigorous tour of Cape of Good Hope. Luvo retired to the living room television to watch a soccer match. Maynard took a glass of cabernet and draped his long body on a settee on the patio.

Eager to join Maynard and apologize for her thoughtless behavior the previous evening, Lysi finished her wine, stacked the dishes and carried them to the dishwasher. Grace gathered the condiments and leftover soup then joined Luvo for the rest of the soccer match.

At the patio door Lysi paused a moment, her eyes on Maynard who sat gazing into the night. He didn't stir. It seemed as if the sky had hypnotized him with its millions of luminous stars shimmering in the dark canopy of indigo blue. Lysi remembered that same look on his face when she'd sat with him on the big homestead porch at the Outback sheep station he loved.

She took a few seconds to study him. He looked the same. The thick, dark Aboriginal hair that contrasted with his light sunburned Swedish skin. The chiseled jaw softened by a chin dimple that gave him a boyish look. Brown eyes that seemed to see into her soul. His long-legged, lean body—she could still remember how good it felt when he pulled her close the first time. What had changed? Why couldn't she just relax and enjoy being with him? Maybe that was the problem. Maybe she enjoyed being with him too much.

A feeling of intense emotion overwhelmed her. Suddenly her legs felt heavy. Her heart palpitated. An uncertainty washed through her. She really didn't know Maynard. She'd only spent a week or so with him in Australia and that was over a year ago. Of the two days he'd been in Cape Town, she'd had very little time alone with him. Not his fault. Hers. Yet, she felt like she'd known him forever. Ridiculous. How could she have such teenage-girl feelings?

When he raised smiling eyes to her she jumped. "Maynard, I'm sorry."

He shook his head and patted the seat next to him. "Sit here, Lysi."

She hesitated. The small settee would force her to sit close to him. Could she handle that?

He patted the seat again. She slid into the small space and breathed in the aromatic heat radiating from his body—a mixture of light cologne and heavy primeval masculinity. Her body's powerful response jolted her.

"I'm the one who should apologize," he said, seemingly unaware of his impact on her. "I behaved like a pouty kid last night. I wanted so much to spend some time with you. I overreacted at the very traits that make you so appealing."

Lysi swallowed. She forced herself to shake the intoxicating effects of his body heat, and focus on his words. Does he like my pushy traits? She resisted an urge to laugh.

Maynard's quiet voice broke into Lysi's thoughts. "Lysi, are you listening?"

She blinked. "Yes, yes. It's okay. I know I'm too persistent verging on compulsive."

"No. You were being you. Curious. Observant. Helpful. You believe you can do anything and aren't afraid to try." He looked thoughtful. "I guess I'm saying I'm sorry I threw a wobbly when you acted true to your character. When you behaved in the way I should expect. Don't change, Lysi. Cri-key, I like you the way you are."

Lysi's mouth went dry. She realized she'd stopped breathing. He said it again. *He likes how I am.* She felt his dizzying heat again. *Oh my God! What do I do next?* Now her stomach churned and unfocused thoughts somersaulted around in her head. Should she slowly back away from him or take the proverbial leap in the dark her mother always talked about?

No. She'd taken an emotional risk once and ended up in a miserable marriage that ended in divorce. She took a big breath. *Wait. He simply said he approved of her character. He hadn't proposed marriage. Get a grip, Lysi girl.*

Maynard touched her arm. "Am I forgiven?"

Lysi's eyes shot to his face and she nodded too many times.

He took her hand. "I do have one request. Spend some time with me."

She gulped and the words raced from her mouth. "Tomorrow. Tomorrow. Come with me on a tour, maybe visit Victoria and Alfred Waterfront or Kirstenbosch Botanical Gardens or Table Mountain or—"

Laughing he said, "Or how about a bag lunch, a stroll on the beach and dinner in a little restaurant later."

"Agreed."

Maynard put his arm around Lysi and leaned toward her.

Unable to control the burning in her cheeks, she just stared at him—lips parted, pulse hammering.

He brushed the corner of her mouth with his lips.

The soft pad of footsteps jerked Lysi and Maynard's eyes to the patio door. "I hope I am not interrupting," Amele said, a knowing gleam in her eyes.

Maynard whipped to his feet. "Of course not. Please join us." He gestured to his seat on the settee. "Sit here."

"Thank you, I will be fine here." She sat on a chair that faced the settee. "I want to talk to both of you. Yesterday Lysi and I went to check on Lindani. Do you remember her, Maynard? She works at Themba."

"I don't think I met her." Maynard looked interested.

Amele crossed her legs and folded her arms on her knee. She leaned forward and lowered her voice. "Lindani told us some things that shocked me. Things that may point to a suspect in Sipho's murder."

Maynard looked at Lysi. "You didn't mention any of this."

"This is the first time I'm hearing it. Lindani spoke to Amele in Xhosa."

"That's true. I did not translate for Lysi sooner because I just could not believe it. I told Grace first because I needed her advice." Amele said. "You know, Lindani is...well...a little slow. She gets confused. Sometimes we cannot rely fully on her credibility."

"She's like a sad little girl trying to get people to pay attention to her. To like her," Lysi said.

Amele nodded. "Lindani told me she missed her period a couple of months ago. She thought this meant she was pregnant. She is very innocent. She has not had a mother to teach her about life."

"Poor thing," Lysi said.

"Her brother Thabo loves her and is very protective of her." Amele's eyes hardened. "Also he has a temper. Lindani was afraid he would be angry with her if he thought she had run the streets and gotten pregnant so she lied. She told Thabo that Sipho was the father."

Lysi's hand flew to her chest. "What? Do you think Sipho *is* the father? Maybe Lindani wasn't lying."

53

Amele held up her hand to silence Lysi. "Wait. There is more. Lindani told Thabo that Sipho promised to marry her. She actually believed he would marry her. She is very naive. She thought Sipho was in love with her because he was kind to her and often comforted her with warm hugs at times when she cried over the cruel things people say to her."

Maynard who had been listening without comment asked, "How did Thabo react?"

"Thabo flew into a rage. He said he would make sure Sipho kept his word. A few days later, Lindani got her period but Thabo had already confronted Sipho." Amele shook her head and sighed. "Then they found Sipho dead. Lindani blames herself."

Lysi turned to Maynard. "Mandisa said she'd talked with eight-year-old Philani—Remember? I told you about him—and he told her he'd seen Thabo punch Sipho and knock him down. Now it makes sense."

Lysi looked at Maynard's expressionless face. Did he suspect Thabo of murder?

Chapter 16

The card game ended. Eight-year-old Philani threw up his hands, hooted, dropped down on all fours and bounced around the playroom snorting like a baboon.

Grace rolled her eyes. "Okay, okay kid. Cool it." She tousled Philani's curly black hair. "You win this time but I'll get you next round." The game filled the time while Saba and Philani the last two Themba Center kids to be picked up, waited for their mom to arrive.

At first Grace wasn't sure she wanted to spend the day talking kiddie talk with a bunch of 5-year-olds but Amele had talked her into it. Amele argued Grace would have nothing to do if she stayed at the Butshingi house since Lysi was off with Maynard. Besides someone needed to monitor the kids while Amele took Mandisa to the police station to hear about the formal autopsy report on her son, Sipho. The day had gone better than Grace expected. She'd followed the checklist Mandisa had left her. Lindani had managed to get the toddlers through their afternoon snack and into play activities while Grace supervised the returning school kids as they stampeded through the door accompanied by a cloud of gray dust.

Grace gazed at Saba in her pink ruffled play shirt and big matching hair bows perched on two pony tails that flipped adorably whenever she turned her head. Grace had to admit she enjoyed the little scampers. Kids have some good traits; they're honest, straightforward, spontaneous, affectionate and wonderfully transparent. She liked that. Maybe she might want kids of her own some day. Whoops! She kicked that thought out of her head. What would she do with kids? Nope. She's got a good life. Why complicate things?

"Mama Grace." Saba pointed toward the playroom. "Lindani."

Grace looked up at Lindani standing in the doorway between the office and the playroom waiting for Grace to acknowledge her.

Grace pushed up from the floor and brushed dust off her pants. "Lindani girl, what do you need?"

Lindani stumbled into the room—long skinny arms dangling at her sides, mouth open, eyes begging for approval. "Miss Grace, all the children in my room have been picked up."

Grace consulted Mandisa's checklist. "Did you tidy up the playroom and wash the juice glasses?"

"Yes." Lindani nodded several times. Grace thought she looked like a little girl eager for a pat on the head.

"Good job, kid. Can you take over the game? I need to finish some paperwork."

Grace went to the office, sat at the old cast-off teacher's desk in front of a black, dog-eared roll book and began marking off the names of picked-up children. When the door opened she looked up, expecting to see Philani and Saba's mom. Instead, Thabo Deyi's tall physique filled the doorway. He scowled at Grace from under a black stocking cap pulled low on his forehead. His eyes asked where Mandisa was, but he said, "I've come to pick up my sister."

"Hello Thabo. Lindani's pretty much ready."

Thabo blinked his surprise when Grace said his name.

She stood. "Hey, just want to let you know, Lindani really helped me get through the day. She had to show me what to do because I was here alone. Mandisa left with Amele a couple of hours ago."

Thabo's face softened. He removed his stocking cap and shoved it under his arm. "Lindani was a help to you?"

"Oh yeah. I couldn't have managed without her. Right now she's tending two kids so I can finish this paperwork." She pointed to the tattered roll book on the desk. "Do you mind if she stays a bit longer?"

Thabo blinked. "No, no. I can wait. I…" He looked around, spotted a broom in the corner and added, "I will sweep the front entrance."

Grace flashed an aren't-you-the-sweetest-little-old-thing-smile and said in her Mississippi southern-belle drawl, "Why thank you, Thabo. That's just lovely."

Thabo's cheeks turned plummy and a half smile crossed his lips. He nodded, took the broom and walked outside. "I will sweep the entry walk while I am about it."

Grace's admiring eyes followed Thabo out. Oh yeah. Broad shoulders. Muscular arms. Firm glutes. If only she were 10 years younger…

About twenty minutes later Saba gave Grace a big hug and Philani high-fived her just before leaving with their mother. After Thabo finished sweeping, he collected Lindani, nodded goodbye to Grace and left.

Grace watched Thabo take Lindani's hand and lead her down the sandy lane. How has that boy managed the role of mother, father and big brother to a sister who will never mature beyond the age of ten? Under that belligerent exterior he's got a real soft spot for Lindani.

Grace turned back to her paperwork; satisfied she'd made a friend in Thabo by simply being kind to Lindani.

The sun was a dull red blotch on the black horizon when a brisk rap on the door jolted Grace from her concentration. Now who could that be? Not Amele and Mandisa. They wouldn't knock. Not a parent. All the kids had gone home. Thabo? Had Lindani forgotten something?

She went to the door, opened it a crack and peeked out. A cinnamon-colored face with thickly lashed dark eyes stared back at her. Officer Billy Joe Mbeki looked pleasantly surprised to see Grace.

"Excuse me," he said, easing his over six-foot frame through the door. "I expected Mandisa." The appreciative look on his face told Grace he was not disappointed to see her instead.

After an instant, he pulled his eyes from Grace and looked around. "Where is she?"

Even though Mbeki had exchanged his uniform for chinos, a pale blue sport shirt and sandals, Grace recognized him as the officer with the southern drawl Amele had spoken with at the police station. "Amele took her to the police station to hear the autopsy results on her son."

"Oh yes, the autopsy report." Officer Mbeki raised one eyebrow brow.

Officer Mbeki's expression caught Grace's attention and curiosity. She wanted to probe a bit but decided it wasn't any of her business. Instead she said, "I'm finishing up some work for Mandisa. Can I help you?"

Officer Mbeki's eyes swept over Grace's face. "I believe I saw you at the police station. Grace Wright isn't it?"

Grace's eyes widened. "How did you know my name?"

Officer Mbeki looked her over with unconcealed lascivious interest. "I make it my business to know the names of all the desirable women in my precinct."

Grace kicked into sexual harassment training mode. The use of the word "desirable" has a sexual connotation. She should object to his comment. On the other hand…it may be a cultural difference. Yes, that's probably it.

"Officer Mbeki. Of course. I do remember you from the police station."

His smile broadened. "I'm flattered you noticed me." Mbeki looked deep into Grace's eyes. "You definitely caught my attention." For an instant the air between them crackled with electricity.

Again Grace considered objecting to Mbeki's comment. Not so much his words but what accompanied his words—his intense stare, sensual voice and his body leaning toward her invading her personal space. She knew he deliberately moved too close to her. Oh yeah, he verged on overstepping the boundaries. She should caution him about harassing women. She should tell him not to make any other similar comments to her or any other woman. Could she chalk his behavior up to cultural differences? Maybe a part of her wanted to do just that.

Mbeki's eyes turned casual. "From your accent I see you are American."

"That's right. And I can tell from your drawl you've spent some time in America's deep south."

"Mississippi."

"Mississippi?" Grace said. What part?"

"Clarksdale. My father worked at Coahoma Community College."

"Really? My Grandmother lives in Clarksdale and I used to spend summers with her when I was a kid. My best friend lived in Lula."

The face of Grace's childhood friend, Marita Rendeau, drifted through her mind. Grace still hadn't fully recovered from finding Marita's battered body in a dirty alley far away from Lula in Sydney, Australia. Deep down Grace knew she would always grieve for Marita.

Officer Mbeki studied the change in Grace's face. "Is it something I said?"

"No, no. It's just such a surprise to meet someone from Clarksdale clear across the world."

"Well, as you say in America, 'It's a small world.'" Mbeki scanned the room one more time. He sighed and turned towards the door. "I guess I'll try to catch Mandisa tomorrow."

Grace opened the door for him. "I'll let her know you were here. Is there a message I can give her?"

"No. Thanks anyway." Mbeki hesitated before leaving. "I would very much enjoy reminiscing about Mississippi with you. Perhaps tomorrow evening—over a glass of our good Constantia Valley wine."

Grace's lips fell open. "I…" Thoughts whirled in her head. This boy doesn't waste any time. Guess nothing's wrong with having a drink with a police officer. After all, Lysi's off with her Australian sheep farmer. No use sitting around moping waiting to live vicariously through Lysi's adventures. She touched her hand to her heart and said in a thick southern drawl, "Why Officer Mbeki what a very generous offer."

"Please, please—Billy Joe. And I will take that as a 'yes.'"

Officer Mbeki opened the door. He looked back over his shoulder at Grace. "I will pick you up at the Butshingi home at 8:00. Oh…" He smiled—a slow stretch of amusement…"And the southern drawl is very cute especially mixed with that strong New York accent."

The door closed behind Officer Mbeki leaving Grace's grin turned slightly wicked. Nothing's wrong with a little vacation adventure.

Grace finished the last attendance sheet input and dropped the pen on the desk. How does Mandisa manage all this record keeping for so many kids? It would make me crazy.

She did a quick walk-through of the Themba Center to check that all exterior doors and windows were locked and all lights off.

The sun had completely set when Grace left the Center and started towards Sara's B&B. It was much darker than she'd expected and she had to use her small purse flashlight to avoid the potholes in the road.

She didn't see people milling around like back home in Harlem. No one on the street. She walked by the Shebeen and noticed a couple of men seated at a table nursing drinks. She ignored their hoots and whistles as she passed. Same as guys back home, she thought.

The darkness didn't worry her but the feeling of being alone did. Good thing she didn't have far to go to Sara's B&B.

About a block from the B&B uneasiness clutched at her chest. She felt the footsteps behind her before she heard them. She hastened her pace.

Chapter 17

Lysi took a sip of latte and hoped Maynard would broach the topic of Sipho's murder. All day she'd resisted mentioning the Sipho case. Sitting on a bench in the Kirstenbosch Botanical Garden surrounded by yellow fynbos, she'd swallowed the urge to bring up Sipho. Later, watching the panorama of Cape Town from the Table Mountain Café, 900 meters above the city, she'd struggled against slipping Sipho's name into the conversation. And now, sipping lattes on the sun-drenched terrace of La Playa Café at the Victoria & Alfred Waterfront she had to bite her tongue to keep Sipho's name from escaping. The effort exhausted her but she felt some pride in her success. What was it her dad always said when she demanded immediate action or answers? "Your mother and I should've made your first name Impatient, your middle one Urgent and your nickname Insistent." His words had annoyed her as a child but now she got the point.

Lysi knew Maynard wanted a day alone with her. A day to reminisce about their good times together in Sydney and Alice Springs. A day to catch up on what had happened in their lives since they'd last seen each other more than a year ago. And a day to talk about their future—a topic she wasn't ready to even think about. Her unfocused gaze wandered from the shimmering blue Atlantic to the feathery cirrus clouds floating high above. On a day like this, why think about anything?

She leaned back in the cushioned chair, closed her eyes, breathed in the warm sea air and allowed her mind to drift on the delicate sea breeze into pure contentment.

A moment later she opened her eyes at Maynard's intense voice. "Cri-key Lysi. You *are* a beauty."

Lysi blinked several times in surprise. Maynard's words embarrassed her. She understood men tended to exaggerate in an effort to please. Still it made her uncomfortable. She guessed he charitably ignored her unmanageable curls, long thin neck and somewhat prominent ears. Instead he focused on her engaging smile, bedroom eyes and flawless complexion—attributes in which she, herself, took pride. Lysi considered herself presentable, but certainly no beauty.

Before she had time to recover from her surprise and respond, he averted his gaze, cleared his throat, took a small spiral notebook from his pocket and slapped it on the table in front of her. Lysi's eyes devoured the notebook but she clenched her jaws, determined not to mention Sipho even though she knew Maynard was finally ready to talk about the case.

He tapped the notebook. "Okay. You've done a good job controlling your insatiable urge to question me about your murder. So, I'll take a few minutes to tell you what I saw at the crime scene—but that's all." He dipped his chin at her and raised his brows as if to ascertain that she understood before continuing. "As I said before, Ikhaya is not in my jurisdiction. Besides I'm on holiday."

He pulled a small bag from his daypack and set it next to the notebook. Lysi held her breath and tried not to appear as eager as she felt. "Yes?"

Maynard's faint grin gave her the distinct feeling he could see right through to her thinly disguised curiosity. So much for an attempt at subtlety.

A waiter who looked about twelve-years-old to Lysi took her empty cup, placed it on his tray and glanced at Maynard. Maynard held up two fingers. "Two more."

The waiter nodded. "Yes. Thank you, sir."

Maynard flipped open the notebook and eyed his written comments. "Behind Qamata's hut the long grass was smashed down like someone had knelt there more than once. I found a pencil-sized peephole in the hut wall and—"

Lysi lurched forward. "Was there a bush near the hole?"

Maynard tilted his head back and looked at her. "How about letting me finish before you start asking questions. Yes, there was a bush."

"I just thought you should know that a man named Paki said he hid there…behind a bush."

Maynard scribbled the name in his notebook.

Lysi watched Maynard ponder the name. He may not have jurisdiction over this crime, she thought, but he certainly has interest. He might just decide to help solve it.

Maynard circled the name and looked up. "Who's Paki?"

"I don't know much about him except Amele said he's gay and wouldn't exactly win a popularity contest in Ikhaya."

"Uh huh." Maynard reached into his daypack and removed a bag. He opened it and pulled out the tissue-wrapped, multi-colored stone bracelet Lysi had found in Qamata's hut. He picked up the broken latch he'd scratched from the soil of the dirt floor and held it up to the bracelet. "Now I think we know the owner of this bracelet. What we don't know is what this…" Maynard looked down at his notebook. "…this Paki was doing outside that hut and why he hid behind it? Sounds pretty clandestine to me." Maynard paused for a few beats then, holding up the bracelet, he continued. "You found this inside the hut. That means Paki had to have gone inside. The question is why?"

Maynard fingered the broken latch. "Someone ripped this off Paki's wrist. I think we know why given the attitude toward gays in Ikhaya. What we don't know is who."

Lysi's eyebrows contracted in a thoughtful frown. "What if that crazy witch doctor yanked it off…or…or Sipho pulled it off in a struggle with Paki? What if Paki murdered Sipho? Maybe—"

"Lysi. Slow down. Detectives don't pick a perp out of the blue and then find evidence to prove his guilt. We examine the evidence first and it leads us to suspects. That's what I'm trying to do."

Lysi gave herself a mental smack. She knew that. She'd learned that basic tenet of crime investigation in her Criminal Justice Studies at San Francisco State University before she switched her major to education. "You're right. I got ahead of myself."

Maynard flipped to the next page in his notebook and spoke in a erudite tone. "I recognized some of the contents of the bottles on Qamata's shelves. Ground ochre—red, yellow and white. Various herbs. They're similar to what's used by the tribal people near Alice Springs in their traditional healing rituals. Their ceremonies consist mostly of singing songs, chanting and shaking string amulets but they also paint designs on the body of the sick person with colored ochre. They do use herbs." Maynard closed the notebook and gave it a slap. "Most of the stuff on the shelves was pretty harmless."

Lysi remembered the short dark-skinned Aborigines she'd seen in Australia and tried to envision their healing rituals of chants and body painting art. Pretty harmless maybe but some herbs could be dangerous. They could cause problems leading to death. An image of Qamata popped into her mind.

Maynard reached into his bag and pulled out another tissue. He opened it and shoved it closer to Lysi. She squinted at a round object that looked like a flat plastic disk about half inch in diameter. "What's that?"

"It looks like a cap used to seal the mouth of a small bottle or vial of some kind. I'd like to know what that vial contained," Maynard said.

The twelve-year-old waiter set two lattes on the table. He wiped his hands on his apron and turned to Maynard. "May I offer anything more?"

Before Maynard could answer Lysi jumped in, "Maynard dear, would you like anything more?"

Maynard suppressed a grin. "Nothing for me."

Lysi cast her sweetest smile at the waiter. "Nothing more thank you."

The waiter did a double take, thanked Lysi and hurried off. Lysi frowned at the waiter's back. What is it with these waiters? Are women invisible to them?

Maynard returned to his notebook as if nothing had happened. "A partial imprint in the shape of a rectangle tells us the table had toppled. Someone had taken the time to set it back up. Curious. Sounds like someone who cared about the condition of the hut."

"Qamata!" Lysi said.

Maynard ignored her comment. He thought for a moment then said, "By the way, has Mandisa had any news on the autopsy findings?"

Lysi nodded. "No information yet. I think the report comes out today."

"That report will answer a lot of questions if you're given access to it."

"I'm sure Nambeko or Mandisa will share it," Lysi said.

Maynard nodded then pulled out a tissue with a small amount of soil on it and another one with finer soil. He set them on the table in front of Lysi. "See the difference between these two soil samples? The one on the left is untouched soil from the floor of the hut."

He pointed to the sample on the right. "Look closely at this one. Do you see them?"

Lysi scrutinized the two samples and strained to see differences. She remembered Maynard showing them to her in Qamata's hut. "The color is kind of pale yellowish in this one. The grains are more coarse."

"Good eye, Lysi."

The waiter approached the table carrying a small silver tray with the check on it. He started to set the tray in front of Maynard, paused, glanced at Lysi and set the tray on her side of the table. She smiled, gave the waiter a "thumbs up" and placed her credit card on the tray.

"I think I know what those grains might be," Maynard continued.

Lysi waited for him to tell her the significance of the soil samples but instead he repacked his daypack and ended the discussion.

Chapter 18

Grace could see the faint light from the low wattage bulb on the front porch of Sara's B&B. Less than a city block to go. The footsteps behind her drew closer. She glanced over her shoulder, stumbled into a wet pothole and almost landed on her knees. A sound between a squeak and a gasp escaped her lips.

Strange, she never felt this kind of fear walking the night streets of Harlem. Here it was different. Here the black night beyond the little circle of light from her purse-size flashlight seemed to envelope her, thick as tar. Another glance over her shoulder revealed three dark shadows trailing behind her. She felt an unaccustomed chill wash over her body.

Now Grace could hear whispering and sniggering. She didn't understand the words but knew from the tone what they were after. When she looked back again, they hooted, slapped each other on the back and rammed each other's shoulders. That was when she felt a rock form in her chest.

Back home in Harlem she'd encountered roughnecks behaving like adolescents on the prowl. Most of the time she'd rise to her 6-foot height, confront them and they'd back off. If they didn't, she could knock on almost any door in her neighborhood and get help. Everyone knew her father, Big Natchez Wright and no one wanted to walk on his dark side. He may have owned a quiet bookstore, but he'd also owned the streets of the hood since he was sixteen.

Growing up under the watchful eye of big Natchez, Grace rubbed shoulders with her Harlem neighborhood homies and those from El Barrio where her Puerto Rican mother was raised and her Grandmother Graciela still lived. From the homies, her father and her Harlem sisters, she learned what to do and what not to do to stay safe on the streets.

It wasn't the same in Ikhaya. Here she felt alone, exposed, vulnerable.

Grace had to make a decision. Should she run for the B&B? She calculated the distance to the Inn and the closeness of her pursuers. No use running. She'd never make it before they caught her. She had to face them. Her father had always warned her never to turn her back on an attacker. Never give them the advantage. Pearls of sweat formed on her forehead.

When the footsteps increased in speed Grace halted and whirled around to face them.

The three men stopped. She could feel their surprise, hear their uneasy laughter. Two of them started pushing the short, wiry guy toward her. He shuffled nearer measuring her height with his eyes. She towered over him by almost a foot. He hesitated and continued his approach with caution—chin tucked, head low, fists clenched.

Grace thrust up her open hand, as if she was stopping a car, and shouted, "Back off!"

He stopped. His two companions yelled words that must have goaded him forward because he sidled closer.

When he closed in and tried to grab her, Grace seized his boney shoulders and at the same time kneed him in the groin so hard that he collapsed in the dust. His two companions stared in wide-eyed silence.

The man on the ground's features distorted in pain. He screamed something to the other two men. A moment later they began to slink toward Grace. She knew she couldn't take both of them. She had to run. She took a step backward and whirled.

Too late.

Strong arms grasped her around the waist. A sickening beer breath stench nearly gagged her. Hands tightened around her throat. Fear turned to tearful humiliation followed by fierce anger. She kicked and punched and scratched and clawed. She screamed and uttered guttural sounds. She struggled to stay on her feet. She would inflict as much agony and injury as possible. She would maim, cripple, mutilate. She knew she would lose this battle, but she would make sure they never forgot this Harlem girl.

Grace's muscles turned to gelatin as two heavy bodies forced her to her knees. Never in her life had she experienced this kind of total subjection. Resigned to her fate, she went limp.

Out of the blackness a deep, menacing voice growled something in Xhosa. An instant later Grace was free. She dropped to a sitting position and scooted backwards as the two attackers slithered away and faded into the dark.

Thabo sauntered over to the skinny man on the ground who had managed to rise to his knees. Thabo kicked him in the chest, throwing him back into the dust and yelled something at him. The man lay on the ground in the fetal position. Grace found her flashlight in the dust and shined it in the man's face. She flinched at his terrified expression, stifled a sob and brushed her hair back from her eyes.

"Thank you." She recognized Thabo who studied her in silence.

He nodded.

"Where did you…? How did you…?"

"I saw you as you passed the shebeen. When I saw them get up and trail after you, I left my drink and decided to check on you. I followed. I watched. I saw you cripple Uuka so I did nothing. When I saw the others go after you, I did something."

The man on the ground started to crawl into the darkness on the side of the road. Grace managed to stand. She brushed the dust off her pants and gestured with her chin towards the man. "What did you say to him?"

"I told him he is a dead man and if I ever see him again I will prove it." Thabo didn't smile. He watched in disgust as Uuka hobbled to his feet.

"I think he believed you."

Thabo glanced at the man then shifted his eyes to Grace. "You should not walk alone at night in Ikhaya. I will see you back to your car."

"I don't have a car. I came with Amele Butshingi. We're staying at Sara's B&B and will return to Cape Town tomorrow."

If Thabo recognized the Butshingi name he gave no indication.

"I will see you to the B&B. But I must finish my drink before the barman throws it out and closes the shebeen. You will join me. It will restore you." He turned toward the shebeen.

Surprise flooded Grace's face. A drink? All she wanted to do was get to her room in the B&B, lock the door and crawl into bed. Still, he might be right. A drink after her ordeal might calm her rattled nerves. "Okay, just one."

The shebeen was empty except for an old man nursing a tall sorghum beer and the proprietor draped over the bar. Thabo's beer sat half full on a table in the middle of the room. He ordered a sorghum for Grace as they settled into chairs.

Thabo took a swig of his drink and wiped his lips with the back of his hand. "Thank you for your kind words about Lindani."

"Kindness? No." Grace shook her head. "Gratitude? Yes. I told you she helped me get through the day."

The hard lines around Thabo's mouth softened. "Life has not been kind to Lindani. You may know her mother died when she was little." He tapped his temple with his index finger. "She is not right in the head."

"Thabo, Lindani can learn, but at a slower rate than others." Grace knew kids in her high school who went to special classes because they needed more time and support to master concepts that came quick and easy to other students. Many of them graduated.

As if he hadn't heard her Thabo said, "Did she tell you she miscarried a baby?"

"Miscarried?" Grace swallowed. Lindani forgot to tell Lysi and Amele that part of the story. Lindani may have thought she was pregnant when she missed her period, but she out and out lied to Thabo about a miscarriage.

"Two weeks ago Lindani told me she was pregnant," Thabo said. "She told me Sipho was the father and that he said he would marry her but changed his mind."

Thabo took a gulp of beer as if he needed to put out flames of anger. "I confronted him. He denied having sex with Lindani. Denied the baby was his. Swore he was not the father."

Grace felt torn. Should she tell Thabo that Lindani had lied to him about Sipho? About the miscarriage? Would he hurt Lindani? Better leave well enough alone. Best to stay out of it. She took a sip of beer and wiped at the condensation on the outside of her glass.

Thabo's face hardened. "I grabbed Sipho's shirt, clenched my fist and held it in front of his face. He closed his eyes. I knew he was thinking up a lie."

The bartender wrapped the counter with his knuckles and said something in Xhosa. Grace figured he wanted to close up. The old man mumbled a couple of slurred words, pushed his chair back and staggered out the door. The bartender glared at Thabo.

Thabo cast him a threatening don't-push-me look then continued talking to Grace. "Sipho said he remembered a night he came home late from a party in Cape Town. He had had too much to drink. He found Lindani sitting outside the school crying. He said he put his arm around her to comfort her. He swore he did not remember what happened next." Thabo's mouth twisted into a revulsive scowl. "Then he admitted his guilt."

"How so?" Grace wasn't sure she really wanted to hear the rest of Thabo's story. What would she have to do with that information?

"He told me that it seemed impossible, but he might have taken Lindani to his bed. He said he only wanted to comfort her. Lies! A man knows why he takes a woman to his bed." Thabo slammed his fist on the table.

Grace jumped at the sudden bang.

"I wanted to crush his face at that moment."

The hatred in Thabo's eyes sent a chill down Grace's spine. She realized he had made up his mind even before confronting Sipho and nothing Sipho could have said would have changed it.

"I told him he had to marry her. He refused." Thabo punched the palm of his hand. "I hit him—hard."

Lysi's words passed through Grace's mind. "The boy, Philani told the truth. He did see Thabo slug Sipho."

Thabo swallowed the last of his beer. "A week later Sipho died. God forgive me, I'm glad Lindani miscarried. We could not have raised a baby without Sipho."

"Thabo, how did Sipho die?" Grace waited for what seemed like a long time for a response. Maybe she shouldn't have asked that question.

Thabo looked at Grace with cold eyes. "It is good he is dead. He deserved to die."
Grace stared at Thabo. Could this angry, violent man be a killer?

Chapter 19

Lysi sifted the white, granitic Clifton Beach sand through her fingers. Her gaze followed the fiery sun's slow descent into the cold Atlantic. She shivered in a gust of ocean breeze and pulled a lacy knitted shawl over the shoulders of her gauzy blue dress. It was the same dress she'd worn in Yulara when she dined with Maynard in the romantic candlelight of the Kuniya Restaurant. Grace had picked out the cleavage-revealing dress and insisted she wear it.

When Lysi walked into the Butshingi living room, Maynard gave the same appreciative whistle he'd given in Yulara only this time he didn't make any effort to keep his eyes off her deep décolletage. Somehow she didn't mind.

Lysi shivered again and Maynard moved closer. He put his arm around her without interrupting the description of his progress in converting his Northern Territory sheep station into a tourist spot. "We've painted the cottages and installed air conditioning in the homestead. Even built that rustic stone barbie you suggested. You wouldn't recognize the old place."

His contagious enthusiasm brought a smile to Lysi's face.

He caught the smile and gave her shoulders a little squeeze, his eyes hopeful. "You seemed at home at the station when you visited."

Lysi picked up another handful of pearly sand and watched it flow through her fingers.

"The visit to Alice Springs and the sheep station was a highlight of my trip to Australia," she said. She didn't add she had no idea how she felt about the station. She hadn't sorted out those feelings in her own mind. Raised in San Francisco, she couldn't relate to the vast, dry land of Australia's sun-blasted Outback in any other way than a tourist attraction. One thing she knew for sure, the sheep station was an important part of Maynard's life.

He took her hand and held it in both of his. "Remember that night on the front porch of the homestead."

Lysi stopped breathing. She remembered. The clearest star-filled sky she'd ever seen. The intoxicating scent of purple wisteria. The sweet taste of desert mango sparkling wine. Maynard's lips caressing hers. She drew a long, slow breath and whispered, "I do."

"I'll never forget that kiss." He pressed his lips to her palm. It felt like a low-voltage current was suffusing up her arm into her chest. She tried to interpret those smoldering signals that made the air crackle between them.

"Lysi, do you realize I haven't even given you a real kiss since I've been here."

Lysi lifted her eyes to him. She considered reminding him of the kiss at the airport but before she could utter a word his lips touching hers blurred everything and eliminated all rational thought. When the kiss ended, every nerve in her body longed for another one. She felt color rise in her hot cheeks and she didn't care if he noticed.

Maynard took a long breath and exhaled. "Nice start." His thumbs stroked her cheekbones. His eyes wandered over her face and a slow, smooth smile crossed his lips. "We need to finish what that kiss started. And soon."

At the steadiness of his gaze and the firmness of his expression, she dropped her eyes. "Mmm. Soon."

Maynard pulled the car into the Butshingi's driveway. He cut the engine but made no move to open the door. Instead he turned to Lysi. "I need to fly to Namibia."

Lysi's eyebrows shot up and her mouth fell open. "What?"

"I got an e-mail from my son Joel telling me he has a "special person" he wants me to meet." Maynard set the emergency brake and leaned back in the seat.

"I see." Lysi swallowed. "Of course you have to go." She hoped Maynard wouldn't notice her disappointment. She'd hoped to spend more time with him. Now he would probably fly back to Australia from Namibia.

"Kids!" He slapped the steering with his fist. "I don't know why he didn't bring her around when I was there. I told him I planned to fly home from South Africa." He turned to Lysi, his expression frustrated and unhappy. "Anyway, I'm leaving for Namibia Thursday."

Lysi knitted her brow and groped for something to say. She didn't want him to go. She knew it was needy, selfish even childish but she couldn't help it. Danger signals ignited in her brain. Emotion clouded her ability to think rationally. She'd been around that corner before and it was disastrous. She knew she had to rein in her passion, her dependence and get back in control.

If Maynard noticed her disappointment, he didn't show it. "Joel volunteers in a small village school some miles outside of Windhoek, the capital. Since his school is a rough, dirt-road drive from the Hosea Kutako Airport, he and his special person decided they should meet me in Windhoek. That'll save quite a bit of time."

After a hard swallow Lysi said, "When will you be back?"

"I'll spend the day with them. Maybe have dinner. Stay the night. Then fly back the next morning."

Lysi forced a smile. At least he would not fly home from Namibia. He would come back to South Africa. That was more than she'd hoped for. She tried to disguise her upset by expressing interest in Namibia. "Namibia is a country I know very little about. Isn't it the land of orange sand dunes?"

"It is that and much more." Maynard looked serious. "You could learn more about Namibia if you'd come with me." He stretched his arm along the back of the seat, caught a ringlet of her hair and slipped it through his fingers.

Before she could obey her brain's warnings, Lysi heard her mouth say, "I'd love to go."

"You would?" Now it was Maynard's turn for surprise. "I'll book a seat for you straight away. Can you be ready by early Thursday morning?"

"I could be ready in two hours."

Maynard shook his head. "You amaze me. Deep inside that conservative soul of yours lurks an almost unquenchable thirst for adventure."

Chapter 20

Lysi poured steaming Rooibus tea into Grace's cup then yanked out a chair, flounced into it and glared at her from across the table. A spray of morning sunlight drifting through the Butshingi's kitchen window didn't soften Lysi's anger. "What in Heaven's name were you thinking—walking out alone in Ikhaya last night?"

"Look, Lysi. Correct me if I'm wrong but haven't we been around this block already?" Grace looked at the ceiling. "Let me run through it barefoot for you. I have never had big concerns about being out alone at night. I know how to defend myself and if I find myself in trouble I have a scream that can be heard all the way from New York to L.A. I—"

"You weren't in New York."

"I know. I know. Let me finish. I realize the difference between Harlem and Ikhaya. In Harlem I can always find help if I need it. In Ikhaya no one will risk helping me. Lesson learned. I won't walk the streets of Ikhaya alone at night ever, ever, ever again." She stamped her feet in rhythm with the ev-er, ev-er, ev-er then slapped her hand on the table. "Subject closed."

Lysi stared into her cup. Cristin Holden's happy self-confident face passed through her mind. Lysi still felt some responsibility for her colleague's murder in Montana three years ago. If only she'd gone to Cristin's room right after checking into the motel. If only she'd looked after her. If only...

She clasped her hands together so tightly the knuckles turned white. "It's just that I've already lost one colleague. I..." She sighed. "I just can't bear the thought of losing another one."

"Hey Soul Sister." Grace gazed at her through understanding eyes. "Please believe me, I do understand the dangers in Ikhaya."

Grace paused. When Lysi didn't respond she continued in a compassionate voice. "I'm sorry I was short with you. I promise you I will not take a stupid risk like that again."

Lysi looked up, eyes watery. "I guess that's all I need to know."

"Good." Grace patted her hand. They smiled and clinked teacups to seal their agreement.

"I'm afraid I do have one more worry." Lysi clenched her teeth. "Now don't get me wrong."

Grace narrowed her eyes in suspicion. "Spit it out."

"Well, I'm glad Thabo came along at the right time last night." Lysi spooned some sugar into her tea and swirled the spoon around in her cup several times while trying to order her thoughts about Thabo. What she'd learned about him confused her—he resents women yet he came to the aide of Grace; he has a propensity to solve problems with his fists yet he cares for Lindani like she was a delicate flower; he has an arrogant disdain for authority yet he works in health services acting on orders eight hours a day. Still the bottom line remains. Thabo is a dangerous man. Lysi added another spoon of sugar to her tea and watched it dissolve.

"Stop with the sugar, Lysi. You hate sweet tea." Grace's chastising words jolted Lysi out of her reverie. "Quit stalling. Tell me what's on your mind and get it over with."

"What concerns me is...you spent time alone with a murder suspect."

Grace tucked her chin into a where-did-that-come-from pose. "Murder suspect? Who suspects him? You, Lysi?"

Lysi took a slow sip of tea and tried to think of how to express her suspicions about Thabo. "He has a pretty strong motive—Lindani's pregnancy. And he did assault Sipho."

Grace opened her mouth to say something then clamped it shut as if determined not to let any words escape.

"Uh oh." Lysi leaned over the table towards Grace "What haven't you told me?"

Grace blasted air through her lips. "Thabo told me Sipho admitted he might have had sex with Lindani. It seems late one night Sipho came back from a Cape Town booze party and found Lindani alone and sad outside the child center. Get this, he took her to his bed to…comfort her." Grace spoke the last two words in a staccato beat.

"What!" Lysi said. "That gives Thabo an even stronger motive."

"There's more." Grace took a resigned breath. "Lindani told Thabo she miscarried the baby. Seems to me that would have weakened Thabo's motive a bit."

Lysi recovered quickly from surprise. "That depends on when Lindani told Thabo she'd miscarried—before or after Sipho's death. We have to find out the answer to that question."

"Not we, Lysi. You. I'm on vacation." Grace leaned back in her chair, locked her hands behind her head and closed her eyes.

"Uh huh," Lysi said in an absent-minded tone. She made a note in her mental files. Maynard needs to know about this.

Through a fake yawn Grace said, "On to a more interesting topic." A big smile spread across her lips. "I have some fun news. I have a date tonight with a totally fine South African fox."

Lysi decided not to press Grace for more details about Sipho. Why rain on her parade? "All right! Who's the lucky guy?"

"Officer Billy Joe Mbeki."

"The Ikhaya cop with the southern drawl?" Lysi winked. "I guess you'll be safe enough with one of Ikhaya's finest."

"He's going to show me a little African nightlife." Grace got up and shimmied her hips around the kitchen as she hummed a little rhumba beat.

"Sounds like a dreamy date." Lysi enjoyed Grace's pleasure.

"You know, we'll explore Cape Town." Grace's voice turned impish. "Then later I might explore him."

"That's my Gracie." Lysi swallowed another sip of tea. "Now that I know you'll be in good hands, I guess I can share my newsy item." She enjoyed watching curiosity flood Grace's face. Maybe she'd make her suffer a little bit.

Lysi let her eyes wander around the room. "Are there any cookies? They'd be great with this tea." She got up and moved in slow motion to search the cupboard. She shuffled boxes, opened the silverware drawer, checked under the sink and behind the window curtains.

"Cookies. Who cares about cookies? I know what you're doing. Set your little tush back on that chair and talk to me," Grace said.

Lysi meandered back to the table. She relished watching Grace's curiosity swell to the bursting point. Lysi smoothed under her chin with an index finger. "Well…"

"Get to it, girl."

"Thursday Maynard and I leave for Namibia."

"Namibia! Whoa, the land of orange sand deserts—the Kalahari, the Namib. Better take some bottled water and sunblock." Grace shook the teapot and refilled her cup. "When will you get back?"

"I'll be back Friday. I plan to do a little exploring myself."

"Why Lysi Weston you little devil you." Grace stared at Lysi like her prissy friend had just morphed into Linda Lovelace. "You've decided to risk a stroll on the wild side. And with an Australian stud. I'm proud of you, honey."

At that moment, Amele swished through the door and dropped into a chair. "This chat sounds interesting. What is our on-site little devil up to?"

Lysi's cheeks started to burn. She couldn't predict what Grace would say next but she knew it would embarrass her.

"Lysi's heading off to Namibia with her sheep farmer cop. She plans to explore more than just the country."

Amele looked at Grace and raised her eyebrows as a velvety laugh rumbled up from her belly. Grace's low throaty guffaws joined her in a resounding duet Lysi swore could be heard as faraway as the top of Table Mountain.

In a weak voice Lysi said, "I told you he's a grazier on a sheep station."

After another chortle, Amele wiped her eyes with a napkin. She got up and took a cup from the cupboard, sat and poured some tea.

"On a more serious side," she said, her voice quiet. "I've got more information about Sipho's cause of death."

Amele stirred two spoonfuls of sugar into her tea and took a sip of the syrupy liquid. "You remember Nambeko, Sipho's sister? My goddaughter?"

Grace and Lysi both nodded.

"Well, Mandisa and I met her at the police station and she shared her final autopsy report with us. Sipho did die of an overdose of Xhosa Dream Root as she suspected."

Lysi's interest spiked. "Xhosa Dream Root? What's that?"

"It comes from the root of a flower that is native to our Eastern Cape. Some traditional Xhosa people consider it a sacred plant." Amele pursed her lips and added in a disdainful tone. "Witch doctors believe it induces prophetic dreams."

"Silene Capensis?" Lysi remembered the discussion she and Grace had had about their African Studies class where they'd first heard of the plant.

"That is the scientific name," Amele said. "Xhosa people call it Dream Root. Its primary purpose is to purify and initiate shamans,".

"Interesting." Lysi twisted a lock of hair around her fingers as she often did when she pondered new information. "So Sipho planned to become a shaman?"

"No. Heavens no." Amele wrinkled her brow. "Sipho wanted to become a school teacher."

Lysi looked puzzled. "Then why would he take the dream root?"

Chapter 21

The clock on the Butshingi mantle chimed eight times. Four pairs of eyes shifted to the clock. A minute later the doorbell rang. Lysi, seated on the couch next to Maynard, nodded at Luvo and Amele. Billy Joe's right on time, she thought. Good sign. She started to stand up. "I'll get Grace."

"Please stay seated Lysi," Amele said. "You know Grace." Amele spread her arms and curtsied. "She will make her grand appearance when she is good and ready."

Luvo went to the door and ushered Officer Mbeki into the living room. "Billy Joe, you know my wife, Amele."

Billy Joe removed his leather African Bush hat. Lysi thought it looked slightly out of place with a navy blue blazer, starched white shirt and sharply creased slacks.

"Of course. Nice to see you, Amele." Billy Joe flashed a mischievous smile. "Your gourmet nibbles are the main reason we keep Luvo in our poker group." He slapped Luvo on the back.

Amele gave a curt nod that signaled she was still irritated about the conversation she'd had with Officer Mbeki at the police station. Lysi read Amele's unspoken message, Mbeki might be Luvo's poker mate, but he didn't impress Amele.

Luvo gestured toward Lysi and Maynard still seated on the couch. "Please meet Lysi Weston from California and her boyfriend Detective Maynard Christie from Australia."

Lysi hoped she wouldn't redden at that boyfriend comment as her cheeks heated up. Why did she feel so uncomfortable with the term "boyfriend?"

Billy Joe took Lysi's fingers in his two big hands. "I had heard California is the land of beautiful women. Now I am convinced it is true." He pressed her fingers to his lips and regaled her with an endearing dimpled grin.

Charming, Lysi thought. She loved his mix of Xhosa accent and Mississippi drawl. His spontanious smile put her at ease. She appreciated his air of understated confidence. A reliable man. A man you could trust. She liked Billy Joe. He would indeeed be good for Grace.

Billy Joe extended his hand to Maynard. "It is a pleasure to meet you Detective Christie from the land down under. Luvo tells me you have a sheep station."

"I do. Three hundred thousand acres near Alice Springs in Northern Territory."

Lysi could tell by Maynard's tone he appreciated Billy Joe knowing the difference between a farm and a station.

Billy Joe eyes grew round and he whistled. "That is half the size of Cape Town. How do you manage a place that big?"

"Free range sheep don't need much managing. One of my sons runs the place with the help of some Aborigines and seasonal jackaroo workers—most of them college students. Even though I work in Sydney, I get out to the station about once a month." Maynard's pride was evident in his voice.

"You look robust and healthy. Those wide open spaces must suit you." Billy Joe had the same deep laugh as Luvo.

"I love everything about Northern Territory. My sons and I are in the process of converting a section of our place into a working sheep station for tourists." He looked at Lysi. "We're using some of Lysi's ideas."

74

Billy Joe turned approving eyes to Lysi. "Not only beautiful, but a smart business woman, too. That is as much as a man could want."

"I agree." Maynard touched Lysi's hand.

"I saw a recent T.V. program about Australia's sheep and cattle industry. Very informative. So many of your sheep and cattle stations are closing down." Billy Joe shook his head. "I fear it is the end of an era."

Lysi saw a brief shadow of regret pass over Maynard's face. She knew he would fight to keep his sheep station financially viable. The tourist visits would help.

"The world will always demand prime wool and good mutton. Only sheep can meet those demands," Maynard said. "Sheep stations will be around for awhile."

Amele reached for Billy Joe's hat. "Please sit down. Grace may be a while." She set the hat on the coffee table and turned toward the hall door. "I guess I'd better go and hurry her a bit." Over her shoulder she said, "Luvo dear, please get Billy Joe a drink."

As soon as Officer Mbeki settled into an overstuffed armchair Lysi seized the opportunity to bring up the Sipho murder case. "Billy Joe, Maynard is a homicide detective in Sydney. He's taken a professional interest in the Sipho case."

Maynard did a double take and looked at Lysi, a surprised then annoyed expression on his face. Lysi felt his eyes on her but didn't look at him. She'd done it again. Overstepped. Interfered. She would take back her words if she could but too late, now. She determined not to say another word about the case.

Luvo set a scotch on the coffee table in front of Billy Joe and took a seat in a matching armchair next to him. Luvo's amused expression reinforced Lysi's resolve to keep her comments to herself.

Maynard shifted his eyes back to Billy Joe. "I…I would like to talk with you about the case when you have time…if it wouldn't be intruding."

"Not intruding at all. Always good to hear other professional points of view." Billy Joe spoke in a straightforward tone. Lysi began to relax.

"I am sure you know I am working two murders right now." Billy Joe leaned forward propping his forearms on his thighs. "A teenager and his dog found the body of witch doctor Qamata in some thick shrubs not far from his hut. Someone had bludgeoned him with a heavy rock. It would interest me to discuss both murders with another homicide detective."

Maynard cast a reproachful glance at Lysi. When she saw his jaw tighten she averted her eyes again. Why is he upset? Billie Joe seems to have an interest in his input.

"I went to Qamata's hut a couple days ago." Maynard sounded confessional. "There was nothing to indicate it was a crime scene so I took the liberty of having a look around."

Guilt stung Lysi's conscience when she realized she'd put Maynard on the spot. She inserted herself into the discussion. "Billy Joe, I have to confess that Maynard went to Qamata's hut at my insistence."

A knowing grin crinkled the corners of Billy Joe's eyes. Maynard got the message and returned the grin. *Women.*

Lysi caught their silent communication and decided she'd learn more if she listened and didn't kibitz.

"Crime scenes in Ikhaya are a bit more loose than crime scenes in Cape Town," Billy Joe said. "Sipho's death was not reported as a possible homicide until later. By the time I got to it, the scene was badly corrupted. I will be most interested in hearing your discoveries when we have more time."

Lysi leaned forward, curiosity trumping her decision to listen and not kibitz. "I understand Sipho's autopsy indicated the cause of death was overdose of Xhosa Dream Root."

Billy Joe folded his arms across his chest, leaned against the armchair back and took a labored breath before speaking. "The cause of death is a bit in question at the moment. An overdose of Xhosa Dream Root or Silene Capensis, can make you very sick. However, it is quite unusual for it to lead to death unless the victim has some kind of illness that would render him susceptible. This does not appear to have been the case with young Sipho."

Lysi looked at Maynard who appeared deep in thought. Why doesn't he ask about the cause of death? She waited a couple of beats then asked, "Are you saying Dream Root didn't kill Sipho?"

Billy Joe's observant eyes moved from Maynard's frustrated face to Lysi's inquisitive one. "Dr. Mkiva, a colleague of Dr. Nambeko Nala, reviewed the report right after its completion to confirm it. Standard procedure. What he found led him to conduct another autopsy immediately. He discovered what he considered to be a more likely cause of death. It seems—"

A rustle of satin and click of high heels announced Grace's grand entrance into the living room. All three men bounded to their feet. Grace swirled in her red satin dress. Her long hair glistened like black onyx under the subdued lighting. Four-inch stilettos put her eye-to-eye with Maynard. She formed her full red lips into a soft kissable pucker. "Maynard honey. The way your eyes are bugging out I must look okay."

"More than okay," Maynard said through what Lysi considered a silly grin.

"You hear that Lysi. You better treat your man right or I will."

Lysi did hear. She slipped her hand into Maynard's. The unaccustomed tinge of jealousy she experienced annoyed her. Maynard gave her hand an affectionate squeeze that annoyed her even more because it meant he noted her need for reassurance.

Grace turned to Luvo. "Your turn, darling."

"You look like a Watusi queen." Luvo bowed low. "Your majesty's beauty is exceeded only by that of my lovely wife."

Amele laughed. "Okay Queen Grace. Enough. You will knock poor Billy Joe right off his feet." She smiled at Billy Joe. "Grace is holding court, Billy Joe. Perhaps you would like to comment on her elegant beauty."

Billy Joe's eyes slid slowly over Grace's body leisurely undressing her as if they were alone in a bedroom.

Luvo coughed. "A...thank you, Billy Joe. You have made your appreciation of our queen abundantly clear."

Lysi had drifted into a deep sleep when Grace tiptoed to the side of the bed and whispered, "Are you awake?" She gently squeezed Lysi's shoulder. "Lysi, honey, are you awake."

"Now I am." Lysi rolled over and looked at the luminescent clock dial. "Three o'clock. Go to bed, Grace."

"Okay. Okay. Just wanted to tell you you're borrowing my red dress for your trip to Namibia."

Now wide-awake, Lysi sat up. "What? No. You woke me up to tell me that?" She squinted at Grace. "No. Not just that," Grace said.

Lysi clicked her toungue. "Well, I'm awake now. Tell me how it went tonight. Or dare I ask?"

"Let me put it this way. This dress had Billy Joe panting like a hungry puppy. Unfortunately he remained a perfect gentleman all evening. We're getting together again on Friday."

The excitement in Grace's voice assured Lysi she was right. Billie Joe was very good for her. "And your plans for Friday?"

"He has the weekend off. We're going to Cape Point and we'll hit some Constantia Valley wineries on the way back." Grace slid out of her dress and hung it in the closet.

Lysi yawned. "Sounds like you and Billy Joe are an item. Now can I go back to sleep?" She lay back on the pillow. "No red dress in Namibia. There's no place to wear it." She closed her eyes.

Grace shook Lysi's shoulder. "Wake up Lysi. Didn't you see the look on Maynard's face when I walked in wearing this dress? Honey, red is the color of fiery heat. It symbolizes passion and desire. It stimulates men's most profound urges and impulses. All those base instincts we women love so much."

Lysi noticed Grace's breathing rate had accelerated. She figured Billy Joe might be on her mind.

"Time for you to start pleasing your man," Grace said. "You will take my dress and you will wear it—even if you have to wear it in a tent."

Lysi rolled away from Grace. She did remember Maynard's face. Maybe Grace had a point. Maybe she needed to woo Maynard a little more. Maybe she wanted to. "Okay Grace. If I take the dress will you let me sleep?"

"And wear it." Grace pulled on a pair of flannel pajamas and bounced into bed.

"And wear it. Now can I please go to sleep?"

Chapter 22

Lysi stood outside the Themba Preschool and watched the VW disappear in a cloud of dust. She wanted to go with Maynard to review the Sipho case with Detective Billy Joe Mbeki but knew it was out of the question. She hadn't even bothered to ask. Maynard insisted she wait at the daycare center and not wander the Ikhaya streets. He told her he figured his meeting might take a couple of hours or even longer if Billy Joe wanted to go to the crime scene. He said he'd phone her cell fifteen minutes before picking her up. They planned to explore Ikhaya's Monwabisi Beach after the meeting. Lysi brushed the light dust off her yellow sundress and turned to the Themba Center.

The Center door stood ajar. Lysi knocked and stuck her head through the opening. Mandisa looked up from a desk littered with papers and envelopes. "Lysi, what a surprise. What brings you here?

"Oh, I thought I'd spend a few hours helping out with the kids." She didn't mention she had time to kill while Maynard met with Mbeki. She knew Mandisa wouldn't pry.

"I can certainly use the help." Mandisa's tired face brightened. "Without Sipho…" She swallowed. "Well, I never catch up."

Dark bags under Mandisa's eyes, her sunken cheeks and the sagging neckline of her cotton dress attested to the toll on her health that her son's death had exacted.

"Whatever you need." Lysi patted Mandisa's shoulder.

Mandisa gestured towards the piles of paper on her desk. "With the older children in school I have some time to catch up on my supply orders, deposits and invoices. I do not like this part of owning a daycare center."

"I don't blame you," Lysi said. "Where's Lindani?"

"She is in the nursery room. I cannot get my work done because I have to run into the playroom every few minutes to check on her. It would help so much if you could monitor the toddlers with her." Mandisa's wan smile didn't reach her eyes.

Lysi walked into the toddler room. For a few moments she was back in Robin Hood Nursery School where she'd worked summers during her college years. Fifteen wriggling, giggling two to four-year-olds filled the small room. Some sat on a threadbare carpet working puzzles and scribbling pictures. Some zoomed toy cars across the room while others built block towers and sent them crashing to the floor. A few girls wearing big grownup hats perched at a little table in the playhouse pretending tea party with dolls and teddy bears.

Lindani sat on a chair in the center of the room and rocked a crying toddler. She held a washcloth under his chubby chin. Lysi noticed Lindani's gentle touch and soft cooing. If Lindani had a baby, it would never want for affection and care, Lysi thought.

"Hi Lindani, I'm here to help out for awhile. What would you like me to do?"

Taut lines around Lindani's mouth revealed exhaustion. It occurred to Lysi that Lindani didn't usually work the toddler room by herself and probably found it a bit overwhelming.

Lindani gave the little butterball on her lap a hug and kissed his chin. She said something in Xhosa, put the washcloth in his dimpled fist and pressed it against his bruised chin. He slid off her lap sniffling and tottered to the carpet.

78

"Lysi. I can use your help." Lindani stood and took both Lysi's hands. "You can help put the children in a circle so they can eat their lunch—" She looked around as if trying to remember details. "But first they have to pick up toys. After lunch you can help put out the nap mats." She hesitated, a worried look on her face. "Is…that too much for you to do?"

"Of course not. I'm happy to do it." Again Lysi noticed Lindani's natural considerate manner. Such a sweet girl. She would never intentionally hurt anyone. Lindani may have lied about Sipho, but she had no idea of the seriousness of her allegations. Like a child she simply made up a quick story she thought would solve her immediate problem. Poor thing.

Lysi had forgotten the challenge of cleanup time with toddlers. The kids reminded her of a pack of good-natured puppies romping in all directions. She corralled all fifteen little perpetual motion creatures and herded them into a lopsided circle on the threadbare carpet. Lindani joined the circle and led the tots in a Xhosa nursery song.

Lysi went to the kitchen nook to assemble the lunch tray—a stack of peanut butter sandwiches and carrot sticks. She took a knife and began to quarter apples and place them on a plate.

The side door opened and Nambeko Nala, still in hospital scrubs, entered the kitchen carrying two net bags of groceries. Her clean antiseptic scent accompanied her. "Lysi, good to see you. Mother told me you were here. You must enjoy working with the children."

"Actually I do." Lysi continued quartering apples. "I used to be a teacher."

Lysi hadn't seen Nambeko since Sipho's funeral. The hard tension lines had softened around her mouth and Lysi thought she smiled more spontaneously.

"I must say it surprised me when Mother told me you were here." Nambeko set two large jars of peanut butter on a shelf.

"Really. Why?"

"After Grace's bad experience with Uuka Dlomo and his two brothers, I just did not expect either of you to ever set foot in Ikhaya again," Nambeko said speaking as though Uuka was a casual acquaintance not her brother. Lysi wanted to question Nambeko about Uuka but she had a feeling Nambeko did not take pride in the sibling relationship.

"I came with Maynard." Lysi quartered two more apples.

"Aw, your Australian detective. Those Dlomo boys would run like rats if he so much as frowned at them." Nambeko placed three loaves of bread on the shelf then turned to face Lysi. "Please tell Grace that daytime is safe in Ikhaya. Nighttime? No. I live here and I never go out alone at night."

"Grace did a foolish thing," Lysi said. "She learned her lesson."

"My mother says you and Grace have been a great help to her." Nambeko looked at Lysi with approval. "For that I thank you."

Lysi nodded. She had a lot of questions she wanted to ask Nambeko but decided to just ask one. She placed the quartered apples on the plate then looked up.

"Nambeko, did you know Lindani accused Sipho of seducing her and making her pregnant?"

Nambeko's pleasant smile morphed into a hard frown. "That's ridiculous. What would a bright boy like Sipho want with a girl like Lindani? She is sweet, but slow-witted."

"I see your point." Lysi placed the plate of apples on the tray and added a stack of napkins. Maybe she could probe just a little bit deeper. "You mentioned the cause of Sipho's death was an overdose of Xhosa Dream root."

"Yes." Nambeko looked guarded.

"Did you know there is an additional possible cause?" Lysi picked up the tray without looking at Nambeko. Maybe she shouldn't have mentioned the other cause of death. Oh well, too late now.

"Did Detective Mbeki tell you this?" Nambeko said.

"I overheard him talking to another detective about the autopsy." Lysi hoped she hadn't insulted Nambeko's professionalism.

"Detective Christie, of course. Yes, I knew about the other possible cause." Nambeko started to empty the second grocery bag. "I did not mention it because I did not wish to heap more pain on my mother's already heavy heart."

"I certainly understand." Lysi waited for Nambeko to reveal the other cause of death.

"I am sorry but I should not talk about the investigation. I only hope they find the person who took my brother's young life." Nambeko placed apples in a bowl on the counter and shoved the carrots and milk into an already crowded mini refrigerator. "You will forgive me for rushing. I must finish putting these groceries away and get back to the clinic."

Nambeko emptied the last bag and smiled at Lysi. "Thank you for all you do for my mother." She left the center without another word.

Lysi swallowed her disappointment. She understood Nambeko's desire to minimize her mother's suffering. She almost wished she hadn't burdened Nambeko with comments about the second cause of death. Memo to self, Lysi thought, control your insatiable need for instant answers to questions.

Lysi carried the loaded lunch tray back to the nursery. She returned to the kitchen, filled another tray with plastic glasses and a pitcher of milk, then helped distribute lunch. After lunch she settled the children on their nap mats.

Lysi covered the last child then went to draw the dark curtains on the front windows. As she closed the curtains over the middle window, she glanced out at the street and saw a familiar figure stopped in front of the school. She watched him look over his shoulder then continue on his way casting frequent furtive glances left and right. She studied him for a moment. He didn't look like a typical Ikhaya resident. He wore form-fitting slacks and a blue turtleneck. A silver chain dangled around his neck. Where had she seen that man before? Lysi closed her eyes and tried to jog her memory. Of course, the police station. He talked to Mandisa. The photo in Nambeko's bag. Paki, the gay guy. What was he doing in Ikhaya a place where everybody seemed so hostile to him. And where was he going?

Chapter 23

Maynard pulled to the side of the narrow road and parked in front of a low gray building with a red corrugated steel roof. Sun-faded black letters on the wall spelled out Ikhaya Police Station. He grabbed his backpack and entered the building through a single door with a barred window that matched the bars on three other windows. The pretty young desk officer looked up through thick lashes and scrutinized Maynard for a beat before she spoke. Maynard figured she didn't see many white men in her job. She said something to him in Xhosa. When he looked confused, full red lips curved into an inviting smile. "I can help you?"

Her flirtatious eyes softened Maynard's professional frown into an appreciative grin. "I have an appointment with Officer Mbeki."

"Please to sit on bench." She pointed toward a rough wood bench under a large clock a few steps from the desk. "I will get him."

Maynard thought her throaty voice and thick Xhosa accent had a sensual quality. Her salon hairstyle and makeup, dangling bracelets and fashionable earrings seemed out of place in the Spartan station environment.

He sat on the bench and watched her ample hips swivel to a small cubicle in the corner of the building where Mbeki sat at a desk, head bent over a stack of papers. She leaned over to speak to Mbeki. Maynard couldn't help but enjoy the view.

Officer Billy Joe Mbeki stood, his big body blocking out a gray steel filing cabinet behind his desk. His large physique made the desk look like a piece of playhouse furniture. He motioned Maynard to the cubicle. "Come in, come in."

Maynard stood and walked toward the desk. He smiled at the clerk as she passed.

"Maynard, what a pleasure." Billy Joe shook Maynard's hand then gestured toward the desk officer. "I see you are enjoying our office décor."

"Very attractive." It crossed Maynard's mind that Lysi would be furious if she heard Billy Joe's demeaning remark about the clerk.

"I hope I'm not intruding. Lysi…that is I…was anxious to talk with you about the case."

"Not at all." Billy Joe's lips curved into an understanding grin. He motioned to one of two mismatched chairs in front of the desk. "Please, sit."

"I'll be brief." Maynard knew he wasn't fooling anyone. He was on an errand for Lysi more than for himself. He'd get through the meeting as quickly as possible. However, unable to stop the quickening of his pulse as his investigative instincts kicked in, he had to admit the nature of the case did spark his professional interest. "At the house yesterday evening you mentioned an autopsy result that indicated another possible cause of death."

"Yes. As I told you, Dr. Mkiva reviewed Dr. Nala's report. It puzzled him to find Xhosa Dream Root listed as the cause of death." Billy Joe pulled a manila folder from a wire file on his desk. He opened it and translated Dr. Mkiva's comments. "It is rare for ingestion of the Dream Root to cause anything much more than a stomachache…maybe a bad case of vomiting."

He raised pensive eyes to Maynard. "In my own experience, there have never been any reported fatalities from the root. Shamans have used it for centuries with few ill effects."

"What do the shamans use it for?" Out of habit Maynard started jotting down notes in a notebook he always carried with him.

"As a divination tool to help their patients solve problems," Billy Joe said.

"Sounds like the Australian Aborigine traditional healers," Maynard said.

"I guess there are some similarities among most traditional healers." Billy Joe closed the folder and placed it back in the wire file. "In the case of the Xhosa healers, the witch doctor's patient focuses on a question he wants answered before going to sleep. Then, purportedly, ancestors appear to him in the root-induced dream and provide a response. Is that how it works in Australia?"

"Yes, pretty much. The Aborigines have the same emphasis on ancestor involvement," Maynard said.

Maynard printed "cause of death" on his notebook then looked at Billy Joe. "If the Dream Root didn't kill Sipho, what did?"

"Upon further examination, Dr. Mkiva found Cobra venom in Sipho's body."

Maynard's eyes widened. "You mean he died of a snakebite?" Maynard knew about snakes. In Northern Territory he'd seen some of the most dangerous snakes in the world—the Mulga, Gwarder, Northern Death Adder and the Brown Snake.

"Not a cobra *bite*," Billy Joe said. "Cobra venom. Dr. Mkiva found more venom than could be injected by one cobra. His immediate thought was Sipho might have encountered a quiver of Cape cobras. He dismissed that theory because he didn't find a single fang mark on the body. In his professional opinion, someone injected Sipho with the venom."

Maynard leaned back in his chair and crossed his arms, a posture he often took when analyzing a situation. "Cobra venom. Cri-key!"

"The Cape cobra venom affects the nervous system," Billy Joe said. "Very painful. The victim has trouble breathing and suffocates."

Maynard gritted his teeth as if he could feel the pain. He thought for a moment. Now things were beginning to make sense.

He pulled a brown evidence bag from his daypack, set it on the desk and opened the tissue of soil he'd collected at the crime scene. "I found these crystals on the floor of Qamata's hut."

Billy Joe leaned forward and squinted at the yellowish crystals then shot Maynard a so-what expression.

"In Australia we have snake farms. Australian Reptile Park for one," Maynard said. "The farm snake milkers extract venom and freeze dry it into crystals for shipping to medical research centers where the venom is reconstituted with sterile water and used in the production of antivenins."

"Tell me more," Billy Joe said still eyeing the crystals. "I am investigating how someone would get hold of snake venom."

"I had occasion to visit a research lab on a business trip to Melbourne." Maynard spread the crystals with a finger. "These look a lot like the crystals I saw at the Melbourne lab. They could be venom crystals. I'll leave them with you to check out."

Billy Joe rolled up the tissue containing the crystals, placed it in a baggie and dropped it into an evidence box on the floor behind his desk.

Maynard reached into his bag and pulled out another tissue and unwrapped a small white cap. "I wondered about this. I figured it was the lid for a prescription drug container of some kind. Now I think it could be the cap to a vial used to ship freeze-dried venom." He handed it to Billy Joe.

"If we could locate the vial it might be labeled." Billy Joe slipped the cap from the tissue into a plastic bag and added it to the evidence box.

"I have one more thing." Maynard took the multi-colored stone bracelet from his bag and laid it on the desk. "Do you know a man who goes by the name of Paki?"

"Paki? Oh yes. Poor fellow." Billy Joe's jaws tightened. "The *good* township citizens drummed him out of Ikhaya because he is openly homosexual."

Lysi was right, Maynard thought. Paki is gay and this is his bracelet. "Well, I think this bracelet may belong to him."

"Where did you find it and why do you think it belongs to Paki?" Billy Joe picked up the bracelet and examined it.

"First, this is a Rainbow Pride bracelet. The kind that originated in the U.S. in memory of the '76 San Francisco Gay Pride Parade.

"The Gay Rights Movement. I know about that. I was a small child living in Mississippi when that whole crusade started." Billy Joe turned the bracelet over and scrutinized it. "No inscription. It could be Paki's—or any other gay guy's."

"True, but I found it in Qamata's hut. Paki told Mandisa he had gone to the hut."

Billy Joe's eyebrows drew together. "I am surprised Paki would set foot in Ikhaya much less risk going into that isolated area given his fear of bullies like the Dlomo boys. If those homophobic little bastards caught him, they would probably beat him to death. "

Maynard pointed to the broken latch. "See how the metal is stretched. Someone had to yank pretty hard to get it off Paki's wrist. Also there were signs of struggle inside Qamata's hut. A toppled table. Maybe an overturned seat of some kind. I think a check of Paki's wrist might still show signs of bruising."

"The next question is whether Paki struggled with Qamata or Sipho?" Billy Joe wrote the question on his tablet.

Maynard leaned back in his chair again. He hadn't considered the possibility of a struggle between Qamata and Paki. He figured the bracelet ripped off in a tussle between Paki and Sipho. Unfortunately, the answer to that question may have died with Qamata.

"I understand the dead boy's mother is a person of interest in the murder of the witch doctor," Maynard said.

"Not a serious one. Mandisa has always hated Qamata—with cause. Years ago she might have had the strength to murder him. Today arthritis has made her incapable of lifting a rock the size of the murder weapon. More important, Mandisa's values would not allow her to kill anyone." Billy Joe ran his fingers through his hair in frustration. "On the other hand Mandisa is convinced Qamata is responsible for the death of her son. A vengeful mother can find a way."

"It happens," Maynard said.

"Of course my question would be what was Sipho doing in Qamata's hut? Surely not for a healing," Billy Joe said. "Why would an educated young man like Sipho resort to traditional practice to solve some kind of problem?" Billy Joe tapped his pen on a tablet page full of scribbled notes and commented more to himself then to Maynard, "Maybe Qamata was killed because he knew the answer to that question."

Maynard flipped back a few pages in his notebook. "The name Thabo has come up several times. Where does he fit into all this?"

Billy Joe shook his head. "That young man breaks my heart. I knew him before his mother died. She had such high hopes for him. He shared her dreams. When she died, his future crashed. He insisted on raising his little handicapped sister, Lindani. Bitterness replaced his aspirations. I have no doubt you already know the story about Lindani and Sipho."

Maynard nodded. "So he's a suspect?"

"Yes, we're looking at him for both murders."

"You think there's a connection between the two murders? The same killer?" Maynard hadn't thought of that because the causes of death were so different. "Bludgeoning with a rock is far different from death by snake venom. Doesn't sound like the same killer to me. Evidence?"

Billy Joe sighed. "No evidence. Motive, yes. Opportunity, maybe. The list of suspects is pretty sparse."

Chapter 24

Lysi did a quick visual check of the Themba students lying on their nap mats. Several had fallen asleep and the rest lay quietly, eyes drooping. She turned back to the window just in time to catch a glimpse of Paki as he passed behind a large shipping container painted deep orange with the words "Community Chat" printed above its door. What is he up to? Not my business, she thought. Stay out of it.

Lindani returned from the kitchen and sat on a chair by the window to watch the children during their nap. Lysi tiptoed over to her and told her she wanted to run out for a quick bite while the children were resting. It crossed Lysi's mind that she would have to follow Paki a little ways since he was heading in the same direction as the snack bar.

Without waiting for an answer, Lysi rushed out the door just in time to see Paki turn onto the path toward Qamata's hut. Where is he going and why? She forgot about food in her determination to find out.

She trailed Paki at a distance. A couple of skinny dogs of uncertain pedigree fell in line behind her and sniffed at her feet with their wet noses. She wanted to clap her hands, shout and send them running but Paki would have heard her. She forced herself to ignore the annoying canines until they turned and galumphed back toward the street.

Lysi slowed her pace as Qamata's hut came into view. She ducked behind the large yellowwood tree and watched Paki disappear into the shack. What business did he have in there?

She stood by the tree trying to decide what to do. Could Paki be dangerous? He seemed pretty harmless when he approached Mandisa at the police station. On the other hand, murderers are always dangerous. He might have a weapon. She decided not to confront him. She'd just observe.

Lysi sneaked around the back and found the peephole Maynard had told her about. She peeked through the hole at Paki. He rustled about the hut glancing at the door every few seconds. He shoved jars and boxes around on the shelves and peered behind them. He searched the corners of the hut. He scraped at the dusty soil with his shoe.

Lysi watched him with an inquisitive eye. What was he searching for? Curiosity trumped caution. She edged along the perimeter of the hut to the front. She could see Paki through the crack in the partially opened door. He rubbed his hand over the walls, eyed the ceiling and emitted a loud sigh. Lysi figured he'd reached a point of desperation in his search.

She slid the door open a little wider. It produced a painful creak.

Paki whipped around.

Lysi's body wrenched and she let out a little squeak.

Paki slapped his hand over his heart. "You scared me to death!" He stared big-eyed at Lysi. "You are Mandisa's white sister from the police station."

"You remember me?" Lysi stepped over the threshold into the hut.

"Yes, you are the only white sister Mandisa has." He frowned. "What are you doing here?"

"I might ask you the same question," Lysi said.

"Nothing."

"Stop it, Paki. I watched you. You were searching for something." So much for not confronting him, she thought.

"No, I was not." His voice sounded like a whiney child trying to lie himself out of a spanking.

Lysi knew what Paki was searching for. The bracelet. She decided not to challenge him about it immediately. She'd accuse him of something else first. Worry him a little then throw the bracelet at him.

"You came to find the cap, didn't you?" Lysi sounded like an angry parent even to herself.

"Cap? What is that? I know nothing of a cap. I never wear hats." Paki fluffed his well-coifed hair.

"Do you want me to report you to Officer Mbeki?" Lysi said even though she had no intention of letting Billy Joe know she'd gone to Qamata's hut.

Paki shrugged and thrust out his lower lip in a childish pout. Lysi got the message. He had no fear of Mbeki. What now?

Lysi remembered Thabo's angry interrogation of Nambeko about Paki's presence at Sipho's funeral. She figured Paki remembered it, too.

"Or maybe you'd rather I tell Thabo."

Paki's eyes widened and he swallowed hard. Lysi had guessed right. Paki was much more afraid of Thabo than Officer Mbeki. Why?

"Paki, tell me what you were searching for."

"Nothing you would care about." He turned his face away from Lysi.

Lysi knitted her brows. "If you won't tell me, maybe you'll tell Thabo."

"I...I..." Paki dropped his eyes. "A bracelet. That is all."

"The rainbow bracelet?" Lysi asked.

Paki nodded. He looked curious but didn't ask how she knew.

Just as Lysi thought, Paki came back to the crime scene to remove evidence that would connect him to Sipho's death. Now she knew she faced a murderer.

"You lost your bracelet in a struggle with Sipho. He grabbed it off your arm when you beat up on him." Now Lysi's palms began to sweat. She knew better than to press a desperate killer. She started to back toward the door but stopped because something inside her couldn't quite picture Paki as a dangerous killer.

"No. No. I would never hurt Sipho." Paki sounded shocked at her accusation.

"Enough, Paki. Let's see what Thabo has to say about this." Lysi pretended to punch in Thabo's number on her cell phone.

"Please. Do not call Thabo. The bracelet is not mine."

"What?" Lysi stopped dialing. "Whose is it?"

"I cannot tell you." Paki's eyes watered. "What does it matter now that Sipho is dead? Now that Qamata, his killer, is dead?"

"It does matter." Lysi didn't know what to believe. Her voice hardened. "Maybe Thabo can get you to talk." She raised her phone.

"No, please," Paki said in a high-pitched pleading voice. He swallowed hard. He laid his hand on Lysi's phone, hung his head and spoke to the floor. "It belonged to Sipho."

Lysi stood for a moment her mouth agape staring at Paki. In a small voice she said, "Sipho was gay?"

Paki's shoulders slumped. "We were lovers. I gave him the bracelet. It matches mine." Paki pulled up his shirtsleeve and showed a twin to the Rainbow Coalition bracelet Lysi had found in the hut. "Please do not tell anyone. Sipho is dead now. People in Ikhaya are not very tolerant. If they find out he was gay it will hurt Mandisa and Nambeko."

Lysi's eyes fluttered. It was almost too much. Her brain began trekking through the information she already knew about Paki and Sipho. Nothing fit. She knew Paki was gay because Amele had revealed that at the Police station. That fit. Grace told her Sipho had admitted he'd slept with Lindani. If he was gay, that didn't fit.

"I came for the bracelet because I saw Sipho did not have it on in his casket," Paki said. "I wanted to have it as a token of our lost happiness."

An avalanche of words tumbled from Paki's mouth as if he needed to reveal everything at once. "Sipho stayed with me in Cape Town every Thursday and Friday. He telephoned me every night from Ikhaya. When he did not call for two nights I knew something was wrong. I went to Themba to speak to him. That day Lindani told me he had just left to go to see Qamata. I caught up with him. I asked why he was going to see a witch doctor. He told me he had fathered a child with Lindani. He had to marry her to make it right." Paki hung his head.

Lysi guessed Paki didn't know the whole story. "What happened then?"

"I loved Sipho." Paki locked the fingers of both hands into a beseeching mode and pressed them against his chest. "I begged him not to throw his life away on an empty-headed girl. He insisted he had to do the right thing. He said he could not allow his child to be raised without a father. He could not allow his child to be raised by Lindani and Thabo." Tears filled Paki's eyes. "I told him it would never work."

"Sipho wanted to do what he thought was right," Lysi said in a sympathetic tone.

"True, but It went against his nature. Still, he insisted he would go to Qamata for a cure for his homosexuality. I begged him not to go. I couldn't stop him. I followed him, hid behind the hut and watched Qamata feed him the Xhosa Dream Root elixir. He got terribly sick and passed out. I couldn't watch anymore. I ran and ran."

"Paki, you said you saw Thabo outside Qamata's hut on the day of Sipho's murder. Did he have something to do with Sipho's death?"

Just as quickly as Paki's avalanche of words began—it stopped. He wouldn't look at Lysi. "I have said too much. I must go."

Paki stuck his head through the door opening and looked both ways then slipped out. Lysi stood at the threshold and watched him disappear into the woods. His grief seemed so intense. She hoped he would find a way to deal with it.

A crack and a swish sound pulled Lysi's stare to the back wall of the hut. What was that? A wild animal? She stood like a statue. She heard the swish sound again. Something was moving behind the hut. What should she do? Her head swam and her heart pounded. She choked when she tried to breathe. Run. Wait, no. What if it's a lion or leopard? Cats love to chase. Where had she heard that? Wild animals try to avoid humans. Give them space. That's it, she thought. Be quiet. Maybe it won't notice me.

She inched further into the hut and closed the door. She moved close to the small hole on the back wall and tried to peek out. Something blocked the hole. Something with a pine soapy smell. Were there pine trees in Ikhaya? Had the animal rubbed up against some pine boughs? She backed away from the hole. She could hear her blood pounding in her ears, feel her heart thudding against her chest wall. She watched. She listened. She waited.

Minutes crept by. No more sounds came from behind the hut. The sudden ring of Lysi's cellphone exploded the silence sending a bolt of fear shooting through her body.

Maynard's voice slowed her rapid heartbeat until he said, "I'll see you in about fifteen minutes."

Lysi streaked out the door.

Chapter 25

The sun climbed above Namibia's dry Eros Mountains and started driving the day's temperature toward the 90-degree mark. When the plane landed at Windhoek's International Airport, Lysi followed Maynard down the plane's portable steps and onto the tarmac. As they walked to the terminal Lysi surveyed the dry gray-gold terrain carpeted with low-growing shrubs.

"This landscape reminds me of Alice Springs, she said.

"Uh huh. Maybe a little." Maynard already had his phone out calling his son, Joel.

"We're here. Are we meeting in the parking lot same as before?"

Pause.

"Okay, see you there. Oh, I brought Lysi Weston along." He winked at Lysi as he clicked off his phone.

That was short and to the point, Lysi thought. Men aren't given to chitchat.

They hurried straight through the sterile terminal building past cafes and shops to the parking lot exit.

"Dad, over here." The shout came from a gangly young man draped over a dusty, eighties something Volkswagen. His straight brown hair hung longer than the blonde locks of the equally tall, curly-headed girl beside him. Their suntanned faces were almost as dark as the twin khaki cargo pants and long-sleeved shirts they wore.

Lysi eyed Joel. It struck her he was a younger version of his father. Same soft brown eyes and easy smile. Same appealing laid-back personality. Same lean, hard body. Lysi's breathing quickened. What woman wouldn't want a man like Maynard?

Lysi's eyes widened in surprise. Whoa, she thought. A man like *Maynard*? How had she leaped from Joel to Maynard? She glanced at Maynard then quickly looked away fearful he might read her thoughts. She sighed in relief when Joel threw his arms around his dad and slapped him on the back a couple of times, drawing Maynard's total attention.

Joel grinned at Lysi over his dad's shoulder. He stepped forward and gave her a kiss on each cheek. "At last I get to meet the lady who turned my dad into a wee bit of a dill."

Lysi's eyes twinkled and she risked a questioning glance at Maynard.

"Don't ask." Maynard said and gave his son an amicable punch on the shoulder.

"All right, all right. Enough of that," Joel said. His perennial grin grew bigger as he put his arm around the girl's slim waist and nudged her forward. "Dad. Lysi. Meet Kimberly." He kissed her cheek. "My wife."

Maynard's mouth dropped open.

Lysi did a double-take.

Kimberly's smile faded.

Joel's grin stretched bigger, all the way to his ears.

After what seemed like an eternity of silence, Lysi thrust her hand forward. "So…so nice to meet you Kimberly.

"You're American." Kimberly pumped Lysi's hand and her smile returned. "Me too."

"You didn't tell me…" Maynard swallowed then opened his arms to Kimberly. "I…I…always wanted a daughter."

The Onkala Lodge was only 35 kilometers from the airport but it took 45 minutes to get there. The VW sailed along on B 6, a macadam highway. It slowed on the clay and gravel D 1502 then crawled the final 14 kilometers on the dust and dirt of M 53.

The Volkswagen bumped past the two-story natural stone Onkala Lodge. It halted in front of a thatched-roof bungalow tucked away in a forest of knee-high, gray green bush shrubs.

"I think we're home," Lysi said. She uncurled from the backseat and stretched. Maynard wedged himself out the door and stood beside her.

"Right," Joel said. "This is your bungalow." He pointed to another about a quarter of a mile further up the lane. "That one's ours." He pressed the accelerator and shouted out the window. "We'll pick you up at eight for our honeymoon dinner in the lodge."

Maynard watched the VW's dust cloud putt forward then settle at the next bungalow.

Lysi watched Maynard and saw consternation cloud his face.

"Married? That's it? No discussion? No explanation? No—" He shook his head.

Lysi forced her hand into Maynard's clenched fist. "They seem happy. I'm glad you didn't press him into a discussion of why he didn't tell you he was getting married. We'll learn more at dinner tonight." She pulled Maynard toward the bungalow. "Come on, let's have a look."

They crossed the stone wrap-around veranda, passed two wicker viewing chairs and walked inside.

"Very nice," Lysi said checking out the tan and gold color scheme, the beige lounge chairs and the modern bathroom.

She walked into a small alcove and saw a canopy bed with a tied back mosquito net. Oversized pillows perched on a thick comforter.

Only one bed, she thought. She felt Maynard's eyes on her. She didn't turn to face him. What is he thinking? Surely he understands they have no future together. She would never move to Australia and she was certain he would never move to San Francisco. Did she have to say it? When she did look at him his eyes crinkled with amusement.

"Nice big bed. Plenty of room." He flashed Lysi a roguish grin. "Cri-key, I like this place already."

A warm breeze rippled through the thatched-roof lapa of the Onkala Lodge Restaurant. Lysi could see the pride in Maynard's eyes as he listened to Joel and Kimberly talk non-stop about their activities in a small Namibian village school where they both volunteered. She figured the restaurant's subdued lighting, soft classical music and the restful earth tones of the surrounding wilderness helped calm earlier tensions. Lysi could see why Joel and Kimberly had chosen Onkala Lodge for their honeymoon.

A well-fed black waiter came to the table. Joel spoke to him in Oshiwambo, a Khomas local language. The waiter chuckled and scribbled on his notepad.

"Hey Dad, you're going to love what I chose. A real Namibian delicacy."

Maynard knitted his brow. "And that would be?"

"Mopane." Joel winked at Kimberly. She giggled.

"And that is?" Maynard said.

"Fried caterpillars cooked with chili and onions."

The furrow between Maynard's brows deepened and his lips stretched away from his teeth.

"Dad, don't look so green. They're not the furry kind."

Joel punched his dad's arm. "No, I ordered omajowa mushroom soup followed by a hearty springbok steak. You'll think you're back in Alice Springs having a big prime rib dinner."

The well-fed black waiter flourished a bottle of champagne Lysi had ordered from the host earlier. "Very good champagne. Go good with mopane." A dimpled smile accompanied his little joke. He filled four flutes and placed the bottle in a stainless steel ice bucket next to the table.

Lysi raised her glass to Joel and Kimberly. "To a wonderful future."

Joel took a gulp of champagne and gazed first at Kimberly then Lysi. "Dad, how did we manage to capture these incredibly gorgeous goddesses? Kimberly, a man's fantasy come true in heavenly blue. Lysi a voluptuous vision in brilliant red."

"You should have been a poet, son." Maynard's eyes rested on Lysi. "I couldn't have said it better myself."

Maynard swallowed his champagne and looked at Joel. "So you captured Kimberly then married her just after I left for Cape Town. Seems you were a wee bit secretive about it."

"Not secretive, Dad. It just didn't come up," Joel said.

"Oh! It just didn't come up. I see. Well—"

"Where will you live?" Lysi interrupted, determined to keep the honeymoon dinner light.

"Alice Springs," Kimberly said. "I plan to help out on the sheep station."

Maynard coughed on his second sip of champagne. "Have you ever been to Alice Springs? The heat is—"

"Oh yes, I worked for six weeks as a jillaroo at Napperby Cattle Station last year. That's where I met Joel."

Maynard stared at Joel. "When you trained jills and jacks there last summer?"

"Right," Joel said.

"Heat?" Kimberly giggled. "I grew up in Death Valley, California. My dad's a ranger at Furnace Creek Campground and my mom runs the camp visitors' center. How does 46 degrees C. grab you? 114 Fahrenheit to us Yanks."

"I'd say you'll do fine in the Alice, that is if you don't catch a chill," Lysi said.

"Uh…yeah." Maynard bobbed his chin several times. "Yeah, I think so."

Joel put his arm around Kimberly and kissed her cheek. "You bet she will."

The more Maynard learned about Kimberly the lower his anxiety dipped. The excellent meal, good wine and congenial conversation coupled with the natural ambience of the dining room seemed to relax him.

Joel downed the last of his, stood and stretched. "I'm beat." Again he flashed that endearing grin that reminded Lysi so much of Maynard.

"Yeah, me too," Kimberly said and bounced up next to Joel.

"Good night you two. I'll leave the VW for you," Joel said handing Maynard the keys. "We'd rather walk back to the bungalow. Don't be out too late." He punched his dad's upper arm.

Only a few guests remained in the restaurant as Maynard finished off a beer. Lysi swirled the dregs of her wine then reached for his hand. "They're married. They'll be fine. Young people are flexible." She didn't add …unlike us.

Maynard gazed at Lysi. He sighed. "I guess it'll all work out. She seems like a good match for Joel."

Lysi nodded. She really believed the marriage would work. "Kimberly's life experiences have prepared her for the Outback. She'll feel right at home with Joel on the sheep station."

They sat without speaking for a few minutes. Lysi broke the silence. She needed to talk to Maynard about the murder case and decided this might be a good time.

"Maynard there's something I need to tell you."

"What?" Maynard jiggled his eyebrows and grinned. "That you desire me? That you want me to hold you? That you want me to kiss you?"

Lysi's eyes widened. She caught the real meaning behind Maynard's attempt at humor. He was telling her how he felt. This was not the time to bring up the murder.

Maynard leaned back in his chair. "Go ahead. Let's get it over with."

"No. It's not important."

"Lysi, please. Say what you want to say and then we'll set it aside until we get back to Cape Town. Deal?"

"Deal."

Lysi toyed with her fork. "I'm not sure where to begin. I don't know how much you learned from Billy Joe."

Maynard said nothing.

"I guess I'll just dive in." She dropped her fork and spoke in a serious tone. "After Lindani told Thabo she was pregnant and Sipho was the father, Thabo confronted Sipho. Sipho admitted he might have had sex with Lindani after returning from a drinking party in Cape Town."

Maynard opened his mouth to say something but Lysi stopped him. "Wait, there's more. Later Lindani told Thabo she'd miscarried. She lied. She wasn't pregnant at all."

Maynard folded his arms across his chest. "And how did you come upon this bit of information."

Lysi hesitated. "Thabo told Grace that night in Ikhaya when he beat off her attackers."

"Is that it?"

"No."

"Go on." Maynard showed a mild professional interest.

"You know the rainbow bracelet? It didn't belong to Paki."

Now Maynard leaned forward on his elbows. "And how do you know this?"

"Because I…"

"Yes?"

Lysi did not want to answer Maynard's question. She picked up her napkin and dabbed at her lips while she spoke, muffling her words. "I followed Paki to Qamata's hut while you met with Billy Joe."

"You what?"

"You heard me." Lysi suppressed a flare of irritation at having to explain herself. After all, Maynard wasn't her mother. "Paki admitted he went there to find the bracelet. He said the bracelet belonged to Sipho. Paki has one just like it. He showed it to me." Lysi took a breath. "Maynard, Sipho was gay."

"What?" Maynard's jaw dropped. "That changes the whole case."

"Paki told me when Sipho thought he'd fathered a child with Lindani, he went to Qamata for a cure. He thought Qamata could make him straight. He actually planned to marry Lindani."

"Poor bastard," Maynard said.

"There's more." Maynard's interest encouraged Lysi. "Paki said he saw Thabo Deyi in Qamata's hut on the day Qamata was murdered."

Maynard didn't respond for what felt like a very long time to Lysi. Finally he said, "Do you believe Paki saw Thabo in the hut?"

The question surprised Lysi. She had assumed Paki had told the truth. "I guess I do. I mean why wouldn't I?"

Maynard's eyes focused somewhere in a middle distance. "Something isn't right. I believe he saw someone. I'm just not sure it was Thabo."

Chapter 26

Lysi and Maynard lingered on the dusky veranda of the bungalow and listened to the whispery breeze and quiet movements of nocturnal animals and insects just beyond the their field of vision. A mix of delicate scents wafted from myriads of plants surrounding the bungalow. Lysi moved closer to Maynard. He put his arm around her without taking his eyes off the black-velvet sky, studded with glistening rhinestones. Lysi had seen him gaze at the sky in the same way while sitting on the homestead veranda evenings in Alice Springs.

"The stars are so bright," she whispered.

"Look up there." Maynard pointed to a constellation. "That's Andromeda. The ancients praised her incomparable beauty." He looked down at Lysi. "I wouldn't be surprised if she looked a lot like you."

"Of course you're exaggerating, but keep it up," Lysi said.

"No, I mean it. And by the way, that dress is bonza," Maynard said. "Turn around and let me feast my eyes a bit."

Lysi laughed and spun around. Her skirt flared, revealing long, tanned legs.

"Whoa! I can feel my temperature rising." Maynard grinned and pretended to wipe his brow with the back of his arm.

"Really? Well, let's see just how high it'll soar." Lysi spun around two more times. Grace was right. The red dress was a perfect choice. The effect on Maynard pleased her more than she'd expected.

When Lysi turned back to Maynard, his fleeting smile had transformed into an intense expression. "I nearly dropped to my knees when you appeared in that dress tonight."

He stared at her in silence for a long second. Then, he slid his warm hands down the silky sides of the dress to her slim waist. "It cinches nicely here…" His hands continued down her body and cupped the curve of her hips. "…and drapes smoothly here."

Lysi's pulse quickened. She had trouble breathing.

Maynard's palms glided around to the small of her back. "They say a woman who wears red possesses a simmering inner spark waiting to be ignited."

Lysi caught her breath. She knew what Maynard wanted. Fear fluttered in her chest. A long time ago she had possessed that inner spark. She had allowed her former husband to kindle it. But he also snuffed it out. No. She couldn't risk a repeat of that pain. She should tell Maynard the fire was dead. She should cut this right now. Not lead him on. She should tell him they have no future. She should—

His arms tightened around her. He drew her into an intimate embrace. She could feel every part of his body pressing against her through the thin dress. The kiss was not tentative like his previous kisses. It was long and hungry. Lysi's heart pounded. She felt that inner spark explode into an all-consuming blaze. Her mind emptied of all thought. Now it was just feeling, pure sensation. She didn't want the kiss to end.

Suddenly Maynard released her, stepped back and held her at arms length. Breathing fast and heavy, his eyes searched her face. He lingered for only a moment then kissed her forehead, turned and walked into the bungalow.

Lysi stared after him. She knew he wanted her. Why didn't he take her hand and lead her inside? Why did he just leave her standing there? Did she do something wrong?

Weak with jagged emotion, Lysi ordered her limp legs to carry her into the bungalow. Maynard glanced at her when she entered then he went to the bed, picked up one of the pillows and plopped it on an armchair. He went to the closet and pulled an extra blanket off the shelf.

At first Lysi wanted to question him. Why the change in mood? Why the sudden coolness? But she didn't ask those questions because she already knew the answers. He wanted her, but he thought she didn't want him. Her cheeks felt hot. What to do? Without thinking of an answer she strolled to the chair, picked up the pillow, dropped it back on the bed and fluffed it with exaggerated care. She walked over to Maynard, took the blanket from him, replaced it on the closet shelf and closed the closet door. She turned and dusted her hands past each other as if to say, "There, that's done. Let's move on."

Lysi flashed Maynard her most scintillating smile.

He stared at her, mouth agape.

"Maynard." She smoothed her hands down the sides of her dress in one slow sensual movement. "Can you help me out of this dress?"

Maynard didn't move. His feet seemed to be anchored to the floor. "Lysi, I need to be honest with you. I...We...This...Are you sure?"

"Maynard, don't talk. Just feel." She snickered inside. How many times had Maynard said those very words to her?

She backed up to him and pointed to her zipper.

He slowly unzipped it. He slid his warm hands inside the dress and caressed her waist while his lips skimmed over her neck, shoulders and back igniting millions of little tingles throughout her body.

Nerves somersaulted in her stomach. She swallowed. She was feeling.

As her dress slipped to the floor he turned her around to him. His pupils darkened. His eyes seemed to caress and explore her body the way his hands and mouth promised to do. He said in a hoarse whisper, "Lysi."

He scooped her up and laid her on the bed. He lay down gently beside her and pulled her into a tender embrace. He nuzzled her lips with his own. He kissed her forehead, temple, chin.

His muscular body, the musky scent of his neck, and the roughness of his day's beard growth—his total maleness—sent her hormones rocketing out of control.

His lips cruised over the hollow of her throat, shoulders, and chest finding his way to her most intimate parts—long lingering kisses that made her lose all sense of anything except his lips. All she could hear were heartbeats and sighs.

When he was above her, his tongue skimming over her lips to part them, her arms crept around his neck pulling him to her. In that instant their bodies dissolved into each other in a rhythmic ritual of primeval pleasure.

In the stillness that followed, Lysi lay in his arms. Her last thought before drifting off to sleep was that San Francisco was still a world away from Alice Springs.

Chapter 27

Lysi groaned when the abrasive jangle of the house phone shattered the soothing silence of the Butshingi deck. Less than fifteen minutes ago Grace and Billy Joe Mbeki had left the house for an evening out, mercifully ending their barrage of questions about Namibia. Exhausted from the three-hour delayed flight, Lysi had just started to unwind on the deck, a glass of wine in one hand the other resting on Maynard's hard thigh. She breathed in the sweet soap-like fragrance of potted freesias, took a sip of wine and snuggled closer to him. He felt so good. Forget the phone. Let it ring.

The annoying jangle persisted.

"You better answer it." Maynard pecked her cheek. "Might be important. Maybe Amele reporting on her mother's condition."

Lysi feigned a wounded expression. "Thanks for the great suggestion."

Maynard gave her a little nudge, stretched and ended a big yawn with an equally big grin.

Lysi exhaled and dragged into the house. Maynard was right. It might be Amele. Grace had told her Amele and Luvo had gone to Vredendal to spend a few days with her mother who had stepped off her porch and broken an arm. Since it was a four-hour drive they decided to stay there rather than drive back and forth.

"Hello."

"Amele." The voice on the line choked. "Amele, Uuka tried to hurt me. And so did—"

"Who is this?" Lysi had to strain to understand the panicky words on the other end of the phone.

"Who is this? The voice became a squeaky whisper. "Where is Amele?"

"She's out." The voice was vaguely familiar but Lysi couldn't place it. "This is Lysi Weston."

"Lysi, it is me. Lindani. From Themba. You remember?"

"Of course, Lindani. What happened? Are you all right?" Lysi spoke in an even tone and waited several seconds for Lindani to answer. She could hear her sob and gasp for air.

"Oh Lysi, Uuka tried to hurt me like he hurt Grace. I said 'no' but he would not stop. His brothers tried, too." Lindani's voice broke into childlike whimpering. "I said to stop but they would not they—"

"Lindani, I can help you. Where are—"

"Paki came." Lindani kept talking as though she hadn't heard Lysi. "I ran to Sara's."

"Paki?" Lysi blinked several times. "Is Paki with you?"

Lysi could picture Sara's Bed and Breakfast where she and Grace had spent the night, but she couldn't picture Paki on the dangerous streets of Ikhaya at night. What was he doing there?

"They took Paki." Lindani choked on the words.

Lysi had difficulty following Lindani's disconnected sentences. A cold, questioning fear slithered through her. Why had Lindani been out by herself? Thabo never left her alone at night. What had Uuka done to her?

"Where's Thabo?" Lysi said.

"Thabo? No. You cannot tell Thabo. You cannot tell anyone. It is my shame, not Thabo's."

A wave of sympathy mixed with anger flooded Lysi's thoughts. So typical for the victim of a sexual assault to blame herself—her clothes, voice, eyes or smile invited the attack. Lysi needed to reassure Lindani nothing was her fault. All the blame belonged to Uuka. But first she needed to make certain Lindani was safe. "Lindani, listen to me. Where is Thabo?"

"He went somewhere. A job, I think. Cape Town maybe. I…I don't know." Lindani's helpless whine worried Lysi.

Lysi wanted to ask more questions but as Lindani's fear and confusion seemed to escalate she remembered Lindani had a little girl's mind in a woman's body. She needed help and comfort, not the third degree.

97

Lysi squeezed her eyes shut. What to do? She could phone Officer Billy Joe Mbeki, but would he believe Lindani? She'd already lied about Sipho fathering a child with her. Maybe Thabo? No he'd hunt down Uuka and kill him. He'd probably end up in prison leaving Lindani with no one to look after her. She couldn't reach him anyway. The important thing right now was to get to Lindani.

"Stay where you are. Detective Christie and I will come to you."

"Detective Christie? Oh. I remember him. He is nice. He can keep my secret?" The plaintive, childlike voice sounded eager to trust someone.

Lysi and Maynard sat across the oilcloth-covered table from Lindani in the warm spicy-scented Bed and Breakfast kitchen. Sara, the round-faced innkeeper, had wrapped a shawl around Lindani who sat with shaking hands clutching a mug of rooibos tea. Sara hovered over her like a doting grandma.

"Lindani, you remember Detective Christie. He came to visit Themba pre-school last week," Lysi said.

"Yes. Yes. Your son works in a school in Africa." Lindani stared wide-eyed at Maynard.

"That's right. He's a teacher. Like you," Maynard said.

Lysi admired Maynard's compassionate approach to Lindani. The same approach she had seen him use with Grace over a year ago the night Grace discovered the dead body of her girlhood friend in an alley in Sydney. As the lead detective on the case he could have assigned her interrogation to his partner. Instead he took the time to sit with her in a police car and attend to the delicate task himself.

"I'm not a real teacher," Lindani said with a nervous giggle. "I'm just a helper."

"Children learn from you. Your job is important," Maynard said.

Lysi watched Lindani's face beam into a shy smile. How does Maynard do it? Lysi had to resist an urge to throw her arms around him to show her gratitude for his kindness to this unfortunate girl.

"I'm a police officer," Maynard continued. "My job is to catch people who do bad things and put them in jail."

"That is good. A job like that." Lindani used a big-girl voice to return the compliment Maynard had given her.

"Bad people like Uuka and his brothers." Maynard moved seamlessly into critical interrogation. "I need your help to catch Uuka." He reached across the table and took Lindani's hand in both of his. "Tell me what you remember."

"I can help you." Lindani looked up at the ceiling as if her story were written on it. "Mandisa went to see Dr. Nala. That is her daughter. Do you know her?"

"Yes, I do. She's a fine doctor," Maynard said. "Please go on with your story."

"It is not a story. It is true." Lindani looked worried.

"Detective Christie doesn't think you're telling stories. It's just police talk for telling what happened." Lysi figured Thabo or Mandisa had accused her of telling stories. Lysi looked at Maynard.

"That's right," he said. "Please. Lindani, finish what you wanted to say."

"Where was I?" Lindani scrunched up her face. "Oh, I finished picking up the playroom. I washed the juice glasses and dried them, too. I closed the windows and locked all the doors and I turned off the lights before I left Themba." Her voice exuded pride at completing all her assigned duties.

Maynard listened with patience to the irrelevant information.

"When I passed the shebeen on the way home, Uuka and his brothers came out. Uuka called to me. I asked, 'What do you want?' That is when he…he…" A tear slid down Lindani's cheek.

"Maybe you'd like to tell Lysi what happened." Maynard patted Lindani's hand and stood. "I'll wait in the living room."

Lindani nodded and tried to smile.

Sara put her plump cheek next to Lindani's and said something in Xhosa that Lysi thought sounded like it might mean, "Now, now. Don't cry."

Lysi moved to a chair next to Lindani. She watched Lindani's eyes follow Maynard through the door to the small living room. When the door closed, Lindani took a deep breath.

"He pulled my new blouse and broke the buttons," she said, her voice full of resentment. She smoothed her hand down the front of a pink cotton blouse and stuck her fingers in the tear holes left by the ripped out buttons.

Lysi suspected Lindani didn't get new clothes often. It would take a long time for her to earn enough money to replace the cherished blouse. Would it be acceptable to buy one for her? Lysi wondered. She would ask Amele. Xhosa culture still puzzled her. She wouldn't risk offending again.

"He touched me here." Lindani pointed to her chest. "I told him to stop." Lindani's dark eyes sent the unspoken message that she feared Lysi might think she had encouraged Uuka.

"Lindani, listen to me," Lysi took hold of Lindani's shoulders, turned her and looked hard into her eyes. "He had no right to touch you. You did nothing wrong. Uuka will go to jail for what he tried to do to you."

Lindani nodded several times. Lysi hoped she understood.

"Then his brothers held my arms. Uuka untied my skirt and tried to pull down my… you know." Lindani seemed to be reliving the terror she'd experienced. "I screamed. Then Paki came. He jumped on Uuka's back. Uuka's brothers let go of me. They pulled Paki off Uuka. They kicked him and punched him and pulled him into the dark. I ran to Sara's."

Lysi knew how much courage it must have taken for Paki to attack the Dlomo brothers. She wondered if he might be out there in the dark beaten with serious injuries.

After Lysi told Maynard Lindani's story, he asked Lindani if she saw what happened to Paki after the beating.

"No. I think they took him away," Lindani said.

Maynard cast a worried look at Lysi. "I'd better have a look around." He opened the door. "Paki may need help."

Maynard returned a half hour later with Paki draped over his shoulder. Blood smeared Paki's nose. His lips had swollen into two huge sausages. He couldn't open his right eye. He kept his hands pressed to his ribs.

"I found him behind a woodpile next to the road." Maynard slid Paki onto a chair.

Disgust clouded Sara's face when she looked at Paki. Lysi noticed Sara's expression. Could Sara share the intolerance for homosexuals common in Ikhaya?

Whatever anti-gay sentiments Sara felt, she set them aside and started administering first aid. She dabbed at the blood on Paki's nose and mouth with a cold damp cloth. She provided him with a glass of water and two aspirin. She did not offer him the same warmth she had showered on Lindani.

"Paki, do you know where Uuka and his brothers might have gone?" Maynard said.

Paki nodded. "I know where they are. In the shebeen getting drunk. They said next time they would finish the job on Lindani to pay Thabo back for what he did to them. They are filthy hyenas."

Sara placed a plastic bag of frozen peas wrapped in a clean cloth against Paki's eye. "Ouch," he said.

"Do not whine. You are not a baby." Sara grabbed Paki's hand and pressed it against the bag of peas. "You will hold this against your eye until I tell you to stop."

Paki stared at Sara and nodded without speaking.

Lysi and Maynard exchanged glances. Don't mess with Sara.

"Paki, I thought you had returned to Cape Town," Lysi said. "What were you doing back in Ikhaya?"

"I went to Themba to get some things from Sipho's room. Things I had given him. Small things but important to me. I just—"

A gust of night wind rushed in as the front door of the bed and breakfast swung open. Heavy footsteps banged through the living room. A second later, Thabo's towering figure filled the kitchen doorway.

Thabo stared at Lindani—mouth wide open, shoulders drooping, breath coming in short gasps. He made no effort to hide the deep pain that devoured his whole body. Lysi could imagine the barrage of emotions thundering through him—pity, shame, sorrow, confusion. He had failed to protect Lindani.

Anger spread across Thabo's face. His fiery glare burned into Paki then Lysi and Maynard. He looked back at Lindani, eyes squeezed to lizard-like slits. "Why are you here with them?" he said his voice an ominous growl.

Tears filled Lindani's eyes. She got up, ran to Thabo and threw her arms around him, her head reaching just above his waist. "Where were you?"

Thabo's face softened and the painful expression returned. He put an arm around Lindani and drew her to him. With his hand he cradled her head against his chest. "We go home."

"Not yet." Lindani pulled her head away from Thabo's chest and looked up at him.

It amazed Lysi how this skinny little girl had no fear of this big, hulking man whose very presence could reduce a mob of scoundrels into a gelatinous mass.

"They helped me. Uuka and his brothers tried to hurt me. Paki saved me. They hurt Paki." She pointed to Paki's battered face. "See what they did."

Thabo's eyes ignited. "Uuka?"

From the corner of her eye Lysi saw Paki rise and edge towards the door. Should she stop him? No use. He's terrified of Thabo. He's much better off in Cape Town. The question is will he make it out of Ikhaya tonight?

Lysi stood. At least she could distract Thabo to allow Paki a little head start.

"Thabo, we've not met formally. I'm Lysi Weston. I want to thank you for helping my friend Grace Wright."

Thabo nodded but didn't speak. His angry eyes lost some of their fire.

"This is Detective Maynard Christie. He's working with Detective Mbeki on the Sipho case."

"Why is Mbeki not here?" The growl returned to Thabo's voice.

"It's his night off. He's in Cape Town. When Lindani called Amele for help, I answered the phone. That's why we're here."

Lysi watched the tension in Thabo's jaws relax a little. She figured he felt gratitude for the help she and Paki had provided for Lindani.

100

"What about you Thabo? Where were you?" An unplanned note of criticism seeped into Lysi's voice.

"Cape Town. A job interview. When I returned and Lindani was not home, I went to Themba. I searched everywhere for her. A boy leaving the shebeen said he saw her run to Sara's. Now I know why."

"Thabo," Maynard said. "We'll find them."

"No." Thabo punched his open hand with a hard fist. "I will find them."

Chapter 28

Lysi flinched when Thabo slammed out the B&B door taking Lindani with him. One look at Maynard's frustrated, worn-out face told her they needed to head home. She picked up her purse and extended a hand to Sara. "Thank you for all your help tonight. We couldn't have managed without you."

Maynard nodded goodbye to the innkeeper and took a couple of tired steps towards the door.

Sara pursed her lips and pointed at the overstuffed couch in the sitting area. "Sit. You must recover before you drive back to Cape Town. A cup of Rooibos will restore you."

Lysi and Maynard looked at each other. Too exhausted to argue, they obediently sank into the afghan-covered couch. Lysi squeezed Maynard's hand but didn't speak. They watched Sara fussing in the kitchen.

An aromatic scent wafted from the kitchen followed by Sara carrying a tray with three large mugs of tea. She set the tray on a laminated coffee table in front of Lysi and Maynard, picked up a cup for herself and settled into a sagging, mustard-colored armchair facing them.

A small sip of Rooibus tea convinced Lysi Sara knew best. The hot liquid soothed the weariness that flooded her body.

"Do not mind Thabo's rude behavior," Sara said. "He has always been a hot-tempered boy. Always he settles problems with these." Sara held up clenched fists. "Then he is sorry." She shook her head. "Always too late."

Lysi saw concern on Sara's face. Did Lindani tell Sara that Sipho seduced her? Does Sara think Thabo's hot temper drove him to kill Sipho? "Thabo seemed angry, not just rude."

"I have known Thabo for a long time." Sara cradled her cup between her two hands. "He was a little boy who loved to help me bake biscuits and tidy up the Inn. When he grew bigger, he kept the township ruffians out of my flower garden. I have spanked him and hugged away his hurts. When his mother died, he cried in my arms. Thabo is a good boy who does stupid things."

Lysi wanted to ask if one of those stupid things was killing Sipho. Instead she said, "Thabo's life hasn't been easy."

"No, not easy." Sara swallowed the last of her tea, picked up the tea tray and returned to the kitchen.

Lysi rose. Maynard seemed to wait for Sara to dismiss him.

"Sit, please." Sara's polite request didn't hide the expectation of immediate compliance with her directive.

Lysi dropped back onto the couch. Her eyes followed Sara moving around the kitchen. Sara finished washing the last teacup, wiped damp hands on her sunflower print apron, and bent down to open the oven of a 1960's vintage electric stove. The scent of chocolate filled the room. Sara glanced over her shoulder at Lysi. A warm smile crinkled the corners of her deep brown eyes and dimpled her shiny teak colored cheeks.

"In just a short time I will serve *you all* a piece of Billy Joe's famous Mississippi Mud Cake." Sara seasoned her Xhosa accent with an abortive attempt at a southern drawl.

Lysi and Maynard grinned at the unusual cacophony of sounds.

"I can hardly wait, *honey child*." Maynard peppered his Australian accent with an equally inept southern twang.

Sara's round belly jiggled with baritone chortles. "You sound just like Billy Joe."

A giggle bubbled up from Lysi's chest. What an extraordinary experience to sit here in South Africa and listen to attempts at American southern drawls from a Xhosa and an Australian. She couldn't resist joining in the lighthearted fun. "You should hear Grace do a drawl. It's even funnier than you two." Lysi paused for dramatic impact. "Better yet, you should hear her do Harlem. She—"

From outside, angry shouts and the sound of breaking glass shattered the quiet night and cut Lysi's words.

"The shebeen just down the street," Sara said. "Drunks. Lazy young men with no jobs. They look for trouble every night."

A litany of angry Xhosa shouts ended with a sickening thud followed by a painful groan. Raucous laughter punctuated more thuds and groans.

Maynard bounded to his feet. "Wait here." In two steps he was out the door.

"Maynard, no." Lysi looked at Sara, raised one eyebrow, lowered her chin and said, "Right, like I'm just going to stay here and wait." Then before Sara could stop her, she tore after Maynard.

Lysi reached the shebeen's open door in time to hear Maynard's guttural growl. "Let him go."

Lysi's eyes leaped from Maynard to two men holding Thabo's arms while a third kicked and punched him. The bartender's bushy Afro hair peeked from behind the bar and an old man resembling a scarecrow crouched under a wooden picnic-type table.

"I said let him g—" Maynard didn't get a chance to finish his sentence. The sinewy puncher whirled and slugged Maynard in the face.

Lysi winced. Seeing the punishing blow was too much to bear. Pain then anger surged in her chest.

Maynard's surprised eyes flared. He recoiled from the blow and threw a left-hand punch at his attacker's head. When the man drew back Maynard's lightning fist struck him in the heart. After an astonished blink the man dropped to his knees.

Way to go, Lysi thought. Not smart to mess with my brawny Outback Australian.

The other two men let go of Thabo and he crumbled to the dirt floor.

One of the two men built like a big rig truck uttered a determined grunt and rushed head down towards Maynard who side-stepped. Too late to stop himself the man rammed his head into the bar and slid lazily to the ground. Maynard glanced at the limp body.

When Lysi saw the fat guy grab a bottle from the bar and brandish it above his head, a high-pitched yelp escaped from her throat. "Maynard!"

Before Maynard could react Lysi jumped on the man's back, locked her arms around his neck and her legs around his waist like a bear ready to scale a thick tree trunk. She leaned back trying to increase the pressure on his trachea. He dropped the bottle and clutched at her locked arms making choking sounds. He spun around like a whirling dervish but Lysi held on with every ounce of strength she could muster. She didn't let go until Maynard whipped in, grabbed a hunk of his hair and kneed him in his most vulnerable spot. The fat guy grabbed himself and hit a soprano note. Lysi jumped off just as he fell to the floor and curled into a fetal position.

The three men struggled to their feet and stumbled out the door. The sinewy puncher glared back at Maynard through angry, vengeful eyes and uttered Xhosa words that sounded like threats.

Maynard looked at Lysi. "Are you alright?"

"Me? I'm fine. But you…"

Maynard's nose streamed blood down the front of his shirt.

Lysi ran her hand over his forehead into his hair. She pulled a wad of tissues from her pocket and blotted his nose and mouth. Beads of red grew into blotches on the sodden tissues.

"Maynard. My God. He really hurt you." She took another tissue and dabbed at her teary eyes.

"They're hurt worse. Help me get Thabo up," Maynard said. He grinned at Lysi and added as they left the shebeen, "Glad you're on my team, mate."

Lysi opened Sara's door and Maynard staggered through dragging Thabo. With one hand he gripped Thabo's arm across his shoulder. He had his other arm around Thabo's waist.

"Sara," Lysi said. "Help me with these two battered warriors."

Her comment reflected the fear Lysi felt for both men. What if Thabo had broken ribs that could puncture his lungs? What if Maynard had a concussion that would produce symptoms later? What if Thabo dies? What if Maynard...She gave herself a mental slap that halted her mounting panic.

Sara grabbed Thabo around the waist and draped his left arm over her shoulder. Maynard supported his right side. They eased him onto a chair.

Lysi lifted Thabo's chin and looked for broken teeth. She found none. She ran her finger and thumb over the bridge of his nose. "Not broken," she said.

A jagged red gash creased the back of Thabo's head. He touched it with his fingers and flinched. Sara yanked his hand away from his head. "Do not touch. Your hands are filthy."

"They were waiting for me in the shebeen," Thabo said. Uuka hit me in the back of the head with a bottle. Then his two brothers held me while Uuka beat on me."

"Uuka?" Lysi said. "The one who assaulted Grace?"

"And Lindani," Thabo said. "I will make Uuka pay."

"Shush." Sara pulled a first aid kit from a top shelf in the cupboard, took gauze pads from it and swabbed at Thabo's face. She ordered him to hold the same plastic bag of frozen peas on his swollen black eye that she'd used on Paki. Thabo obeyed and sat in compliant silence while she finished his face. He winced when she began to pick at the glass in his head.

"Ouch, that hurts." Thabo pulled away from Sara's tweezers.

Sara grabbed his hair and held him with determined firmness. "Stop yowling. It will hurt you a lot more if I do not get all these glass splinters. Your head will turn red and mushy like a rotting watermelon and you will die a slow, agonizing death."

Thabo's eyes widened. His mouth remained closed except for an occasional grunt when Sara had to dig at an entrenched glass splinter.

Lysi thought the deep-throated threat in Sara's voice could scare the devil into acquiescence, but Thabo's submissive demeanor still surprised her. Could some people cut through his hard exterior to a fragile inner core? First Lindani then Sara. Maybe Grace?

Sara finished cleaning Thabo's wounds then asked Maynard what happened in the shebeen.

Maynard dampened a tissue at the sink, cleared the blood from the rest of his face and tossed the tissues into a cardboard box used for trash. "When I got there two men held Thabo while another guy punched him. I yelled at them. One of them landed a punch in my face. Wrong move. I educated him." Maynard rubbed red, swollen knuckles on his left hand. "Lysi decked one of them. The other little bastard knocked himself out."

"Well," Lysi said. "I didn't exactly—"

"You should have seen her. The guy didn't have a chance." Maynard spoke with admiration. "She jumped on his back and clamped her arms around his neck like the jaws of a crocodile."

"You are a strong woman. You will make a man a good wife." Sara shifted her eyes to Maynard.

"You think so, huh?" Maynard grinned at Lysi.

Lysi avoided comment by leaning over Thabo's head. "He needs to see a doctor. No sign of a concussion but the cut is deep. He may need stitches."

Thabo shook his head. "I do not need—"

"Shush. You will see a doctor." Sara's voice brooked no further discussion.

Lysi turned to Sara. "Is Site B Community Health Center the closest medical facility? Is there someone on duty at night?"

Thabo answered for Sara, his chin on his chest. "It is the nearest. There is a night duty doctor."

"Thabo works there as an ambulance driver." Lysi answered Maynard's questioning expression.

"We'll take our car," Lysi said. "Thabo, you'll need to guide us. I've been there but I don't think I can find it at night."

Chapter 29

A blaze of light in the dark night announced the Health Center. Inside men, women and children filled all the chairs in the waiting room. Coughing, sniffing, wheezing, crying and impatient patter blasted Lysi's ears. She winced at the stomach-churning odors emanating from sick people crowded into a small stuffy space. A woman in labor wailed with a sudden contraction. Listless children whimpered in mothers' laps. Young men clutching at wounds stared through bitter eyes. It felt like a bad dream.

"This is no surprise," Thabo said as if he read her mind. "It is like this most nights. People cannot come for treatment during the day because they must work and they have a long, slow commute from Cape Town."

The middle-aged desk clerk summoned Thabo over with a bored crook of her index finger. Her neat white uniform spoke medical professional but her gruff treatment of patients spoke of anything but a warm bedside manner.

"What happened to you, Thabo? Another big bad fight?" She didn't wait for his reply. It was obvious she'd been around this block with Thabo many times before. "We need you to drive the ambulance tonight. Dr. Nala better fix you up quick. Wait by number 3 door."

Nambeko Nala, the physician on duty, charged up to Thabo. "Looks like this time you got the worst of the fight." She shook her head and shoved him toward the exam room. "No time to waste. We already have three calls awaiting drivers. Get yourself into the exam room." She followed close on his heels giving Lysi and Maynard a cursory nod.

Nambeko returned a minute later, scribbling on a clipboard. She spoke to a paper-thin nurse standing guard over the exam room entrances. "He will need stitches."

"Yes, doctor," the nurse said.

Nambeko ran her finger down the clipboard and issued terse instructions to the nurse. "Prepare Thabo but first move number twenty-seven to the top of the list. Time twenty-seven's contractions. Take number seventeen into the small cubicle. Give him a tetanus shot."

"Right away, doctor." The nurse walked over to the woman in labor and said something. The woman got up and tottered after her. At the same time the nurse shouted over the din, "Number seventeen come."

Nambeko shifted her face to the waiting patients. "Number eighteen please."

A young woman holding the hand of a sniffling little girl about seven years old rose and walked up to Nambeko. Four red finger marks covered the little girl's small cheek. Her right eye had swelled shut. "Her father hit her again, Dr. Nala," the woman said in a sad, resigned voice.

Nambeko smoothed her hand over the welts. She grasped the girl's chin and moved it back and forth. She flashed a light into the child's eyes.

"The eyes and jaw are okay. Take her home and apply cold cloths to her cheek until the redness goes away." Nambeko reached into her pocket, took out a piece of wrapped candy and gave it to the little girl. The candy brought a slight smile to the child's lips but did not extinguish the fear in her eyes.

Sadness swept through Lysi when she saw the child put the candy in her mouth and turn to the exit with her mother. How could Nambeko send the little girl back to an abusive father?

Nambeko turned to Lysi and Maynard. "Thabo will be fine. The nurse will administer a local anesthetic. In a few minutes it will numb his wound. I will clean it, stitch it up and put him to work. No need for you to stay."

Lysi couldn't hide her surprise. "Can Thabo work after such a beating? Shouldn't we take him home?"

Nambeko's response to Lysi was simple and clear. "We need him here tonight."

She started to turn back to her clipboard then glanced at Maynard. "Detective Christie, I understand you are assisting Detective Mbeki on finding the murderer of my brother."

"Yes. "

"What progress have you made?"

"We know the cause of death," Maynard said. "Cobra venom. Administered by injection."

"We have cobras in Ikhaya. How would a killer access their venom?"

"We're working on that question. I think I know the answer. I've uncovered some pieces of evidence that may lead to the killer."

Nambeko nodded, her expression heavy.

"I want my brother's murderer punished." Her words were resolute.

Chapter 30

Lysi rolled down the car window to let the cool, moist night air vanquish her increasing lethargy. She glanced at Maynard. He leaned back in the driver's seat with one arm resting on the open window frame. He seemed at ease with their silent drive from Ikhaya. So much had happened since their return from Namibia that they'd hardly had a moment for serious conversation.

The VW merged onto N2. In a few more minutes they'd be back in Oranjezicht. If Lysi wanted to share her thoughts about the events of the evening she'd have to do it now. She turned toward Maynard. Did he feel like talking? Maybe she should wait. On the other hand, maybe she'd just make a quick comment and not pursue it. She shifted her body to face Maynard.

"Thabo did it." She would leave it at that.

Maynard shrugged but kept his eyes on the road. He didn't respond. Lysi decided to add just one more very brief comment.

"His angry, impulsive behavior tonight left no doubt in my mind," she said. "The evidence is clear. Paki saw him in Qamata's hut. Thabo still believes Sipho is the father of the baby he thinks Lindani aborted." Lysi gritted her teeth. That wasn't a brief comment.

Still no response from Maynard.

Maybe she'd just add one more thought then end the topic.

"Did you see how protective Thabo was of Lindani tonight? When he found out Uuka had tried to assault her, he bolted off after him. I...I think he would have killed him if he'd had the chance."

This time Maynard sighed and straightened up in the seat. "It's just as likely Paki murdered Sipho," he said. "A thwarted lover. He admits being at the hut. More important, he returned to the hut. Probably to destroy evidence."

"Paki is not violent," Lysi said. "Thabo is. He settles his problems with his fists. And...and there's Qamata. Bludgeoned to death. Thabo's name is written all over the two murders."

A car's high beams flooded the interior of the car with light. The car blinked its lights frenetically and Maynard pulled as far to the left as possible to allow the car to pass. Lysi tensed for a moment but her tension faded when she remembered Maynard was used to driving on the left side of the road.

"Paki had more reason to kill Qamata," Maynard said. "The old crackpot was trying to cure Sipho—make him straight."

"Or," Lysi raised her voice for emphasis now that Maynard seemed interested in continuing the discussion. "Thabo killed him because Qamata witnessed him murder Sipho"

A chilling thought raced through Lysi's mind. Maybe Sipho and Qamata's killers weren't the same person. Maybe there were two murderers. She decided to explore this new idea with Maynard.

"Maynard, do you think there's any possibility there were two killers? Maybe Thabo killed Sipho, but could Mandisa have killed Qamata because she believed he caused the death of her son? Is it possible she killed Qamata for revenge?"

Maynard shook his head. "Based on what Billy Joe says—no. But I haven't discounted the possibility. Mother love is powerful."

"Amele says Mandisa isn't well," Lysi said. "Arthritis."

"Still," Maynard said. "A mother is like a lioness. When someone attacks her young, she'll die trying to protect him—or in this case, avenge him." He cranked the wheel and made a sharp turn onto Rugby

Road. The road sign appeared briefly in the headlights and vanished in the darkness behind them. "I'll know more after I meet with Billy Joe."

"But what if—"

"Lysi, I'll know more after I talk to Billy Joe tomorrow. Please show some patience." Maynard's tone sounded tired—and final.

The Butshingi house was dark when they pulled into the driveway. Luvo and Amele, still caring for Amele's mother, wouldn't return home until day after tomorrow.

Lysi fingered the car door handle. Before she could open it she felt Maynard's hand on her arm. Her heart lurched at his touch.

"Lysi, we've been on such a wild camel ride I haven't had the chance to tell you what a fantastic time I had last night." He smoothed the back of his hand over her cheek.

Lysi smiled. She tried to suppress the old ambivalence that crept into her head. Hadn't she enjoyed making love to Maynard? Hadn't he evoked feelings she'd kept buried for years? Couldn't she trust him? Even if she did, would entwining their lives ever work?

"I hope I don't have to take you all the way back to Namibia for a rerun." He put his arm around her shoulders and pulled her close. His lips slid across her cheek to her ear. "If I have to, I'll book a flight tonight," he whispered.

Lysi needed to lighten the moment. She answered his comment in a joking tone. "Why Maynard, I might just take you up on that. I didn't see enough of Namibia."

"Whatever you like. You realize you saved my life tonight. Now I belong to you." Maynard opened his arms in submission. "You can do whatever you want with me."

"I didn't save your life. I just slowed the fat guy down so you could turn him into a tenor." The bit of humor brought a grin to Maynard's face.

"An old Aussie proverb says once someone saves your life, you remain under that person's care until you leave this world." He pulled back and looked directly into her face. His grin faded and his tone turned serious. "Are you ready for that responsibility?"

Before she could reply he tipped her chin up with his index finger and gave her a peck. "I am."

Lysi pressed her teeth against her lower lip. The question sounded too much like a call for commitment. Common sense dictated she say goodnight, get out of the car, go inside the house and go to bed—alone. But galloping hormones trampled her already weak attempts at prudence. Instead she looked up at the dark window of the bedroom she shared with Grace. "It looks like Grace is either still out or already in bed. I'd hate to wake her. Any suggestion?"

Surprise flashed through Maynard's eyes. His lips eased into a slow, smooth, sexy smile.

"I think I can come up with one."

He gave her a slow, deep kiss that turned hot, needy and urgent. He drew back and on a ragged breath said, "Aw yes I've got it."

Like two teenagers arriving home after curfew they slid from the car, crept up the steps hand in hand and entered the house on tiptoes.

"What's the suggestion?" Lysi whispered.

He beamed, led her through the living room, across the deck into his room and closed the door.

110

Chapter 31

Sultry saxophone blues floated from a small band, smooth and heady as fine scotch. Flickering candles on cabaret tables surrounding the dance floor intensified the intoxicating effect of the velvety blues sound. Grace snuggled close to Billy Joe Mbeki as they slow danced in perfect unison in the dimly lit room. He pressed his lips to her ear and whispered words about the beauty of her hair, her face, her body. Good sense warned her his words were well-practiced lines that she should ignore. Her body didn't care.

"Mmm," she sighed. "Why Billy Joe, you could turn a girl's head."

"I hope I turn yours," Billy Joe said.

He swung her out in a circle. The skirt of her gold lamé dress whirled above her knees. He pulled her back, let go of her hand and enfolded her in both his arms. "I had almost forgotten how erotic it is to caress an American woman's voluptuous body," he murmured. His embrace tightened and she felt a faint stirring.

Grace caught her breath at his candor. "You silver-tongued devil, you."

It seemed like they'd talked nonstop all evening—so much to share, so easy with each other. Now talk had ended replaced by whispered sensual messages raising Grace's body temperature to an almost unbearable level.

In the heat of his arms Grace felt less in control. Maybe she should have ended the evening after dinner. She should have said goodnight and gotten out of the car. She should have said "No" when Billy Joe murmured the evening was still young, and invited her to one of his favorite nightspots.

The music ended. Billy Joe kept his arms around her. "Let's not sit down. The music will resume in a few seconds." He nuzzled her neck and found her lips.

Grace felt a little self-conscious but she looked around the dance floor and three other couples seemed locked together in embraces unaware of anyone else.

How do I want to end this evening? She thought. He's one of the sexiest men I've ever known. God, sensuality exudes from his pores like musk. She didn't want to squelch the ardor of this delicious man but he was moving too fast even for her.

Suddenly his breathy whisper tickled her ear. "You may not know I will soon be ready to retire from the police force. I think I would like to move back to Mississippi some day."

Grace leaned her head back and looked into his eyes. "What?"

"Please, Grace." Billy Joe pulled her back into his embrace. "Allow me to finish my thoughts." He pressed his lips close to her ear again and whispered. "If I moved to Mississippi…well, it is just that I would need a good woman there to take care of me."

It took a moment for Grace's dreamy brain to process his words. Then like cold water splashed in the face of a drunk, the rainbow clouds in her head disappeared. This guy's hot for a lay. His lines are not only practiced, but they're creative—pick up and move to Mississippi where he would need a good woman—uh huh. She had to suppress an urge to laugh. Why not play along with him? Have a little fun.

"Why Billy Joe I had no idea you were ready for retirement. You're so young, so virile. So…umm." She nuzzled his ear.

He tightened his embrace as she continued, I would never have guessed you would move to the U.S."

"Well, I…I do not mean right—" Billy Joe's stuttered response confirmed Grace's belief He had no interest in moving to Mississippi but a lot of interest in a good lay.

"Mississippi! You want to move to Mississippi. I always wanted to live there." She kissed his cheek then tipped her head back, gazed into his eyes and managed a perfect ingenuous smile.

"Well I have not made a final—" Billy Joe's amorous tone turned cautious.

"And you need someone to take care of you in Mississippi." Grace widened her eyes and raised the pitch of her voice. "That sounds like a marriage proposal. Are you proposing marriage to me, Billy Joe?"

"Well I—"

Grace pressed her fingers on Billy Joe's lips. "Oh darling, no need to say another word. I accept. I accept."

"Grace—" Billy Joe now held Grace at arms length. All his ardor had disappeared.

"I have to phone Lysi right away and tell her the exciting news. She'll want to be one of our witnesses. Is that okay with you?" Grace quick-stepped to the table and pulled her mobile phone from her pearl studded bag and started to punch in numbers. Billy Joe shot to the table after her and laid his hand on her phone. Perspiration beaded his upper lip and forehead. Grace saw real terror in his eyes. She felt his hand trembling.

"Grace I—" His left foot started bouncing up and down.

"Yes, my beloved fiancé." Whoops, Grace thought, I just exceeded the speed limit here.

When Billy Joe swallowed so hard she could hear the sound in his throat, Grace could no longer keep up the charade. "Billy Joe, honey I wish you could see your face." She threw her head back and laughed so hard she was mopping up tears.

Chapter 32

Lysi bit down hard on the citrus flavored rusk and grimaced. "I think Luvo over baked these biscuits." She dropped the rusk on her saucer and frowned at Maynard munching across the breakfast table from her.

"They're supposed to be hard. Here's the proper way to eat them." Maynard picked up a rusk with his thumb and three fingers, jiggled his extended pinky, dunked the rusk twice in his tea then took a bite. "Mmm. Luvo outdid himself."

A grin played on Lysi's lips when she thought about a tough detective, a rugged Outback, camel-racing grazier jiggling his little finger and conducting lessons on the proper way to eat a rusk. The more she learned about Maynard, the more he grew on her. She'd never responded to a man on such a visceral level. It made no sense. Their worlds were too far apart. And yet it made more sense than ever.

Breakfast on the Butshingi's sunny deck with Maynard suited Lysi and she longed to linger in the ambience of the warm, flower-scented garden. The chimes from the mantle clock in the living room put a quick end to that fantasy.

"Maynard, you have to get going." She reminded him he had a nine o'clock appointment with Billy Joe at Ikhaya police station and was running late.

He reached for another rusk. "I can't leave until I'm sure you won't crack one of your gorgeous pearlies chomping down on a rusk. Maybe I should cancel Billy Joe and spend a little more time educating you in the fine art of rusk munching." He smiled.

Lysi took the rusk from him, gave it two slow dunks in her tea and bit a piece off. "There, I think I have mastery now." She pushed back her chair and stood. "I wish you didn't have to go, but he's expecting you," Lysi said. She didn't mention her intense interest in what Billy Joe would say about the Sipho murder case.

"Okay, okay. I'm going." Maynard hoisted himself from the chair. "But I want you to be wearing that same...what do you call it? Sun dress...when I get back." His eyes wandered over the waist-cinching yellow dress with its tiny spaghetti straps. "Bare shoulders. Nice."

Lysi warmed under his gaze and felt her cheeks flush. What was it about him that always had that same effect on her?

He put on his Australian bush hat, and sauntered to the door. Over his shoulder he said, "You may want to take a little nap. You didn't get much sleep last night." He blew her a kiss, flashed a satisfied grin and left.

Her face caught fire. Was she losing control?

She poured herself another cup of tea. The house seemed so quiet with Amele and Luvo still at the home of Amele's convalescing mother. Lysi took a sip of tea and listened for sounds from Grace's room.

Silence.

Was Grace still asleep? Was she even there? Last night Grace seemed pretty excited about her date with Billy Joe. Lysi knew Grace had pretty much recovered from her tumultuous relationship with Jerome Gardner in Australia. Was she now hungry for a new lighthearted romantic interlude? Billy Joe was a pretty tempting morsel with his broad shoulders, sensual smile and smooth voice. Lysi was glad to see Grace happy again but worried her needy emotions might overpower rational decision-making.

After her last swallow of tea, Lysi let her eyes wander over the garden flowers and shrubs. Even the chirping birds didn't lighten her spirit. She had a lot on her mind—her ambivalent feelings about Maynard, fear Grace might rebound into an premature relationship, Sipho's murder case. She thought about what to do next.

Lysi clenched tight neck muscles and did a couple of neck rolls. No relief. She went to the kitchen and opened the refrigerator. Closed it. Started toward Grace's room. Stopped. Went to the living room and picked up the Cape Argus newspaper. Dropped it on the coffee table.

The depressingly silent house didn't help either. Maybe a short stroll around the neighborhood would sort things out. She stepped onto the sun-drenched street and let the balmy outdoors envelop her. The soft breeze tossed her hair. Somewhere wind chimes emitted a soothing, tinkle.

Lysi headed down Bosch Lane then wound along narrow Rugby Road enjoying the dappled shade of the large old yellowwoods and Cape Ash trees that lined the street. Twittering birds and scurrying grey squirrels animated the serene woodsy scene. She curved past walled yards and wrought iron fences. Cobble stone driveways led to pastel colored houses—salmon, rose, creamy yellow, peach. Around each turn the street opened to panoramic views of the city below and the sea beyond.

Lysi paused for a moment on a small wooden bench labeled "Bus Stop." She closed her eyes and tilted her head skyward and tried to clear her mind. She breathed in a clean medicinal scent and opened her eyes to the shimmering leaves of a tall eucalyptus tree. Something about the whole scene evoked dark thoughts that stained her pleasant reverie. The big tree reminded her of the one near Qamata's hut. Had Qamata stood under that tree when his killer crushed his head with a rock and dragged him into the bushes?

Was the killer Paki or Thabo?

Thabo? The killer had to be a big man, strong enough to drag a limp body. Paki claimed he saw him at the murder scene. Paki fears and hates Thabo. Would he lie? Maynard insists Thabo's not the killer because the murder had to have been planned with precision—timing, place, weapon— both suggested forethought. Thabo seems violent but his impulsiveness precludes premeditated murder. And there's that soft side to him.

Paki? Not a big enough man. Not tough enough. He wouldn't use a rock. He's more the poison type. If not Paki or Thabo, then who? Who?

She had a deep down feeling she already knew something. Something distressing. Something painful. Something she didn't want to know. Something that pointed to the killer. Something…it was no use, she just couldn't get it.

Lysi sighed, took a last sniff of the eucalyptus then rose and continued down Rugby Road. At Marmion Road she turned back toward Bosch Lane.

She slipped inside the house, closed the door without a sound, crossed the dining room and headed for the kitchen. Her mood lifted when she caught the scent of Grace's favorite perfume—Exotic Woman. Grace claimed it could seduce a monk.

"Hey, Lysi." Grace sat at the table, a cup of tea in front of her and a couple of rusks on a saucer.

"You finally woke up." Lysi cocked one eyebrow. "Exotic Woman? Billy Joe? Must have been quite a night." Lysi fanned herself with her hand.

"Me? You're the one who had quite a night. Where's Maynard? Poor guy couldn't make it out of bed this morning, huh?"

"Touché, Grace." Lysi had no interest in discussing last night with Grace.

"Come on Lysi. Tell all." Grace dipped her rusk in tea.

"There's nothing to tell. Maynard has a meeting with Billy Joe this morning. He's in Ikhaya."

"Billy Joe, huh." Grace grinned. "I hope old B.J.'s recovered enough to make it to a meeting."

Lysi sat down across the table from Grace. Curiosity gripped her like a vice. "Recovered? Your night sounds more interesting than mine."

"Let me tell you, that red-blooded African boy has got to be one of the smoothest Casanovas I've ever met." Grace folded her arms on the table and leaned forward. "You should have heard the honey-coated lines that flowed off his silvery tongue. I was almost taken in until he said he was ready to retire and move to Mississippi and needed me to care for him."

"You're kidding."

"No. He tried to make me feel he couldn't survive without me. So…I called his bluff. I accepted his proposal of marriage. I—"

"You what?"

"Now Lysi don't get your knickers in a knot. I was bluffing just like him." A sly grin flitted across Grace's lips. "Hell, I even pretended to call you. Maid of Honor you know."

"Maid of Honor! Grace, You didn't."

"I swear he almost had an attack of apoplexy. The poor guy will never be the same. He couldn't get me home fast enough. Three a.m. is pretty early for me." Grace laughed and dunked a second rusk twice in her tea.

"So Billy Joe is now out of the picture?" Lysi said, eying Grace's rusk strategy.

"Oh no." Grace looked dreamy. "He'll be back."

Chapter 33

Maynard sat across the desk from Officer Billy Joe Mbeki in the busy Ikhaya Police Station. Mbeki's rank alcohol breath assailed Maynard's nostrils. He studied Mbeki's loose tie, rumpled shirt, bloodshot eyes, gray complexion and drawn face. Mbeki must have crashed into bed after his date with Grace and woke with barely enough time to make it to their nine a.m. meeting. Grace could probably do that to an unsuspecting bloke like Mbeki. How much bottle courage had he needed last night to manage a smoking hot woman like her? Maynard wouldn't ask. Why be cruel? Why humiliate him by forcing him to replay the evening he spent with her? Poor, miserable wretch. Better to keep the discussion professional not personal. Spare him. A mischievous grin jiggled the corners of Maynard's mouth.

"Well now." Maynard scratched his head, tucked his chin and tried not to grin. "How was your date with Grace last night?"

Mbeki raised his head from the legal pad he'd just pulled from his desk drawer, accusations of betrayal written all over his face.

A twinge of guilt stung Maynard's conscience. He got the message. Mbeki knew the answer to the question was obvious and thought Maynard had asked it just to rub salt in an already painful wound.

"She is quite a woman," Mbeki mumbled. After a quick glance at the cute desk clerk, probably to assure himself she wasn't listening, he dropped his eyes back to the legal pad and made a couple of random check marks.

Maynard caught the manly don't-want-to-talk-about-it message from Mbeki and changed the subject. Cri-key, his manhood must have taken a hell of a beating.

"Have you narrowed down the number of suspects?" Maynard said.

Mbeki took a couple of big gulps from a quart bottle of cure-the-hangover mineral water and wiped his mouth with the back of his hand.

"I am looking pretty seriously at Thabo Deyi," Mbeki said.

"Thabo Deyi? I don't see it." Maynard was adamant. "He may be a snarly bastard, but not a murderer. Too much to lose. Who'd take care of Lindani if he ended up in prison?" Maynard shook his head. "Nope. I don't think so."

Mbeki rotated his fingers over his temples, popped two aspirin into his mouth and took another gulp of mineral water. He shuffled through a couple of legal pad pages and ran his finger down the sheet.

"Here is why I think I am right," he said. "We contacted S.A. Venom Supplies in Limpopo Province. They sell Cape Cobra venom. Three thousand rand will get you enough venom to do a pretty good job."

"Okay, I'm listening." Maynard looked interested, but didn't see a connection to Thabo Deyi.

"Trouble is it is illegal to buy venom except for medical purposes. Like making antivenin." Mbeki stroked his chin and looked pensive. "Now Thabo might be able to bluff his way through the medical requirement since he works at Site B Community Health Center, but where would he get the R3000?"

"So far you're supporting my view that he didn't do it." Maynard folded his arms and leaned back in the chair.

"So…" Mbeki held up his index finger. "I checked the Internet and discovered a place in China that sells venom to anyone. Cheap."

"Internet?" Maynard's eyes widened in question. "Does Thabo have a computer?"

118

"No, but we have 30 of them in the Ikhaya Community ICT Lab thanks to Dell Computer Corporation," Mbeki said.

Maynard was silent. This new information was still circumstantial evidence. No solid proof Thabo purchased snake venom and even if he did, there was absolutely nothing to indicate he used it to kill Sipho.

Mbeki looked past Maynard and hand motioned an officer to come over. The officer said something in Xhosa, nodded at Maynard and left. Mbeki put his hands on the desk, clenched his teeth and pushed himself up with what sounded to Maynard like a painful groan.

"They just brought Thabo in. You might want to observe the questioning." Mbeki pointed to a cubicle a few yards from his desk. "Just sit on that chair by the door."

Mbeki picked up the mineral water bottle and stepped into the cubicle.

Maynard stood when a police officer led Thabo into the small, windowless cubicle that served as an interrogation room. When Thabo spotted Maynard, he looked confused at first, but the expression on his face soon hardened into an accusation of treachery. Maynard figured Thabo's gratitude for him having come to his aid in the shebeen had changed to anger at seeing him with Mbeki.

"Sit Thabo," Billy Joe said.

"I will stand."

"I said sit." Mbeki's tone left no room for discussion.

Thabo slouched onto the metal folding chair, crossed his arms and looked past Mbeki at the blank gray wall.

"Let's start with what we already know. You killed Sipho because he seduced Lindani. Isn't that right?"

"I would not kill Sipho. He promised to marry Lindani."

Thabo's surly tone made Maynard wince. Couldn't he see that attitude would only alienate Mbeki?

"Come Thabo," Mbeki said. "You knew that would never happen."

Thabo tightened his crossed arms and glowered at Mbeki.

"Well then." Mbeki ignored the hateful scowl. "Where were you on the night of December 13th."

"Why do you want to know?"

"Answer the question Thabo." Mbeki squeezed his eyes shut then opened them wide and blinked them a couple of times. Maynard could almost feel Mbeki's throbbing headache. He bet Grace was just fine.

"I do not remember where I was. Work I guess." Thabo sounded unsure.

"You guess?"

"Check my card."

"We did. You were not there." Mbeki slapped the blank timecard on the table.

"That was Friday? I always work Fridays." Thabo's voice had lost some of its edge.

"Look at the timecard, Thabo. It was Friday. You were not there. Your timecard was not marked."

"I—" Thabo blinked several times.

"In fact, a witness placed you at Qamata's hut."

"Lie." Thabo sprang to his feet. "Who said that?"

Mbeki's eyes narrowed to slits. "Sit down, Thabo. I will tell you when you can get up."

Thabo banged down on the chair.

Maynard remembered Lysi telling him Paki had seen Thabo at Qamata's hut. Would Paki have reason to lie?

"Come on Thabo. You want me to tell you who saw you so you can go beat him up?"

Thabo jumped up from the table again. "I will beat the truth out of him."

Mbeki exhaled a heavy breath. "I said 'sit!'"

Maynard listened to Thabo alienate Mbeki more with every outburst. The evidence was mounting against Thabo and yet Maynard's gut told him Thabo was innocent. Could someone be framing him?

"Where did you get the Cape Cobra venom, Thabo?"

"What? I have no venom."

"Not now. You used it to kill Sipho."

"Sipho died of too much Dream Root." Thabo knitted his eyebrows and his mouth hung open. He looked as though he couldn't believe Mbeki didn't already know this.

Maynard thought Thabo's surprise was genuine. He probably didn't know about the second autopsy report.

"No, Thabo." Mbeki slammed his fist on the table. "You used your medical identity card to purchase venom in China. You followed Sipho to Qamata's hut. You injected cobra venom into him. Then you watched him die."

Thabo's lips trembled. No sound came out. His eyes widened in fear. Gone was the insolent tough-guy demeanor.

Thabo's glazed expression darted to Maynard. Maynard understood his unspoken plea. "Help me. I did not do this thing."

Chapter 34

Interrupted by the familiar "Tie Me Kangaroo Down" ringtone of Maynard's mobile phone, Lysi and Grace put down their after-dinner drinks and watched his eyebrows inch towards his hairline after he answered it.

A late dinner in the Butshingi dining room had provided an opportunity for comfortable conversation. Grace had just filled Lysi and Maynard in on her telephone conversation with Luvo. Amele's mother was better and they would return to Cape Town tomorrow around noon.

Lysi looked at the clock on the fireplace mantle and frowned. Who would call Maynard at this time of night? Maybe something happened to his son, Joel.

"I've already trekked to Ikhaya once today." Maynard's surprised look morphed into a look of troubled curiosity. "This better be important."

Lysi and Grace exchanged questioning glances.

"I see. Where?" Maynard asked after a short pause.

"Who is it?" Lysi mouthed.

Maynard frowned and waved his hand to silence her. He checked his watch. "I can get there by 10:00."

"Where?" Lysi whispered. She moved her head close to Maynard's cell.

Maynard switched the phone to his other ear. "All right. I'll leave right now."

Lysi pursed her lips and squinted at Grace.

Maynard clicked off his phone.

Lysi's curiosity exceeded restraint. "Maynard, who was that? What did they want?"

"Nothing really." He cleared his throat. "Information about the Qamata murder. I have a meeting at his hut at 10:00." Maynard got up from the dining room table and headed towards the living room. Lysi followed close on his heels while Grace sipped her drink and watched.

"A meeting? With whom? Why his hut? Why so late?" Lysi's stomach churned. Something about Maynard's clandestine conversation didn't feel right.

"You ask too many questions." Maynard put an arm around her.

She pulled away from him. "I'm going with you."

"Lysi, no." Maynard took a deep breath. "I've already said too much. It's confidential. Police business." He took the VW keys from the wall key holder, pecked her on the cheek and headed for the door. "It could cause problems for Thabo." He patted her shoulder. "Please."

This was not reassuring. Lysi stared unseeing at the door Maynard had just exited. Problems for Thabo? Why would Thabo want to meet Maynard at Qamata's hut at night? Problems for Thabo? Why? What kind?

Lysi and Grace traded meaningless conversation and watched the hands of the clock move slowly.

"It's 11:30." Lysi paced back and forth in front of the living room sofa. "Why isn't he back?" she said, wringing her hands. "Why doesn't he answer his cell?"

"Lysi, please. Park. Maynard's a big boy. He can take care of himself." Grace paused as if trying to think of what to say next. "He's probably on his way back and doesn't want to answer his phone while driving."

"He would've called." Lysi dropped onto the couch. "Something's wrong. I know it." She jerked out her cell phone. "I'm calling Mbeki."

Grace rolled her eyes. "You're overreacting. Maynard's only been missing for 2 hours."

"Missing! Oh God, you're right. I'll report him missing." Lysi started to punch in a number for the Ikhaya Police station then realized she didn't know it. "What's the number Grace? I know you know it."

"You're misconstruing what I said, Lysi. I didn't mean missing...missing. I meant—"

Before Grace could finish Lysi said, "Never mind. I'll call 10111."

"Emergency? Wait." Grace reached into her purse and pulled out the card Mbeki had given her the first day they met. She handed it to Lysi.

"021-3602300," Lysi said as she dialed.

A deep male voice answered in Xhosa. All Lysi understood was Ikhaya. "Is this the Ikhaya Police Station?"

"Yes. What is your need?" the man replied in English.

"Detective Mbeki, please."

"I am sorry, Detective Mbeki has left for the day. How may I help you?"

"I want to report a missing person."

"I can help you. Please say the name of the person and how long he is missing?"

"Maynard Christie." Lysi paused and felt her face heat up. "How long missing?"

Grace sniggered.

Lysi glared at her. "About 2 hours." She sounded sheepish even to herself.

"Two hours? Did you mean to say twelve hours?" The voice on the phone sounded incredulous.

"No. Two hours."

The voice hardened. "Miss, it is true there is no waiting period for filing a missing persons report in Ikhaya. It is also true any person can file a report as soon as they think something out of the ordinary has happened to a subject. But two hours—"

"Maynard would never go to Ikhaya at night for that long and not at least call and—"

Deep sigh. "You must come to the station and fill out a SAPS 55 form so we can begin a search." The clerk sounded like the thing he most wanted in the world at that moment was to hang up on this neurotic woman. "Goodbye."

"Wait!" Lysi shouted into the phone. "Fill out a what?"

"A SAPS missing person's information form. You will please bring a photo of the missing person."

"I don't have a photo."

"Maybe has he a special mark." All pretense of politeness had disappeared from the clerk's voice. "A beard, mustache, mole, tattoo, bald—"

"Oh, he has a tattoo. A Tasmanian Devil just below his left ribcage and—"

"You may fill it on the form when you get here." As the clerk grew more frustrated his English deteriorated to near gibberish. "Please to say me at time you come at Ikhaya station. Goodbye."

Lysi clicked off her phone.

"A tattoo of a Tasmanian Devil just below his left ribcage?" Grace raised her eyebrows and pressed her lips together as if trying to keep a straight face. Little snorts escaped through her nose.

Lysi glowered at her, daring her to laugh.

Suddenly an explosive burst of air escaped through Grace's tight lips and she threw her head back in a bray of laughter. "Honey, I'm not even going to ask how far below the ribcage that tattoo is or how you found it. I just want to know if he's as good as he looks."

Lysi's face burned. "Let's go, Grace."

"Go? Go where?"

"To Ikhaya."

"Ikhaya. Hmmm…Let me think about that." Grace poked at her cheek with her index finger then shook her head. "No. Hear me, Lysi. Maynard's not missing. He's—"

Lysi started to call for a taxi when her cell phone chirped.

She clicked it open. "Maynard?"

"Lysi? It is Billy Joe Mbeki. I am trying to reach Maynard. He does not answer his cell. I thought I would try you because he is usually sniffing around you." Billy Joe's chuckle sounded forced.

"He's not with me. I can't reach him either." Why didn't Maynard answer his cell? Maybe he forgot to charge it. No, he's too assiduous. Maybe he misplaced it. No, he's too well organized. Maybe he couldn't…

"Do you know where he went?" The chuckle faded from Billy Joe's voice replaced by an almost undetectable note of concern.

"He got a phone call to meet someone at Qamata's hut. I'm worried."

"Who called? What time was that?" Billy Joe demanded.

Lysi detected the urgency in Billy Joe's normally calm professional voice. The lump in her throat dropped to her stomach.

"I don't know who called but the meeting was set for 10:00. I'm going to the Ikhaya police station to file a missing person report."

"No need to go to Ikhaya. If a SAPS is needed I will file it. If Maynard calls, tell him to get back to me on my cell. I am here in Cape Town."

Lysi dropped on the couch next to Grace and answered her unspoken question. "Billy Joe. He'll take care of the missing person report."

Grace grinned. "How'd he sound?"

"I'd say he sounded tired even worn—" The phone interrupted Lysi. "Please let it be Maynard."

"Maynard?" Lysi answered in a pleading voice.

"No. I am calling to Maynard."

"Oh, Lindani." Lysi couldn't hide her disappointment. "Honey, I can't talk right now. I'm expecting Maynard to call."

"He is not back from Qamata's hut?"

A jolt of alarm shot through Lysi's body. "How did you know he went to Qamata's hut?"

"I made the meeting," Lindani said with pride.

"Meeting? Why did you want to meet with Maynard?"

"The meeting was not with me. Someone else."

"Who?"

"I promised not to tell. I am sorry."

Lysi's fist tightened around the phone. "Lindani, you must tell me. He may be in danger. Who was he meeting? Tell me."

124

"I cannot." Lindani's voice turned whiney. "I have to keep my promise."

Lysi feared her frustration might cause her to say something she'd regret so she said nothing and hung up.

"That's strange," she said a puzzled expression on her face. She lifted her chin and her eyes sparked. "Grace, we have to go to Ikhaya."

Grace did a double take. "But Billy Joe's filing the missing person report."

"Not the police station. To Qamata's hut."

"Wait a minute. Stroll through Ikhaya at…" she looked at her watch. "almost midnight by the time we get there? Everything's shut up tight except the shebeens. Civilized people are holed up in their houses. Only goons and thugs'll be prowling the streets."

"I'm going, Grace."

Grace had heard that iron-edge of determination in Lysi's voice before. "Okay," she said. "Let's go."

Chapter 35

The taxi bumped through the dark nameless streets in Ikhaya's informal settlements. Lysi worried that a cab driver from Cape Town couldn't find his way through the maze of dirt roads and shadowy shacks but after a couple of backtracks, he found the Themba Center and pulled up next to Amele's VW. Lysi eyed the red Volkswagen. So Maynard had parked here and taken the same walking trail to Qamata's hut they'd followed the day she'd nagged him into checking out the crime scene. How she wished she hadn't insisted on involving him in the case.

Lysi got out of the cab and handed the irritating East Indian cab driver 300 Rand for the 30-kilometer trip. Grace slid halfway out of the cab and stopped.

"No streetlights in this section of Ikhaya." The driver spoke in a tone reserved for the village idiot. All the way from Cape Town he'd quoted Ikhaya crime statistics providing way more information than Lysi needed especially since Grace hung on his every word.

"You have a torch?" He switched off the headlights. Everything turned black.

His attempt at drama annoyed Lysi. She flicked on a mini keychain flashlight. It formed a little circle of light on the pitch-black street. "This should work."

"That's not a light. That's a 'dark.'" Grace slid the rest of the way out, but didn't close the car door. "Listen, honey. Your talk is way bigger than your walk. We better rethink this."

The cabby stuck his head out the taxi window. "The murder rate in Ikhaya increased by 6.9% last year." He slapped the side of the door. "In or out, ladies?"

Lysi closed the car door. She looked up and down the street for signs of life. The makeshift shacks she knew were there from her daylight visits, were almost invisible now. Even the bright yellow Shebeen was only a gray cube. The only signs of life were the darting movements of phantom-like stray dogs that cast curious shiny eyes in their direction then sprinted off with quiet yips.

Maybe Grace has a point, Lysi thought. There was a reason Ikhayans sequestered themselves behind barred doors after dark. Maybe we should take the taxi to the police station and get help. Maybe—Lysi reached for the door handle.

Before she could open the door, the driver flicked the headlights back on, the taxi engine revved to life and the cab moved down the street limiting their choices to either a very long walk to the police station or a short walk to Qamata's hut. Lysi and Grace watched the cab's red taillights shrink to tiny marbles and disappear. The only light that remained besides the flashlight was a weak sliver of moon struggling to survive in the charcoal, cloud-covered sky.

"Look," Lysi said as she started towards Qamata's hut, "We've come this far. Let's finish the job."

"What job?" Grace said in a clipped tone. "We don't even know what we're doing here. Reality check, girl."

"Grace. Please." Lysi grabbed her arm. "I've got an awful feeling something's terribly wrong. I couldn't live with myself if something happened to Maynard. I—"

Grace's eyes widened and her jaw dropped two inches. "Lysi Weston…you're in love with that sheep farmer!"

"I…I…He's not a sheep farmer." Lysi looked away from Grace. "This is not the time to talk about that. Let's go."

"Oh God." Grace used both hands to shove her long hair back from her forehead and closed her eyes. "You're crazy. I'm even more crazy to listen to you. I—"

Lysi yanked Grace's arm and pulled her towards the path to Qamata's hut. She pointed the penlight toward the ground in front of them and they followed the pale beam along the trail.

Spiky weeds and low shrubs growing on both sides of the narrow trail brushed against their legs. Intermittent animal-like skittering and whooshing sounds jolted them prompting periodic whispered exclamations from Grace.

"What was that?" Grace grabbed Lysi's arm and yanked her to a stop. "Did you hear that?"

"No," Lysi said.

"Listen. There it is again?" Grace locked her feet in place.

"Come on, Big City Girl." Lysi pulled her forward.

"Umph!" Grace tripped into an unexpected dip in the uneven path and almost fell. "Lysi, I can't see my feet. Point the damn light toward my feet."

Lysi switched the light toward Grace. "Now I can't see. Get over here closer to me." Lysi stuck her arm through the crook of Grace's elbow. They skulked along in lock step following the flashlight beam as it bobbed and bounced along.

The wind gusted sending a flurry of crisp leaves scratching over their sandaled feet.

"Did you feel that?" Grace's body shuddered.

"Leaves," Lysi said. She hoped Grace couldn't feel the goose bumps that fear had popped out on her arms.

"Leaves with fur?" Grace said.

"Your imagination's working overtime. Even if it was a little creature, he's a lot more scared of you than you are of him." Lysi's words didn't sound convincing even to herself.

"A little revelation here," Grace whispered. "First, you don't know how scared I am. Second, you don't know how scared he is. Third, you just admitted there might be little scary creatures."

"It's not the little scary creatures you need to worry about. It's the big ones." Lysi finished the paragraph in her head—unless it's a razor-toothed rat or venomous snake or poisonous lizard or a giant scorpion. Her toes twitched at the thought of something suddenly latching onto them.

"Don't talk," Grace said. "I don't need anymore of your reassuring words."

Each time the path dipped or a shrub brushed against her legs, Grace tightened her grip on Lysi and little squeaks and gasps escaped her lips. Lysi started to ask her how she could walk the rat infested Harlem streets without fear and be so nervous here in nature but Grace jabbed Lysi's arm and pointed to the flashlight's diminished circle of light.

"Lysi, when's the last time you changed the batteries in that 'flashdark' of yours?"

"I…don't remember. Not long ago. Why?"

"Because…that little circle has shrunk from a beach ball to a baseball heading towards a pingpong ball. It's getting dimmer, too."

Lysi shook the flashlight. It brightened for a moment then dimmed again.

Grace looked up. "That skinny moon is like a ball of fire compared to that sickly flashlight." Grace gasped. She tugged Lysi's arm and pointed towards the sky. "Lysi, what happened to the moon?"

The flashlight died. The world disappeared.

Lysi's body lurched. Everything halted—her legs, breathing, heart. She could hear Grace panting. Hyperventilating. "Grace. Grace. Squeeze my hand. Close your eyes as tight as you can and keep them closed until I count to ten. Are they closed?"

"I think so. It's so dark I can't tell if they're opened or closed."

Lysi closed her own eyes and counted to ten. "Now open them. Can you see a little better?"

"Yeah," Grace said. "Now everything's a sooty gray."

The yellowwood tree's huge form rose like a black sea monster in front of them blocking out the view of the moon. As they neared the tree eyes appeared in the blackness. The eyes didn't blink. Didn't move. For an instant eternity Lysi and Grace turned into statues.

Lysi stared hard at the eyes. Why didn't they blink or move? The eyes seemed to group in one place. She squinted. A hazy outline appeared around the eyes. Of course. How could she not have figured it out immediately. She whispered to Grace. "Those yellowish specks aren't eyes. They're lights leaking through the holes in Qamata's hut."

Slurred words from the hut rose in strident whispers that erupted intermittently into raucous laughter. Lysi heard a mixture of Xhosa and English. "Big man not big now." Xhosa phrase. "Maybe sorry now." More Xhosa. "Too late."

The hut door swung open. The sudden light extended almost to Grace and Lysi's feet. They both froze. Something flew out and clunked on the gravelly sand about ten inches from Lysi's big toe. A startled mouse sound shot from her lips. When the door closed, she pointed her flashlight towards the ground, shook it and pressed the on button. The light flashed on then off. She caught a glimpse of the object.

"It's a bottle. Got to be at least a magnum." She shook the flashlight again. Nothing. She bent down and ran her hand along the ground, hoping she wouldn't disturb some creepy crawly nocturnal thing. Her fingers touched the glass bottle. She grabbed it and shoved it at Grace. "Let's go."

Lysi and Grace stood nearly nose-to-nose in whispered conversation.

"Where?"

"Around to the back."

"And…when we get there, what? Why don't you ever plan?" Grace spoke in a high- pitched whisper.

"Plan! Look who's talking. Who suddenly plops us on a plane and zips us off to Africa?" Lysi immediately regretted her reaction to Grace's frustrated words. This was not the time to debate personality types. Not the time to get testy. "I'm sorry."

"What now?" Grace's voice softened.

"We look through that hole I told you Maynard found behind the hut and see what they're up to. We move on them if we need to."

Grace cupped her ear and whispered. "Hello? No weapons."

"What do you think that is in your hand?" Lysi gestured toward the liquor bottle.

Lysi started to move forward, Grace on her heels. Suddenly another bottle flew out the door and Lysi froze in a sudden stop. Grace rammed into her forcing Lysi to take a quick step to avoid falling. The flashlight fell from her hand, clanked on a rock and rolled about a foot toward the hut door. The shouting in the hut ceased.

"They heard us," Lysi whispered. "Move." In three gigantic steps they ducked out of sight along the side of the hut just as the hut door widened spotlighting the flashlight.

Cold sweat washed over Lysi's body. Please don't let them see it. Both she and Grace stared at the flashlight and didn't breathe.

A dark head shot through the open door, bobbed unsteadily left and right, paused, whisper-yelled something in Xhosa to the men inside then closed the door.

Lysi mopped her forehead with the back of her hand then motioned Grace to follow her. They inched around to the back of the hut. A small ray of light sprayed through the hole Maynard had discovered when he checked out the scene. Lysi peeked through it. Nothing prepared her for what she saw. The rage that swept through her made her feel nauseous. She gasped for breath. "Grace, look."

"Oh God." Grace shook her head and put her arm around Lysi to steady her.

Maynard sat in a chair, hands tied behind him, head drooping. Three men holding magnum bottles of amber liquid staggered around him kicking, punching and slapping him.

Maynard didn't move.

Lysi felt sick. Was Maynard still alive? How could he survive a beating like this? She wanted to run to him, to shield him, to help him. Her eyes watered. She swiped at them with her fingers.

"Big man not so strong now, eh?" The skinny, wiry guy pushed Maynard's head with the heel of his hand.

"That skinny guy is Uuka," Lysi said, "I remember him from the Shebeen last night. The other two are his brothers." Lysi swallowed hard. Anger and determination dried her eyes.

"I know him. He was one of the creeps who assaulted me," Grace said. "I got a little debt to settle with those three." Grace looked volcanic. She slapped her open palm with the heavy glass bottle. Vengeful anger had supplanted the fear in her voice.

"Grace, look. The big guy's about to pass out."

"We don't know how long that'll take." Grace sounded skeptical.

"I know how long. My all-American drawback ex-husband used to stagger around like that about ten minutes before he'd pass out. They're all getting plastered. I think we can take them after they finish those liter bottles they're chugalugging."

Lysi looked around for something to use as a weapon. If only she could have grabbed the other bottle that flew out the door before that creep stuck his head out.

Eerie shapes emerged around her as her eyes readjusted to the dark after peeking through the hole at the bright interior of the hut. A dead White Karee tree materialized behind her. Lysi picked up a broken branch that resembled a baseball bat. Perfect size and weight for a club.

Time moved at the speed of grass growing as they peered through the small hole waiting for the right moment. Lysi tried to bury worries about the danger that confronted them. They had the element of surprise on their side. They had good strong weapons. The creeps had turned into clumsy drunks, barely able to walk. Still, drunk or not, they were men and strength was on their side. Lysi looked at Grace. Even in the dark she could see the fire in her eyes, the determined line of her jaw and the ready, almost eager bearing. If Grace could turn into a tiger, so could she. She looked at Maynard and her chest ached but her muscles flexed.

Lysi changed into a tiger.

The big guy passed out precipitating howls of laughter from the other two. Uuka gave him a couple of kicks and said something in Xhosa. All pretense of whispering disappeared as the two men slapped each other and downed big swigs from their bottles.

The two women waited and watched the men empty their magnums, open two more and chugalug them. Their stagger turned to a wobble and their wobble dissipated into an inability to stand without holding on to something.

"Now," Lysi whispered.

Chapter 36

Lysi and Grace edged along the wall of Qamata's hut toward the front door. A few yards from the door a panicked screech followed by the flap of wings jolted them to a stop. Lysi's hand flew to her chest. Grace grabbed Lysi around the waist and dug her chin into Lysi's shoulder.

"Just an owl." Lysi's whisper didn't sound as casual as she'd hoped. It sounded more like a gasp. "Come on."

A few steps further and they stood in front of the door. Lysi flashed an are-you-ready look to Grace. At Grace's nod she nudged the door open a couple of inches. Light spilled through the opening. Suddenly a small, clawed creature sprinted across Lysi's feet. She jumped.

"What?" Grace whispered.

"Nothing. I think the light frightened a tiny chipmunk." She didn't say what she really thought—a rat. No use getting Grace into more of a dither.

Lysi peered through the crack. Two men leaned over Maynard, their backs to the hut entrance. Uuka handed the fat one a knife and nodded towards Maynard. The fat one thrust the knife back to Uuka and shook his head. Uuka laughed, punched the fat guy's huge paunch and made a remark in Xhosa.

"Uuka's mine," Grace said. "I'll teach him to put his hands on me." Her hate-filled tone would have brought Goliath to his knees begging for mercy.

"I've got the fat one," Lysi said. Her fingers tightened around the sturdy Karee tree branch.

Uuka grasped the knife with both hands and raised it over his head, wobbling so much he almost lost his balance.

"Go!" Lysi said.

Lysi whipped the door open. They flew through it and lunged at the two surprised men who turned their heads in slow motion and blinked. Too late. Lysi grasped the branch with both hands, swung it like a bat and slammed the fat one on the side of his face. Homer! His head hit his shoulder and he crumbled to the ground. At the same time, Grace, fueled with vengeful fury, bashed Uuka on the head with the bottle so hard he toppled without even a moan.

The big guy on the floor raised his forehead a couple of inches off the dirt, fluttered his eyes open and looked around, wide-eyed as an awakened toddler. He grinned and stretched his hand toward Grace's bright red-painted toenails. "Wha…"

Lysi whirled and slammed him on the back with the branch. His face flopped on the ground and he snored the snore of an out-cold drunk.

Lysi rushed to Maynard. He didn't move. She touched his neck with her fingertips and felt the regular beat of his carotid pulse. She wanted to do something to help him. She just didn't know what.

A moan from one of the men caught her attention. Her eyes jerked to Grace. Then both women moved into quick action. Lysi grabbed Uuka's knife, grasped the rope from which a smelly monkey carcass dangled by its mangy neck. She hacked at the knot under the monkey's hairy chin until the malodorous primate fell to the floor. She cut the other end of the rope from the low ceiling beam and tossed it to Grace.

Lysi sniffed her fingers and uttered a quick, "Yuk." The smell reminded her of the putrid odor of a sewage treatment plant near San Francisco.

Grace tied Uuka's hands and feet together behind his back while Lysi cut two more animal carcasses off ropes, kept one rope and tossed the other one to Grace.

Lysi looked at the tie job Grace had done on Uuka. "How'd you do that?"

"Watch the master, honey."

Grace rolled the fat guy onto his stomach and trussed him up like a rodeo calf, ending with a neat square knot under his chin. "Now, if he moves his legs, he'll tighten the rope around his neck and choke himself—which, by the way would be just fine with me."

Lysi copied each of Grace's rope tying steps and ended with the same square knot under the chin of the dazed big guy. "Done."

Grace stood over Uuka. She smiled down at him then gave a hard yank on Uuka's feet. The rope tightened around his throat squashing his Adam's apple. He emitted a choking sound.

"Aw come on Uuka. You can do better than that." Another yank, another choking sound. Grace smiled with satisfaction. "How's the old libido now, Uuka boy?"

Lysi returned to Maynard. She felt a sharp pain in her throat. His chin still rested on his chest. She raised his chin. His eyes were swollen shut, his nose and lips bruised and bleeding.

Grace took out her cellphone and lifted an index finger to punch in the emergency number, 10111. Before she pressed the first number, she heard engine noise outside the hut and jerked to attention, her index finger still poised over the number one. Two car doors slammed.

Lysi looked at Grace. They listened to the sound of approaching footsteps. Lysi gave Grace an eye message to stand behind the door, her magnum bottle at the ready. Lysi slinked towards the branch she'd dropped on the floor, picked it up and held it with both hands in the air above her head. They stared at the door. Seconds dragged and their fear escalated. As the door inched open, a wavy black shadow materialized. A head emerged.

Lysi swung the branch with a loud grunt.

A big hand grabbed it before it hit the mark and threw it on the ground. Grace stumbled from behind the door ready to swing the magnum but hesitated when she saw who had come through the door.

"You crazy?" Thabo's voice sounded like a deep roar of thunder. "You could kill me."

Thabo's appearance didn't surprise Lysi. He must have lured Maynard here then left Uuka and his brothers to beat him up. What she couldn't grasp was how Thabo and these three thugs got together. She thought they hated each other.

"Thabo, how could you?" Lysi said. "Maynard saved your life."

Grace stood back an expression of hurt and betrayal on her face.

Anger rose up in Lysi. She threw caution to the wind and plowed into Thabo using as much force as she could muster in an attempt to batter him with her shoulder. In the same instant, Grace jumped in and tried to strike him with the bottle.

With one broad sweep of his arm, Thabo deflected the blows and threw both women to the ground. "You are both crazy. Stay away before I have to hurt you."

Lysi stared up at Thabo in confusion. Why hadn't he put more force into his defensive move? He could have injured them with little effort. Why had he held back?

Thabo's dark eyes roamed around the hut. He didn't hide his disgust when he spotted Uuka and his brothers on the floor. He walked over to Uuka and with the toe of his heavy boot lifted him on his side then let him flop back on his stomach. He did the same with Uuka's two brothers. "They will not wake up soon."

He looked at Lysi and Grace, who remained seated on the dirt floor staring up at him, their legs spread eagle. Lysi saw respect in Thabo's eyes not threat. With a cautious expression on his face, he extended a big hand to each woman and pulled them both up in one swoop.

Thabo stepped in front of Maynard, lifted his chin with gentle finger. He scrunched his face at Maynard's swollen eyes, fat lip, bloody nose and bruised cheeks and jaws. He examined the cuts and contusions and smoothed his palms over Maynard's ribs. "The beating is very bad. Maybe a concussion. Maybe damaged ribs. He needs hospital. I will load him into the ambulance."

Thabo stuck his head out the hut door. "Lindani, help me with the gurney."

No sound came from Lindani, but Lysi heard the back door of the ambulance click open. Thabo left the hut and Lysi heard more clicks and then the creak of gurney wheels. Thabo reappeared at the head of the gurney. Lindani pushed from the foot.

Lysi stared at Thabo. This didn't compute. If he wanted to hurt Maynard, why didn't he finish the job? Why would he examine him? Why would he put him in an ambulance and take him to the hospital? Why was he here?

Thabo lowered the gurney and said, "Help lift him." It took all four of them to lift the Maynard's limp, unconscious body onto the gurney. Thabo secured him with well-trained, professional hands. He took the head end of the gurney and gestured to Lindani to take the lighter end. After they secured Maynard in the back of the ambulance he turned to Lysi. "You will drive the ambulance to Site B."

"What? Why me?" She followed Thabo back into the hut. "Thabo, you drive. You're the ambulance tech. You're the one on duty tonight."

"I will stay with these filthy hyenas." Thabo kicked Uuka in the ribs. Uuka groaned but didn't stir.

Lysi didn't know what to do. She wanted to go with Maynard but was fearful. What if she couldn't drive the ambulance? What if she had an accident? What if she lost her way? In desperation Lysi said, "Lindani can—"

"Lindani does not know how to drive," Thabo said. He picked up Maynard's bush hat and jacket and returned to the ambulance. Lysi trailed him out the door. "Thabo, you don't understand. I've never driven an ambulance before. I don't think—"

"You will do it." Thabo climbed into the back of the ambulance, took some gauze from a glass container and dampened it with an antiseptic solution. He swabbed at Maynard's face. Maynard flinched but remained unconscious. Thabo checked that Maynard's body lay straight, wedged small sandbags against each side of his head and taped them in place. He pulled a woolen blanket up to Maynard's chin.

"Grace, you will ride in the back with Detective Christie," Thabo said as he jumped out of the ambulance. "Keep him covered. We must guard against shock,"

"You, get in the cab." He pressed a key into Lysi's hand and nudged her into the ambulance. "Lindani, ride in front. You can give directions to the center." Thabo started back towards the hut.

"Wait, Thabo." Lysi jumped out of the cab. She tried to keep the panic out of her voice. "Where's the ignition? The lights? The windshield wipers? Turn signals?"

Thabo shot air through his lips, grabbed Lysi's arm and shoved her into the ambulance cab. He took her hand and put it on the starter. "Ignition," he said. Then he switched on the headlights. "There is no rain. Now go."

The ambulance lurched foreward.

Thabo entered the hut and flashed a light in Uuka's face. Uuka did not stir. Thabo picked up a half empty bottle and sniffed it. Whiskey? Where did they get money for whiskey? He took a big swig then poured the rest of the liquor on Uuka's face. Uuka shook his head and his eyes fluttered open. When he saw Thabo, his pupils dilated into huge black balls, bulging with fear.

Thabo spoke to him in Xhosa. "I promised you I would kill you the moment I caught you in Ikhaya. I changed my mind."

Uuka exhaled in relief.

"You have earned a special death—a slow death, a painful death."

Uuka's lips stretched across his lips in terror.

"First I will steal your manhood for what you tried to do to Lindani and Grace." He held Uuka's own knife in the air. "I will beat you for what you did to Detective Christie. Then I will crush your head for what you did to Qamata."

"Qamata? No." Uuka shook his head back and forth. He seemed to be grasping at straws. "I did not kill Qamata."

Thabo could tell Uuka's words registered genuine surprise but he didn't care. "I do not believe you."

"Why would I kill Qamata?" Uuka whined. "He is an old man ready to die on his own."

Thabo paused a moment. Why would Uuka bother to kill Qamata? He would gain nothing.

"Thabo, I beg you. You must listen." Tears streamed down Uuka's face. "I did not kill Qamata but I know who crushed his head with a rock."

"Liar. If you did not do it, how do you know a rock killed him?" Thabo shook the knife at Uuka.

"Wait. Wait. I know because I was there. So were they." Uuka's eyes shifted toward his two brothers.

"We held Qamata but we did not kill him."

Chapter 37

In a small exam room at Site B Community Health Center Lysi sat on a stool beside Maynard. He lay on a narrow examination table, a white sheet draped over his body. Sundry medical supplies filled a stainless steel tray on a mobile instrument stand. A nurse swabbed Maynard's facial lacerations with gauze pads she dipped in a container of saline solution sitting on the tray. The light from a bright overhead incandescent bulb beat down on Maynard's face. Lysi felt the urge to shield his eyes from the strong rays though she knew the nurse needed the light to see the areas she had to clean.

At frequent intervals the nurse lifted the sheet to check the blue vinyl cold packs she'd placed on his thighs, arms, chest and abdomen. Lysi didn't take her eyes off Maynard. She winced at the painful red blotches on his body that would soon darken to purple-black. She longed to touch him. It took all her control not to question the nurse about his every movement and sound.

"He is sedated," the nurse said as if she heard Lysi's thoughts. "But he can feel some pain from the cuts and bruises."

The door clicked open and Nambeko came into the room cleansing her hands with an antibacterial wipe. The strong alcohol scent of the antiseptic stung Lysi's nose. Nambeko must have to disinfect her hands a hundred times a day, Lysi thought. That medicinal smell seems to cling to physicians even off duty. She recalled smelling that scent in other places besides medical facilities.

Lysi forced a smile. "Nambeko, I'm so glad you're here. Maynard's—"

"Lysi, I must ask you to leave while I examine the patient's ribs and lower extremities." Nambeko stood by the open door and gestured towards the crowded waiting room. "Just have a seat out there. I shouldn't be long."

Lysi felt tears prick the back of her eyes. She stared at Nambeko but said nothing. She didn't want to leave Maynard. Why should she have to go?

Nambeko pulled on rubber gloves and said something to the nurse who picked up her tray and left the room.

"Lysi, are you listening?" Nambeko's eyes narrowed. "I said you must step out while I examine his ribs and lower extremities." She looked stern, her voice formal. Professional. Authoritative. A command not a request.

Lysi choked back a sob. Of course she should leave and let the doctor do what she needs to do to help Maynard. Lysi rose from the chair, nodded and shuffled from the room.

Grace and Lindani, seated next to each other, raised questioning eyes to Lysi when she approached. Lysi dropped onto a folding chair next to Grace and gazed, unseeing around the packed waiting room.

"He's so badly hurt. I hope they have the medical equipment to take care of him here." Lysi's voice cracked.

Grace put an arm around her. "Nambeko is a fine doctor. Maynard wouldn't have better care anywhere."

"But we don't know what they did to him—broken ribs? Internal damage? Head injury? Brain…" Lysi squeezed her eyes shut and shook her head back and forth. She choked on her words. "Oh, Grace, it's all my fault. I got him into this. If I could only undo it. If I could only un—"

"Hey! Don't think that way." Grace grasped Lysi's arms and shifted her so they were almost nose-to-nose. She tipped up Lysi's chin and looked hard into her eyes. "You listen to me. First, he's a tough Outback sheep farmer. He's probably weathered a lot worse than this. Second, you didn't tell him to come to Cape Town. Truth is, I don't think you could have kept him away." Grace smiled and softened her voice. "Third, he's going to be racing those wild camels again before you know it. You might even be trailing along behind him on a small lady camel."

Lysi wanted to hug Grace. She wanted to believe her. She had to believe her. Only, what if she was wrong? "I want you to be right, but I'm so afraid he—"

Lindani's loud sob cut Lysi's sentence. She stood suddenly then dropped to her knees in front of Lysi. "I am sorry." Sniffles syncopated her words. "I thought the call would help find Sipho's killer. I did not know Detective Christie would get hurt. I am sorry."

Lysi stared at her. "Lindani, I..." She gestured to a chair next to her. "Please sit."

Lindani slumped into the chair.

"Now, tell me what you're talking about." Lysi tried to keep frustration out of her voice. Lindani still thinks like a child and behaves like one. Best not to make her more anxious than she already is.

"The phone call...to Detective Christie." Tears streamed down Lindani's cheeks. "I had to call. I tried to keep the secret but Thabo got mad at me. He said he would tell Detective Mbeki what I did if I did not tell him my secret. He said they might put me in jail. So I told him part of it."

Lysi brow creased in confusion. She groped for the question that would unlock the information Lindani was trying to convey. "What did you tell him?"

"I told him about Detective Christie's meeting at Qamata's hut."

"Wait, Lindani." Lysi pressed her fingers against her temples. Her brain kept repeating, Stay calm. Stay calm. "You wanted to meet May—Detective Christie at Qamata's hut?"

"No, no. Not me." Lindani's voice turned shrill. "Thabo wanted me to tell him who was meeting Detective Christie in the hut, but I had to keep my promise."

Lindani paused. Lysi figured she needed prodding.

"You must tell me what you know, Lindani?" Lysi pressed.

"Yes." Lindani nodded several times. Her thoughts flooded into words. "Thabo told me he would go to Qamata's hut and see for himself. He told me to go home and wait for him but I would not because I wanted to ride in the ambulance with him. He never lets me ride when he is on duty. But he did this time to go to Qamata's hut."

"So that's why Thabo came to the hut?" Grace said. She turned to Lysi. "He wanted to see if Maynard was in danger. He wanted to help him not hurt him. I knew it."

Lysi's breathing accelerated. Her lips compressed in a desperate line and her unblinking eyes focused on Lindani. She grabbed Lindani's shoulders. "You have to tell us who made you make that call to Detective Christie. Who wanted to meet with him? Who, Lindani? Who?"

"I am sorry." Lindani started to cry.

"I don't care how sorry you are," Lysi said. She wanted to shake Lindani. Slap her. "I want a name."

Tears flooded Lindani's cheeks. "It was—"

The clinic door banged open startling all three women. Billy Joe Mbeki flew through it. "Where is Maynard?"

"He...He's in there." Lysi pointed to the room. "Nambeko is examining him."

"No!" At Mbeki's roar every head in the waiting room turned. Startled eyes stared. No one moved. No one spoke. The unasked question was: Who is in trouble?

Mbeki sprinted to the room. Lysi followed on his heels. Mbeki jiggled the knob but the door was latched. With one hard yank the flimsy lock yielded and the door opened. The overwhelming smell of disinfectant in the airless room assaulted Lysi's nasal passages. Where had she smelled that strong odor before? The scent of the eucalyptus tree on Rugby Road flashed through her senses. But that wasn't it. Hospitals, doctors, nurses. Yes, of course. Still not the place that lay hidden just below her conscious memory. Where?

A quick inhale and she knew. Qamata's hut the day she followed Paki. The rustling wild animal sound. It wasn't a wild animal. Someone had hidden behind the hut. Someone who smelled like antiseptic.

"Dr. Nala. Stop," Mbeki shouted.

Nambeko had injected a hypodermic into a vial and turned it upside down to fill the syringe.

"What is the meaning of this?" Her eyes lasered in on Mbeki. "You cannot just walk in here and—"

"I just did." Mbeki grabbed the hypodermic and vial out of her hands. "You are finished here. Dr. Mkiva will take over your treatment."

Lysi stared at Mbeki, her mouth twisted in anguish. A scream stuck in her throat. Why wouldn't Billy Joe let Nambeko help Maynard? The alcohol scent nauseated her. Then the realization crushed her chest. Could Nambeko have been behind Qamata's hut? No. Impossible. What reason would she have had to be there?

"You are interfering with my treatment. You are putting this patient at risk." Nambeko reached for the hypodermic.

"Treatment?" Mbeki held up the hypodermic and examined it. "What is in this syringe?"

"It is a painkiller." Nambeko looked him straight in the eye and didn't flinch.

Lysi wanted to shout at Billy Joe. She wanted to beg him to allow Nambeko to administer the painkiller to Maynard. How could he be so cruel? Couldn't he see Maynard was suffering?

"No, Dr. Nala." Mbeki held the hypodermic up to the light and studied it. "I think we will find that this syringe does not contain a painkiller—unless it is a permanent one."

"If this man dies, I will see you in prison." Dr. Nala clamped her mouth into an angry line her eyes sparked fire.

"Prison? Yes. I think you will." Mbeki's face hardened into iron; his eyes turned to cold black granite as he stared at Nambeko. "Now you may come with me without creating a scene or I can take you out in handcuffs. The choice is yours, Nambeko."

Billy Joe alarmed Lysi by no longer giving Nambeko the respect of calling her "doctor." Lysi's eyes darted from Billy Joe to Nambeko to Maynard and back to Billy Joe. What kind of nightmare had she entered? She still couldn't speak. Her confused gaze slid over to Dr. Mkiva who stood by the door with downcast eyes. Lysi's hand flew to her mouth as Billy Joe Mbeki shoved Nambeko out of the exam room. Lysi could hear shocked whispers emanating from the waiting room as Billy Joe and Nambeko passed to the exterior door. Soon the whispers intensified into a deafening crescendo.

Lysi's breathing accelerated. Her pulse pounded. She looked at Maynard lying sedated and helpless on the exam table. Tears stung her eyes. She hadn't fully grasped until now how horrible it would be to never see him again. She wouldn't, couldn't leave his side.

She turned pleading eyes to Dr. Mkiva. He understood her silent request. "You may sit in that chair while I administer to him."

Lysi nodded in gratitude, sat next to Maynard and lay her hand light as a feather on his bedside.

Through heavy lids Lysi watched the beige hospital draperies lighten as the predawn sky crept from black to navy on its way to azure. Her eyes burned from lack of sleep. She'd stayed by Maynard's bedside since his transfer by ambulance from Site B Community Health Center to Cape Town Hospital shortly after two a.m. Grace dozed in a chair on the opposite side of the bed.

"Please wake up Maynard. I can't lose you now. I need you. Please, don't leave me." Lysi had repeated the same litany over and over. She tried to focus on Maynard as though she could will him to pull through. She struggled to ward off intrusive thoughts about the confusing chain of events that led to Nambeko's arrest, but unanswered questions careened around in her head. For whom had Lindani made the call that sent Maynard to Qamata's hut? Who did Maynard expect to meet there? How did Uuka and his brothers know Maynard would come to the hut? A setup? Did someone set a trap for Maynard? Who? Why? Lysi touched Maynard's cheek with the back of her hand and choked back a painful sob. What was in the syringe?

She scrunched her eyes several times in an attempt to ward off sleep. She sighed and pillowed her cheek on the side of the bed by Maynard's hand. "Please Maynard. Please God. Please…" Her desperate words faded to a whisper as against her will her eyelids drifted closed.

Chapter 38

Billy Joe Mbeki shoved Nambeko into the hot airless Ikhaya P.D. interrogation room and closed the door, making it even more stifling. He sat down, opened his case notebook and flicked on a small recorder. "Sit, Nambeko."

"I prefer to stand since I will be leaving in a few moments." Nambeko folded her arms across her chest and stared unblinking into Mbeki's eyes. Her frown was as brittle as ice

The self-assured attitude of this young woman he'd known since her childhood amazed Mbeki. Nothing seemed to faze her. He supposed that trait made her a good doctor.

"As you like." Mbeki held up the bag containing the hypodermic and syringe. "Would you like to tell me what is in this syringe? Or shall I tell you?"

Nambeko didn't answer. Mbeki's trained eyes caught a slight tick at the corner of her mouth that cracked her hard shell and betrayed deepening fear.

A knock on the door drew Mbeki's attention. "Bring it in," he ordered in a loud voice. "Set it on the table."

A pudgy policewoman set a laptop computer on the table in front of Mbeki, cast a curious look at Nambeko and left the room.

"You do recognize this?" Mbeki smoothed his hand over the laptop. "It's your computer. The one Ikhaya community members ran fundraisers for and donated their hard-earned money to purchase for you when you started to practice medicine after graduating from medical school. I, myself, contributed." Mbeki's voice communicated the disgust and disappointment he felt.

Nambeko stared at the computer, her mouth a tight controlled line.

"You also know what we found on it, don't you?" He fixed her with a steady gaze.

Nambeko's lips parted but she remained silent.

"An order for Cape Cobra venom." Mbeki determined to break her. "Now I ask you again. What is in this syringe?" He jabbed the syringe at her face.

Nambeko blinked several times. Her breaths came in shallow pants. She looked at Mbeki through nervous eyes.

"It's antivenin," she said in a tight croak. "Detective Christie displayed symptoms of snake—"

Mbeki slammed his fist on the table. "Please, Nambeko. Sniveling lies do not become you." He almost felt sorry for her. He thought of the ambitious girl he once knew. How could she have ended her hopes and dreams this way?

"We know you tried to murder Detective Christie. We know you murdered Qamata. Worst of all, we know you murdered your own brother, for God's sake. What we do not know is why, *Doctor* Nala." Mbeki spat out the word doctor as though it had a vile taste.

Nambeko licked her lips. "I had no choice."

"You had no choice?" Mbeki stood. He raised his hand as if to slap her.

Nambeko didn't flinch. She answered in a self-assured voice, as though confident Mbeki would see that what she had to say made perfect sense.

"Sipho was gay. If it got out, it would have destroyed my practice."

140

"This is why you injected your own brother with cobra venom." Mbeki looked incredulous. "To save your practice?"

"And to save my mother the sorrow of having a homosexual son."

Mbeki thought Nambeko added the concern for her mother almost as an afterthought. What kind of person could think murdering a son would save a mother from sorrow?

"Your mother wouldn't have cared if Sipho was gay. She loved her son unconditionally. Just like she loves you."

Nambeko winced.

"Why Qamata?" Mbeki said.

"Lindani caused Qamata's death." Nambeko's response was matter of fact.

"Come now Nambeko. Lindani is a child." Mbeki shook his head. Nambeko lies with such ease—almost as though she believes what she's saying, he thought.

"Lindani is a vicious liar," Nambeko said. "She told Thabo my brother seduced her. Thabo forced Sipho to go to Qamata to cure his homosexuality so Sipho could marry his feeble minded sister. When Qamata's primitive potions failed, Thabo killed him."

"No, Nambeko. Thabo did not know Sipho was gay. He thought Sipho planned to marry Lindani."

Desperation flooded Nambeko's face. She shifted her eyes around the room like a trapped animal seeking a way out. "Paki saw Thabo in Qamata's hut."

"No. Paki lied because he would never hurt your mother. She treated him like a human being when all of Ikhaya had turned on him because he was homosexual. The person Paki saw was not Thabo. It was you, Nambeko."

"Paki told you this?" Nambeko's eyes registered shock.

Mbeki did not answer her question. Why should he? He was the interrogator, not her.

"Thabo did not kill Sipho and he did not kill Qamata, Mbeki said. "Thabo was at work on the nights of both murders."

"No. Thabo's timecards were not marked," Nambeko said.

"Because you substituted new unmarked timecards and destroyed the real ones. You substituted the first timecard the night Sipho was killed. You wanted to blame Thabo for your stepbrother's death in the event your false autopsy report was discovered. Then you did it again when you bashed Qamata's head in with a rock."

Nambeko swallowed. "No. You are wrong. It was—"

"Stop the lies." Mbeki thrust his face close to Nambeko. "Uuka and his brothers betrayed you. They told Thabo they held Qamata while you bashed his head in."

"Why would you believe them instead of me?" Nambeko looked offended. "They are nothing more than rabid dogs."

"Now you try to blame your brothers?"

"They are not my brothers." Nambeko's eyes flamed in anger. "We share genes from the same breeding sow, but not from the same boar. They grew up in a filthy hog wallow. I became a doctor. " She raised her head and looked down on Mbeki as though *he* were nothing more than a hog.

Nambeko's bitter words shocked Mbeki. Her humiliated eyes told him his reference to Nambeko's blood brothers had stripped away every shred of the dignity she had worked so hard to achieve. Had he gone too far? Feeling regret, he looked away from her and sighed. Still, nothing could excuse murder. Nothing.

"Nambeko, it is over." Mbeki said in frustration. "Tell me why you killed Qamata."

Nambeko looked as if she was fabricating then discarding responses.

"I…I—"

"I am losing patience, Nambeko. The truth, please."

The doctor collapsed onto a chair and stared at the table. Her body drooped in defeat. She spoke in an almost inaudible voice. "Sipho went to Qamata for a cure. That is how Qamata found out Sipho was gay. He said he had Sipho's bracelet as proof. Qamata threatened me. He said he would expose Sipho's homosexuality and ruin our family. My practice. He tried to blackmail me. I had to kill him."

"At least there is some truth in you," Mbeki said. "When we searched the Site B Community Health Center dumpster, we found this." He handedNambeko a dirty piece of paper. "Read it aloud."

Nambeko's voice quavered as she read the Xhosa words written in heavy dark pencil. "I know Sipho is homosexual. I will tell everyone unless you give me what I want."

"What did Qamata want, Nambeko?"

"Me. He's always wanted me to follow in his footsteps. Live with him. Belong to him. I could never do that."

Mbeki remembered stories about Qamata stalking Nambeko when she was a child. He heard the tale of the shovel-beating Mandisa had given Qamata for scaring her daughter. The Ikhayans both hated Qamata for his many cruelties and feared him for his occult powers. No one in Ikhaya would regret his death. Nambeko's pitiful plea for understanding saddened Mbeki. He steeled himself to continue the interrogation.

"We can wrap this up if you answer this last question truthfully. 'Why Detective Christie? Why kill him?"

"Because he was getting too close to the truth," Nambeko said. "He figured out about the cobra venom. I knew it was just a matter of time before he tracked it to me."

"How did you know this?"

"I dropped something in Qamata's hut and went back to get it."

"What?" Mbeki placed both hands on the table and leaned into Nambeko.

"The cap to a medical vial."

"You mean the cap to the snake venom vial." Mbeki raised his voice.

Nambeko nodded. "I went to Qamata's hut to find the vial cap. Lysi Weston was in the hut with Paki. I overheard her accuse him of searching for a cap. That's when I knew Christie had figured it all out. I had to stop him."

"Detective Christie did not have to track anything to you. We had already done that."

Nambeko continued as if she hadn't heard Mbeki. "I had Lindani call Detective Christie and tell him to meet me at Qamata's hut, that I had information that might help solve the case. I knew Uuka hated Detective Christie because he had humiliated him in the Shebeen. I told Uuka Detective Christie would be at Qamata's hut at 10:00 p.m. I gave the spineless hyena a case of liquid courage—whiskey— and told him he and his brothers might want to even the score with this white maggot. He did."

Mbeki closed his case notebook and shook his head. "Do you have anything else to say?"

"I take full responsibility for all I did. I loved my stepbrother. I really did. I didn't want to hurt my stepmother. I know she can never forgive me." Nambeko buried her face in her arms on the table. "I cannot bear to see the hurt on her face. I do not want to see her. I am sorry. So very sorry."

Mbeki flicked off the recorder.

Chapter 39

Morning sun brightened the drab beige draperies on the hospital window. Lysi stood, stretched and pulled them open. Brilliant rays filtered through the dancing leaves of a yellowwood tree, flooding the room with shimmering iridescence. Maynard sat in bed propped up by pillows. He'd been a patient in the Cape Town Hospital for two days.

Lysi dropped on a chair next to the bed. Relieved at Maynard's improvement but still fearing a possible relapse, she tried to disguise her lingering worries in weak attempts at humor. "You woke up just in time. I couldn't have stood much more of your bellowing camel snores."

"Now that's cruel." Maynard shot her a wounded look. "Camel mating calls are really quite melodious."

"Maybe, to other camels." Lysi forced a smile. She saw from Maynard's expression he detected the worry beneath the light patter. Instead of commenting, he changed the subject.

"If it hadn't been for Thabo, I would never have awakened at all." Maynard's gaze swept around the crowd of visitors in the room. "Where is that surly hulk?"

"He was here just a few seconds ago," Grace said. "Shall I send my favorite cop to search for him?" She smiled at Billy Joe.

"He may have stepped out for a second," Amele said. "Check in the hall, will you, Luvo dear."

Luvo started for the hall but the door swung open before he got there.

"I am right here, Detective Christie." Thabo stepped in from the corridor, muttered something into his cell phone, tucked it in a shirt pocket and approached the bed. "Now we are even." He gave Maynard a hardy handshake. "A life for a life."

The worry lurking in Lysi's subconscious rose to the surface at sight of Thabo. Was Uuka alive or dead? She wanted to ask him what happened after she left Qamata's hut to drive Maynard to the Site B Community Health Center but this was not a good time. She'd wait and ask later. She didn't have to wait long because Maynard asked the question for her.

"So what happened to that trio of Dlomo baboons?" Maynard looked as though he had the same concern Lysi had.

Thabo's answer relieved the worry that had gnawed at her since she left Thabo alone with the three Dlomo brothers in Qamata's hut. Had Thabo followed through on his threat to kill Uuka?

"I mauled them a little and terrified them a lot." Thabo bared strong white teeth as a big grin spread across his broad face. Clearly he'd enjoyed intimidating Uuka.

"Later, after I told them all the things I planned to do to them and they'd dissolved into slap pap I—"

"Slap pap?" Maynard chuckled.

"Weak, watery, oozy mush." Thabo seemed to relish his description of Uuka's fear. "Later, I called Detective Mbeki. I reported what Uuka said about Dr. Nala crushing Qamata's head with a rock. Mbeki sent two cops to drag the mongrels away."

"First her brother then Qamata." Maynard tucked his chin and arched his brows. "Cri-key, I came close to being her next victim. Nambeko Nala is one scary lady croc."

"I would not like to meet her on a dark night," Thabo said.

A shiver ran down Lysi's spine when she thought about all the clues she'd missed. Clues that pointed right to Nambeko. Clues like Nambeko's hatred of Qamata for terrifying her as a child, the false autopsy report she filed on Sipho, her anger at Paki's presence at Sipho's memorial, her clandestine visit to Qamata's hut, her easy access to cobra venom.

Lysi rubbed her temples. Why had she fixated on Thabo? How could she have been so wrong? If only Paki hadn't lied about seeing Thabo in Qamata's hut. If only Lindani had told her it was Nambeko who asked her to call Maynard. If only she had suspected something when Nambeko insisted on being alone with Maynard at the Site B Center not even allowing the nurse to assist. If...if...if.

Maynard's warm hand on Lysi's cheek swept the painful regrets from her mind. His perceptive gaze seemed to say, "Leave past worries behind."

She would try.

A well-fed nurse padded in wearing plus size scrubs and no nonsense orthopedic shoes. Her thick dreds hung down to a bounteous bosom, the kind a small child could lie on and drift off to sleep within minutes. She had a take-charge manner almost like a drill sergeant. Lysi's eyes followed her as she zigzagged through Maynard's gaggle of visitors leaving the sweet scent of vanilla in her wake. Luvo and Amele backed away from the foot of Maynard's bed to make way for the take-control nurse to pass. Lindani peeked at her from behind Thabo. Grace didn't move from a chair on the opposite side of the bed from Lysi but Billy Joe backed up a couple of steps.

"Eight people crammed into a little hospital room. What is this? A party?" The nurse shook her head and her long braids swung left and right. She spoke in a commanding voice as she fastened an inflatable cuff around Maynard's arm and began taking his blood pressure.

"You are almost ready for a party. You are a big man. Can handle a big beating. You need a strong wife to keep you in line." She surprised everyone when she clicked her tongue, winked and rotated her ample hips. "I am very strong."

Maynard opened his mouth but seemed at a loss for words. Lysi thought he blushed.

Laughter lightened the nervous tension in the room.

"No party yet, but it soon will be," Luvo said. "Christmas South African style means a feast at the beach."

The nurse raised the head of Maynard's bed and straightened his pillows. She shook the still full water pitcher and frowned at Maynard. "When is the last time you peed?" She jiggled her index finger at him. "Drink more water or no South African beach party for you."

This time Lysi saw color creep into Maynard's cheeks. "Yes, ma'am."

Amele stifled a laugh and nodded at the nurse then said, "For Christmas, I will first prepare a special dinner of bobotie, Luvo's favorite lamb casserole, and a big bowl of geel rys, our famous yellow rice. Then we will pack some Hertzog cookies and head for Camps Bay Beach to celebrate with the sundowner crowds."

"So get better fast or you will eat hospital consommé, jello and prune juice while Lysi feasts on South African Christmas fare." Luvo's deep chuckle rocked the room.

The nurse stuck an electronic thermometer under Maynard's arm, checked it then moved to a computer and typed in information. As she left the room she said, "Have no worry. You will party on the beach. But you must drink water to make water."

After the nurse had disappeared, Maynard turned to Amele. "What about Mandisa. How is she?"

Amele looked sad. "Of course she is devastated. She is a strong woman who has overcome many hardships. She will survive. She says she will stand with Nambeko through her trial and prison term."

Everyone in the room remained silent for a long moment. Lysi couldn't imagine how Mandisa could forgive Nambeko.

"Mandisa will not forsake Nambeko because she is her daughter." Amele ended with a heavy sigh.

The white sand of Camps Bay Beach had started to cool. Hundreds of Christmas Sundowner picnickers sat on blankets facing the ocean. Lysi moved closer to Maynard as the sun crept nearer the horizon. She approached him with caution, fearful of hurting him. His black eyes had faded to deep purple and his swollen jaw had shrunk but his facial lacerations still looked raw. Maynard grunted as he lifted his arm to Lysi's shoulders. Afraid of hurting his ribs, Lysi hesitated snuggling to his chest. Maynard pulled her close. It troubled her that it felt so right. She wanted to tell him how comfortable and contented she felt sitting here on the beach with him; how she treasured these moments, how empty she'd felt when she thought she might lose him. She wanted to say those things but she couldn't because she knew it would raise his hopes that they might work out a life together. Instead she gazed out to sea and waited for the moment of sunset, her champagne glass at the ready.

The red sun met the blue sea in a blaze of magenta that turned the Sundowners into pink human cotton candy. Low exclamations echoed over the crowded beach as champagne glasses clinked.

"Quick, do as I do," Luvo said in a histrionic voice, tapping Maynard and Billy Joe on the shoulders. "You must follow the ancient Zulu tradition or you will have bad luck for a whole year." He pulled Amele into his arms and gave her a long kiss. She laughed and hugged him. "Whoa! Our years just keep getting better and better," she said.

"I have not heard of this tradition, Billie Joe said. "But I like it." He leaned towards Grace.

After his kiss, Grace took a deep breath. "Yes. I think I remember this tradition from my African heritage courses. I think we're supposed to do it twice to lock in good luck for the whole year."

Lysi grinned. "Sure, Grace."

"I guess I'll have to sacrifice myself," Maynard said. "We wouldn't want Lysi to have a bad year." He heaved a melodramatic moan. "Is there no end to what I do for this woman?"

Lysi punched his arm. "Not funny." It was all she got out before his lips touched hers. The contact, light and fleeting, thrilled her. He pulled away briefly, his lips barely leaving hers, but before she could catch her breath he kissed her again. She couldn't have moved if she'd wanted to. His kiss took her back to their night in Namibia. The memory made her feel heady.

Grace tapped Lysi's hand with her index finger then blew on it as if she'd touched a hot stove. "Sizzling, girlfriend. That kiss'll bring you ten year's of good luck."

"Speaking of good years," Maynard said, his eyes still on Lysi. "Did you know most years spring and fall weather in Alice Springs are pretty moderate.

Billy Joe leaned across Grace and tapped Lysi's shoulder. "Aussie spring is America's fall, September through November. Their fall is your spring, March through May."

Grace turned Billy Joe's face toward her and gave him a quick kiss. "Mm-ah. There, that's for being so smart. But you're a little late. Lysi already spent hours researching those seasons and everything else about the Outback and Sydney and Australia and…"

Lysi sent Grace a scorching eye message that said, Big Mouth.

Maynard's eyes sparkled and a grin spread across his face. "You researched the seasons in Alice Springs?"

"I had nothing to do while you were lazing around playing wounded water buffalo in that hospital bed." Lysi looked down and mumbled, "So I just did it to kill time."

"Yeah, Maynard. She was bored." Grace chortled. "That's why she spent two hours researching Alice Springs' weather, plants, cultural programs, history, and flight times from San Francisco. Does that sound like she just needed to kill a little time?"

Amele, a wide-eyed innocent look on her face, said, "It does not sound to me like she was killing time."

Luvo took a bite of a cookie, turned his eyes Heavenward and spoke in a divine voice. "There is an old Zulu proverb. 'Love far from home is the best.'"

"A Zulu proverb? You know that is Xhosa," Amele said.

"I am not sure I have ever heard this proverb," Billy Joe said and winked at Grace. "But I now believe it is true."

Grace nudged Billy Joe. "Hey, I've heard that proverb many times in Harlem. It's part of my African heritage."

Maynard jumped into the debate. "So Africa is the origin of that old Australian saying."

Lysi squirmed. She knew the heavy meaning behind the light patter. Marry Maynard. Easy. They just didn't understand. Of course Maynard is the kind of man she could love. Any woman would jump at the chance to spend her life with a man like him. Lysi sunk her teeth into her lower lip. Things weren't that simple. Happily ever after doesn't just happen. Things have to be right. Some things are impossible. She turned sad eyes to Maynard's hopeful face and whispered, "I just can't change my whole life. I'm sorry, Maynard. My plane leaves tomorrow."

Maynard's mouth opened in surprise. His shoulders drooped. Then he shrugged and looked out to sea—silent, brooding, his face taut with anger and hurt.

Everyone's stares followed Lysi as she got up and walked to the car. Grace and Amele rose without a word and trailed after her.

Chapter 40

From his open bedroom window Maynard heard the VW engine growl. To Maynard it sounded like a heavy diesel truck. Heavy like his mood. He'd slept fitfully most of the night and was still in bed. The receding sound of the Volkswagen engine told him Amele had left to drive Lysi and Grace to the airport. He hadn't even said goodbye to Lysi. For the life of him he couldn't understand that woman. He loved her. He knew there were obstacles to their relationship. He'd bent over backwards to compromise. He'd given it his best. Yes, Alice Springs and San Francisco were far apart, but the distance problem was not insurmountable. Yes, the lifestyles were different, but they could share each other's cultures half the year. Yes, there would be adjustments, but he was willing to make concessions and thought she would too. He knew they could have worked out the problems.

He rolled onto his back and massaged his forehead. Something else blocked his efforts. Something in Lysi. Something she hadn't revealed to him. His chest felt heavy and he exhaled in frustration. Lysi had made her choice. He knew he had to accept it. It didn't matter now.

He threw off the covers, dragged himself out of bed and dressed. He had just started to pack his bag when he heard a knock on the door.

He opened it to Luvo who looked past him at the suitcase on the bed. "You are packing already? Your plane does not leave until tomorrow."

"I'm catching an earlier flight." He threw the rest of his clothes into the bag not bothering to fold them, zipped it and started to move it to the door.

Luvo took the bag from his hand. Maynard read sympathy in Luvo's eyes. He didn't need pity. He just wanted Luvo and everyone else to leave him alone. "I'm fine," Maynard said.

"I did not ask, but now that you mention it, you look like hell," Luvo said. "Maynard, listen to me. Do you want to marry that stubborn woman?"

"What does it matter what I want?" He took the bag back from Luvo, set it by the door and went to the closet for his jacket. "She's made it pretty clear she's not interested."

"I have a little bit of a language problem, but I think you meant to say 'yes.'" Luvo looked at Maynard with a satisfied grin.

Maynard dropped on the bed and hung his head. "Look Luvo. I know you mean well, but let it go."

"Go get her." Luvo put his big hands on Maynard's shoulders. "Do not give up so easily."

Maynard looked up. What is it with this guy? Can't he take no for an answer? Can't Luvo see how hard he'd tried already?

"It's too late. Her plane leaves at 9:00," Maynard said in a weak voice.

"It's only 7:30 now." Luvo pointed to his watch. "It will take about 40 minutes to get to the airport in this traffic. They won't board until 8:45."

"Luvo. You don't understand." Maynard shook his head. "It's over."

"No sheep man, forgive me, but you do not understand." He sat down next to Maynard. "Grace told Amele and Amele told me that pigheaded woman is in love with you. It is fear that is making her immobile."

"Fear? Of me?"

"Fear of trying a new relationship. Her former husband abused her with his words. When his abuse turned physical, she walked out on him and vowed never to let it happen again."

147

"She's letting her first marriage destroy any chances for a new life." Maynard's face broadcasted his understanding but he remained reluctant. "Well I can't undo her past." He stood, draped his jacket over his arm, and moved to the door.

"No, you cannot undo her past. But you can create her future. Yes, it will take time. She will need reassurance. Love. There is an old Zulu proverb that says, 'If you win the love of a lioness it will last longer than the love of a kitten.'"

A smile crinkled Maynard's eyes. "I bet Amele would say that was a Xhosa proverb." The smile faded and he picked up his bag.

The noisy hubbub of Cape Town International Airport seemed like a distant murmur to Grace as she sat across the table from Lysi in the Matisse Café. She worried as she watched Lysi mechanically stirring her coffee. Lysi hadn't touched her sweet roll even though they'd skipped breakfast. People bustled past pulling bags behind them like reluctant puppies. Their chatter escalated then faded as they passed the Café tables. Lysi seemed not to notice them. Grace searched for words to cut through Lysi's gloom.

"Lysi, you haven't rubbed two words together since we left Oranjezicht. Perk up girl." Grace patted her hand. "We'll be home soon. Back doing assignments for old Stone Face."

"I know." Lysi said in an almost inaudible tone. She didn't shift her eyes from the swirl in her coffee cup.

Grace knew the reason for Lysi's melancholy but she didn't dare voice it directly. She needed a round about approach. She lightened her voice and chucked Lysi under the chin.

"On the other hand, you could work part time for Stellar. Maybe…say…December through February then June through August." Grace took a bite of her croissant. She looked at the ceiling as though in deep thought and chewed. "But what would you do during your off months in fall and spring?"

"I know where you're going with this, Grace." Lysi's voice was flat. She looked at Grace and sighed. "It just wouldn't work."

"What's not to work?" At least Grace had gotten eye contact and more than a two-word response from Lysi. Encouraged, Grace decided to press a little harder. "You could travel in your off months. Me, being your team partner, I'd take the same months off. I could visit Cape Town and Billy Joe. You? Oh, I don't know. Maybe Australia? I hear the weather's pretty nice there in fall and spring. No blistering heat. Well, that scorching sheep farmer of yours might send your temperature rising a few centigrades."

"He's a grazier," Lysi whispered and dropped her eyes to her coffee cup again.

"Lysi, look at me." Grace's voice turned firm. She felt like reaching across the table and shaking some sense into Lysi. "Girl, he's Maynard Christie—solid, considerate, hard worker—not your ex, Jimmy Nielsen—alcoholic, abuser, jobless. I don't get you. You took a chance thirty years ago on that piece of crap but now you won't even try to make it with a man who adores you, a man who would do anything for you, a man you've admitted your in love with." She shook her head in dismay. "I'm sorry Lysi but I gotta say it. You're acting like a total dipstick."

Lysi swiped at the tears moistening her eyes. She lost the battle and turned her face away from Grace. "I have to go to the bathroom." She got up and walked hastily away nearly running into a couple of pilots rushing to their posts. When she was out of sight, Grace picked up her phone.

Maynard heard his phone ring. He looked around for it—patted his jacket and dug into his pants pockets, unzipped his bag and shuffled the clothes around, lifted the case and felt under it.

Luvo reached behind the bedside lamp, picked up the phone and handed it to Maynard.

"Maynard Christie speaking."

"Maynard, Grace here." Grace's voice trumpeted through the phone so loud Maynard had to hold it away from his ear. "I've got a real pity party going on here. Lysi's a mess. She's not eating. She's depressingly quiet. She's weepy. I've never seen her like this. I tell you, I can't stand it much longer. You better get your cute little buns over here before she completely falls apart."

"She doesn't want to see me." Maynard's eyes lost some of their beaten down, lifelessness. Hope sparked for an instant before he smothered it. He didn't need a rerun of what he'd already been through. "Sorry Grace, I can't help you."

"Believe me, you're the only one who can help."

Luvo could hear Grace's loud harangue. He shook his head and gave Maynard an I-can't-believe-you're-that-dense look.

Maynard grappled with what to do. What if Grace was right? Did Lysi regret her decision to leave him? Could her upset relate to him? He'd never know unless he took the risk of seeing her. He pinched his nose and squeezed his eyes shut. What if Grace was wrong? What if the upset stemmed from the stress of travel? He might get there and Lysi would refuse to talk to him. In his head, a tiny bit of hope battled powerful lingering doubt.

"Even if I wanted to come, I couldn't get there on time." He looked at his watch. "It's 7:30 and the gates close at 8:40 for a nine o'clock pushback."

"Hang up," Luvo said. "We can easily make it if we leave right now."

Maynard obeyed. "Let's go," he said a determined but nervous expression on his face.

They started down the front steps then Luvo stopped short.

No car.

"Oh no." Luvo slammed his forehead with the heel of his hand. "Amele took the VW to drive to the airport. Our other car is still in the shop."

Resignation replaced the determined look on Maynard's face. "Luvo, it's just not meant to be. Let's forget it. I'm going to call a cab. The sooner I arrange for my flight home the better."

Luvo rubbed his chin and gritted his teeth then smiled at Maynard as if he hadn't heard his cab comment. "I'll call Billy Joe."

Twenty minutes later Billy Joe screeched his patrol car to a halt in front of the Butshingi house. Luvo jumped in front. Maynard stood on the sidewalk. "I'm not going."

"Get in the car," Billy Joe said. He jumped out and opened the back door.

"Billy Joe." Maynard looked conciliatory. "I know you came all this way, but I've made my decision."

"Get in the car or…or I will arrest you," Billy Joe said.

"Arrest me? What the hell are you talking about? For what?" Maynard turned and started up the steps.

"For…" Billy Joe scrunched up his face and shifted his eyes left and right. "For compromising the Sipho crime scene."

"What? You said crime scenes in Ikhaya weren't…this is crazy."

Billy Joe pulled handcuffs out of his pocket.

"You're insane," Maynard said but he saw in Billy Joe's expression that he'd best not risk a charge of resisting arrest on top of compromising a crime scene. He hurried down the steps and slid into the backseat.

"Buckle up and hang on," Billy Joe yelled.

Billy Joe used his siren to navigate the back streets to the freeway. At the screeching sound drivers veered to the left curb and stared as if wondering who the cop was chasing. When they hit bumper-to-bumper commuter traffic on the M3 Expressway Billy Joe drummed his fingers on the steering wheel and uttered expletives as he tried to move the car through the throng of commuters. He belted in and out of traffic at every opening, zapping unwary drivers with belts of his siren. Maynard hit an imaginary brake as Billy Joe skidded to a stop when a slow-moving bus cut in front of him. Billy Joe let out a puff of air through his nose, swerved out around the bus and gunned down the street leaving a trail of blaring horns in his wake. Maynard held tight to the armrest.

At 8:25 Billy Joe swerved to the curb in front of the International departures terminal and Maynard burst through the door in the towering glass wall.

He scanned the long line of check-in counters. He had no idea where Lysi might be. Why hadn't he thought to ask Grace? This wasn't his usual style. He patted his jacket pockets for his phone. Not there. He must have left it in the car. Things just happened too fast. Now he'd be too late. What did it matter anyway? This whole thing was probably a colossal waste of his time and effort. She's probably boarding right now. A little ache in his chest told him he had to try.

His eyes flitted around the huge hall and landed on a blue uniformed airport employee standing near a roped off check-in lane. The short Asian woman smiled when he approached her. "Which airline, sir?"

"A…" He hadn't thought to ask which airline. "The one that flies to San Francisco."

"I am sorry sir." The woman smiled again. "Who is going to San Francisco? You sir?"

"No, not me. It doesn't matter who."

"Yes sir. Of course not. Now what exactly do you need?"

Maynard stopped to take a breath. "I need to know which gate is for San Francisco."

"We have several airlines that go to San Francisco. Which one did you want?" The pleasant smile faded from the woman's face.

Maynard looked at his watch 8:30. This wasn't working. What could he do? An idea.

"Miss, is it possible to page someone?"

"I am sorry sir. We do not page people on request. Emergencies only."

"This is extremely important," Maynard said.

She listened sympathetically as he blurted out his desperate need to stop the most important woman in his life from flying away from him.

"Sir, this is an emergency is it not? I cannot page except in emergency." Her eye message told him to answer yes. In case he didn't get it, she also nodded several times.

Grace heard the page first. "Lysi Weston, please go to the iHelp phone nearest you."

Lysi's eyes came to attention. She looked around, a bewildered expression on her face.

Grace sprang from her chair and grabbed Lysi's arm. "That's you. They're paging you. Let's go girl."

Lysi and Grace found a black iHelp phone near area B. When she picked it up, Maynard's voice filled her ear. "Lysi, where are you?"

"Maynard?" Lysi's surprised face morphed into a confused smile.

"Where are you, Lysi?"

"Gotta go." Grace gave Lysi a quick hug. "I'll see you and that sheep farmer in San Francisco some time in January." She laughed and hurried to the boarding gate.

"I'm in boarding area B at an iHelp phone near the Matisse Café. How did—"

"Area B?" Maynard looked around helplessly.

The Asian woman tugged at his sleeve and pointed at an overhead direction sign. "Please follow me."

"Don't move, Lysi. Don't move. I'm on my way."

Umbhako and Hertzoggie recipes from the author

Umbhako

Umbhako, also known as Xhosa Pot Bread, is a traditional food of the Xhosa people, the dominant tribal group in Cape Town. Mandela belongs to the Xhosa tribe. *Umbhako* is called pot bread because it was traditionally cooked in a cast iron pot on an open fire. In my novel, Sarah, a Xhosa innkeeper in Ikhaya Township, prepares *Umbhako* for two of my main characters, Lysi and Grace. *Umbhako* is somewhat similar to cornbread. Sarah served it with jam and butter.

2 cups white flour
1 cup whole-wheat flour
½ cup corn kernals
1 large egg
2 tsp instant yeast
1 ½ TB brown sugar
2 tsp vegetable or palm oil
½ -3/4 cup warm water
½ tsp salt

Directions
1. Combine flours, salt, yeast and sugar in a large bowl. In a separate bowl, combine eggs, oil and warm water.
2. Slowly add the wet ingredients to the dry ingredients, mixing between each addition of liquid.
3. Fold the corn kernels into the batter and pour this mixture into a well-oiled cast-iron pot – the mixture should fill ¾ of the pot.
4. Put pot aside in a warm place until the mixture has risen sufficiently to fill the pot – about 45 minutes.
5. Bake in a pre-heated 350F oven until a skewer comes out cleanly – about an hour.
6. Serve with tea and jam.

Nancy Curteman

Hertzog Cookies

Hertzog cookies, affectionately called Hertzoggies, was named after General Hertzog, who was the Prime minister of South Africa from 1924 to 1939. These were his favorite cookies and for good reason. They are delicious little jam and coconut tartlets topped with meringue. Although South Africans love them all year round, they are traditionally served at Christmas time. The lead characters in Murder Casts A Spell gobble them up as they enjoy a Christmas Sundowner on Camps Beach near Cape Town. By the way, no Hertzog cookie lover will touch Smut cookies named after Jan Smuts who was leader of General Hertzog's opposition party.

The Pastry
1 lb self-raising flour
4 Tbsp sugar
2 Tbsp margarine
3 egg yolks
milk or water (as required)
1 tsp vanilla essence
¼ tsp salt

Directions
1. Beat the margarine and sugar together in a bowl to a light and creamy consistency
2. Stir in the egg yolks and vanilla essence, taking care to blend well.
3. Sift the flour and the salt into the mixture, ensuring that it is thoroughly mixed.
4. Stir in enough milk or water so that a fairly stiff dough is formed.
5. Place the dough on a floured surface and roll out to a ¼ inch thickness. Cut into rounds with a cookie cutter.
6. Line a greased patty tin with the rounds of dough

The filling:
3 egg whites, stiffly beaten
2 cups desiccated coconut
1 cup sugar
apricot jam

Directions
1. Gradually add the sugar to the beaten egg whites, beating well to blend.
2. Fold the coconut into the mixture and mix well.
3. Place a little apricot jam in the center of the rounds in the patties and spoon some of the coconut mixture over the jam.
4. Bake in the oven at 400° F for approximately 15 minutes. The pastry should be a light golden color.
5. Leave to cool slightly in the pan and then place on a rack and let the cookies cool completely.

Makes approximately 60 Hertzog cookies. These may be stored in an airtight container for 2 weeks.

About The Author

Mystery writer, Nancy Curteman, loves to travel and adores reading mystery novels so of course she writes travel mysteries. One of her novels, "Murder in a Teacup," set in Montana, placed second in the California Writers Club Jack London novel contest. "Murder Down Under," set in Australia was #5 in the top ten best mystery novels of 2015. Solstice Publishing recently released her novels, "Murder on the Seine," set in France and "Lethal Lesson" set in California.

Curteman's blog, Global Mysteries, combines information for mystery writers and practical tips on world travel.

A transplant from Idaho, she now lives in the San Francisco Bay Area where she is working on her next Lysi Weston novel set in San Francisco.

Global Mysteries Blog: https://nancycurteman.wordpress.com

www.ingramcontent.com/pod-product-compliance
Lightning Source LLC
Chambersburg PA
CBHW071225260626

47162CB00004B/1424